CORPSE MARKER

The Doctor Who *Monster Collection*

Prisoner of the Daleks
Trevor Baxendale

Touched by an Angel
Jonathan Morris

Illegal Alien
Mike Tucker and Robert Perry

Shakedown
Terrance Dicks

The Scales of Injustice
Gary Russell

Sting of the Zygons
Stephen Cole

Corpse Marker
Chris Boucher

The Sands of Time
Justin Richards

THE MONSTER COLLECTION EDITION

CORPSE MARKER

CHRIS BOUCHER

BOOKS

3 5 7 9 10 8 6 4 2

First published in 1999 by BBC Worldwide Ltd
This edition published in 2014 by BBC Books, an imprint of Ebury Publishing
A Random House Group Company

Copyright © Chris Boucher 1999, 2014

Chris Boucher has asserted his moral right to be identified as the author of the
Work in accordance with Sections 77 and 78 of the Copyright, Designs and
Patents Act 1988

Doctor Who is a BBC Wales production for BBC One.
Executive producers: Steven Moffat and Brian Minchin

BBC, DOCTOR WHO and TARDIS (word marks, logos and devices) are
trademarks of the British Broadcasting Corporation and are used under
licence.

The Random House Group Limited Reg. No. 954009
Addresses for companies within the Random House Group can be found at
www.randomhouse.co.uk

A CIP catalogue record for this book is available from the British Library.

ISBN 978 1 849 90759 0

Editorial director: Albert DePetrillo
Series consultant: Justin Richards
Project editor: Steve Tribe
Cover design: Two Associates © Woodlands Books Ltd, 2014
Production: Alex Goddard

Printed and bound in the USA

To buy books by your favourite authors and register for offers,
visit www.randomhouse.co.uk

INTRODUCTION

Counting on my fingers, my preferred approach to mathematics, I appear to have written this novel fifteen years ago, give or take. My first agent, long before that, told me never to put a date on anything I wrote 'because it tends to date it' but the publisher put a date on this so for once the mistake, if it is a mistake, is not mine. I think it was Harold Wilson, peace be upon him, who said a week is a long time in politics. Well, fifteen years is a long time in anything. It's certainly a long time in terms of memory.

Remembering is a difficult idea anyway, if you think about it. Logically if you wanted to and could give a completely accurate account of, say, the last hour it would take you an hour in real-time. Now having done that, suppose you wanted to and could give a completely accurate account of the last two hours which would necessarily include remembering the hour you have just spent remembering the first hour...

I offer this small digression, which can be a cure for insomnia by the way, merely to justify the fact that when I was asked to come up with an introduction for this new edition of *Corpse Marker*, I couldn't remember enough about the book to do it confidently. I would have to read the book again. So I did. Interestingly, well I hope it's interesting anyway, one of the crucial plot devices turns out to involve remembering. I love a good coincidence don't you? Not as a plot device obviously: coincidence in plotting has to be justified in other ways, at which point it ceases to be a coincidence of course…

Writing any sequel presents problems, if only remembering accurately the details of the original so as not to contradict yourself and look like a fool, but writing the sequel to a television drama as a novel offered some even more interesting difficulties. I use the word interesting as in the Chinese curse: may you live in interesting times. Small things like the costumes, striking but unremarked on television in *The Robots of Death*, required description *and* justification in the sequel novel. If you describe something in prose as opposed to merely seeing it in passing on screen, it does take on slightly more significance: as if a director has thrown the focus. Description seems to say look and look says: hold on what's all that about? Then you have to think it through, which is more fun than it sounds and, I hope, makes for a better and more exciting story. If elements of a story do not make sense then I tend to lose interest and, frequently, consciousness.

As it happens my routine instincts seem to be reductionist: to try to understand by taking apart ideas, feelings and beliefs and examining how they might work as opposed to how they might appear to work. When put like that, it sounds a bit like a god complex, but I think it's more of a complex about gods, and religions, and class systems, and sanity and fashion and death and conspiracies and all the things that scare us all most of the time and amuse us for the rest. Or is that just me? Anyway all that stuff is in the book if you look for it, but my advice is not to look for it but to let it creep up behind you and go boo. And there are jokes and violence and even some small references to sex. Pretty much everything I look for in an entertainment really which is how I've always approached writing anything. If it doesn't amuse me then it's not going to amuse you either and we will both have wasted our time.

When I was commissioned to do this book I remember being grateful for the work and for the money, even though it was more work for less money than writing for TV, or radio for that matter, used to pay. 'Used to' being the key words there. Stephen Cole, the then editor, suggested there was an appetite for a sequel to *The Robots of Death*: the jury might still be out on that one. But I had an appetite for it and my family had an appetite for food and a roof.

When commissioned, the only time I can write at all, I have always worked to a daily word count. I hope it is only obvious to me when in the book I was having trouble meeting my target for any particular day. This introduction was a commission, of course, and today is not going well. Fifty-six words in that bit of the paragraph, none of them of any particular relevance. This must be the moment for you to stop wasting time with this introduction and read the book for yourself. If I'm honest, and usually I try to be honest because lying is such hard work, I found the book slightly disconcerting. Unlike me it doesn't seem to have dated much and I actually rather enjoyed reading it again. I hope you will enjoy it too.

Chris Boucher
October 2013

For Lynda, always

BRIEFING

The vast machine which is Storm Mine Four crawls across the trackless wastes of the Blind Heart. It is hunting unreliable desert weather fronts and the abruptly savage winds which stir up mineral-rich sandstorms and whirl valuable ores into flying seams.

They know all this – why am I bothering with it? I pretend to underestimate them so they feel superior and underestimate me…

A talented captain, backed up by a skilful pilot, can stay with a storm and follow its most productive ore-streams as they swirl and twist past the open mining vents. Robots can do these jobs and any of the others required to operate the mine, but to achieve the full economic potential of the equipment, to really suck the wealth out of the dense, scouring clouds of blasting grit, takes instinct and a subtlety of touch which cannot be programmed into anything less complex than a human being.

But it doesn't matter because they're so far behind the game they have no choice but to underestimate me…

Kiy Uvanov and Lish Toos are one of the best captain and pilot teams the Company currently has on its database. Unfortunately, the rest of the crew of Storm Mine Four do not reach the same standard of excellence and eight months into the two-year tour of duty disaster strikes. There is a suspicious death. Paranoia spreads. Underlying hostilities come to the surface and in an increasingly hysterical

1

atmosphere the crew begin to accuse each other of the killing.

Then one by one they die.

Almost from the first there can be no doubt that someone, or some*thing*, is roaming the empty levels and deserted corridors of the huge mine, murdering randomly and without mercy.

Except that they did doubt it of course. Doubt and paranoia – where would we be without them? Well, I wouldn't be hiding out on this weirdly backward planet…

When it finally becomes clear to the captain what is actually happening, only three of his crew are still alive. Two of them are completely insane and Pilot Toos and even Uvanov himself lose touch with reality and begin to see ghosts and apparitions. In the throes of horror they conjure out of nowhere an oddly dressed man and a primitive girl to fight beside them as they struggle to recognise the unthinkable, the unimaginable.

Impossible as it still seems, what they face are robots, normally functioning, fully inhibited Vocs and Supervocs, which have been modified on site, in the mine itself.

Impossible as it still seems, these robots are de-inhibited so that they are able to kill. With the vents closed and the mine on minimum drive, enough simply to keep it from sinking below the surface of the sand, Captain Uvanov and Pilot Toos begin looking for ways to destroy these killer machines.

A bit over the top, but then a lot of this is melodramatic conjecture so let's see what sort of reaction we can get…

'No.' The voice from the shadows at the back of the conference chamber was imperious. 'I'm sorry, but I don't believe it.'

Carnell froze the images on the demonstration screen and lifted the light level in the room. He looked at the confident man in the crude suit of rough homespun which proclaimed his wealth and aristocratic background, and he sighed inwardly. He would have preferred one of the others, one of the less obviously stupid. He would get as much intellectual rigour from one of the dozen or so humanoid machines which waited, unmoving and unnoticed, to fetch and carry for this secret gathering. He made a mental note to ensure the robots were sent for routine service: he didn't want any of this accidentally retained and accessed.

'I don't believe it, I'm sorry,' the young man repeated.

You've never been sorry in your life, you inbred half-wit, Carnell thought and said: 'Perhaps you could be more specific, Firstmaster Roatson?'

'It could not have happened like that.'

It was a statement of fact, or rather it was a statement of opinion by a man who was too privileged to have to tell the difference. Carnell knew it was pointless to challenge such a person especially in present company but already he was bored. This could have been a mildly interesting game if it weren't for these small-minded fools and their limited desires. Where were the decadent, power-mad psychotics when you needed them? Raising one eyebrow slightly, he smiled a small smile. 'All evidence to the contrary,' he suggested. He paused just long enough then went on, 'It seems you have some intelligence which has obviously been denied to me.'

Several of the representatives of the other founding families and some of the rising stars of the business cartels sniggered openly.

The young aristocrat was not fazed. 'The family,' he said, 'have been in robot development practically from the

3

beginning, and I can tell you that there is no possibility of changing a Voc grade in the way you suggested. No one could do it, not with all the facilities of a fully equipped laboratory at their disposal, and certainly not on a moving storm mine using nothing more elaborate than a standard laserson probe.'

Carnell noted the casual reference to the tool which had been used on the subsystems of the robot brains. It was information so closely restricted that almost no one should have known about it. Certainly this man, a junior member of one of the twenty families, should not have been privy to it. Was it stupidity or simple arrogance, he wondered, which let young Firstmaster Roatson give away how much they already knew of what he was supposedly telling these people for the first time? He was tempted to challenge him on it but this was no time for self-indulgence. 'Normally I would agree with you,' he said mildly. 'But nothing about Taren Capel was normal, least of all his talent for robotics.'

'I don't think Taren Capel ever existed,' Roatson commented.

Carnell smiled. 'If he didn't exist then it would be necessary to invent him.'

'That's exactly it.'

'Yes,' Carnell agreed, still smiling, 'it is.'

He dimmed the lights again and released the demonstration images. This time he took the lights down a little further than before and imperceptibly intensified and saturated the colours on the screen. He hoped to get them all to concentrate long enough for him to finish this largely irrelevant presentation.

With all the unmodified robots closed down using the main deactivation circuits, Uvanov and Toos blow up several of the killer robots with bombs they make by magnetising the base plates of Z9 explosive packs. They further devise a feedback loop in the robot communications links which overloads and burns down through the control levels causing catastrophic brain failures, and then by altering voice recognition systems they manage to turn his hellish creations back on Taren Capel himself. The shadowy genius is the final victim of his robots of death.

By the time the rescuers reach Storm Mine Four it is all over. The survivors – Captain Uvanov, Pilot Toos and the severely disabled Chief Mover Poul – are brought back to civilisation. The mine is abandoned and it sinks into the desert, taking with it the evidence of what happened. A cover story is devised, or perhaps it is just speculated, and because it is what everyone wants to believe it quickly becomes what everyone knows to be the truth. There is no end of civilisation as we know it.

As a finale Carnell ran news footage from the time: the brief chaotic interviews with the survivors; the elaborate reconstruction of the courageous crew's doomed struggle against the ore raiders; the furious public demands for a security crackdown to bring the criminals to justice. When it was over he waited a moment before bringing up the lights. He wanted them to think about it. He wanted to give one of them the chance to ask the obvious question.

'And what exactly does this have to do with the project you were hired for?' The speaker was a tall man in artificial homespun and he was sitting in the front row. 'I'm not interested in the collapse of the economy. If that story gets out everything goes to hell. Where's the profit in that? The cure will be worse than the disease.'

Carnell was a slightly built man, not particularly tall, with

5

blonder hair and a paler complexion than most of those present. His eyes were what really set him apart, however. They were vividly blue and in the right light they could be piercing, like shards of sea ice. He stepped into the right light now and smiled coldly at the man. 'You have to trust me,' he said. 'I'm very expensive precisely because I can be trusted.' He lifted his look to take in the rest of the conference chamber. 'I told you this story because I have to be sure that you can be trusted too. If you are going to panic I want you to do it here and now.' He paused. 'I like panics to be well organised.'

An elaborately coiffured woman swathed in ivory bubblesilk said, 'This strangely dressed man and the primitive girl?'

'Group hallucination,' Carnell said.

'They seemed very positive,' she remarked.

More information you're not supposed to have, Carnell thought, *you've obviously seen the confidential debriefing tapes.* 'False memory,' he said, 'mutually induced and reinforced.'

'They're lying?'

'They believe it.'

From the back, Roatson guffawed. 'A group hallucination,' he scoffed with aristocratic disdain. 'In a group of two.'

Carnell smiled. 'Three. Chief Mover Poul saw them too.'

As he had expected, Roatson could not resist pressing home his point. 'He'd had a breakdown?'

'They all had,' Carnell said. 'That's my point.'

'How do you know the man and the girl were not real?' the woman in the robot-produced confection asked.

'Because it's impossible.'

'Is that a good enough reason?'

'It is to the reasonable. More importantly, they don't matter. They do not materially affect what happened, what is happening, what is going to happen.'

For only the second time in his career as a psycho-strategist Carnell had made a fundamental error.

MARKER

'I still don't remember much about it,' Poul said, a brief frown drifting across his gaunt face. 'All right, let's be honest, I don't remember anything about it at all.' He shifted on the recliner and adjusted his uniform tunic, straightening the blue silk, pulling it down so that it was smooth under his narrow back.

'Even after all this time?' the therapist prompted gently. She was just the front for a mechanical analyst which itself was little more than a sophisticated lie-detector modified for medical use. She was reading her lines from a linked laptop which also gave her precise timing and voice tone cues. As charades went it was crude, and wastefully expensive, but in Ander Poul's case it seemed it was absolutely essential. Without the buffer provided by this average-looking woman with her normally modulated human voice, his rehabilitation could not even have begun. It was clear from the start that for him robot medicine was a contradiction in terms. There was a horror hidden outside the reach of his conscious memory. It was a horror which involved the mechanical humanoids on which the world depended: that much was clear. That much and very little more.

'Even after all this time?' she repeated with the same gentle persistence.

He sighed now and said, 'Especially after all this time.' His face had settled back into a stubborn, stiff blankness.

'Time does not necessarily heal,' the therapist said. 'Or perhaps you feel it does?'

9

'Eventually it does.' Now there was the ghost of a smile. 'Eventually you die and then it does.'

The therapist read from her screen: (*Matter-of-factly*) 'Perhaps. (*Double-beat pause*) You have no idea what happened to you (*Beat pause*) on Storm Mine Four?'

'No idea at all. I thought that's what I just said.'

Following the instructions she was given on the screen, the therapist reached into her pocket and produced a small disc of iridescent red plastic. She reached forward and stuck it on to the back of Poul's hand. 'Do you know what that is?' she asked quietly.

'No,' he said flatly. And then he began to scream.

CHAPTER
ONE

The TARDIS finished balancing the transdimensional flows, pulled an infinity of options together into a single focus and settled into its new place. When the non-sound howling and the unmoving motion had passed and gone, the Doctor stared at the image on the screen above the door and announced: 'This looks disappointingly familiar.'

The picture showed that the TARDIS had come to rest inside an enclosed multi-storey space, the metallic walls of which were lined with gantries and ladders. Nowhere was there any sign of life. At regular intervals along the gantries there were doors, each with an observation port back lit with sharp green light. Nothing moved.

'Of course,' the Doctor went on, 'when you've been around for as long as I have, almost everything does look disappointingly familiar.' He pulled the newly repaired long scarf from the pocket of the coat he always wore and looped it round his neck. 'It's always a happy surprise when it turns out not to be.' From the hat stand he retrieved the wide-brimmed felt he invariably favoured and clamped it over his unruly curls. Routinely unchangeable in the slightly eccentric outfit which would alter finally only when he himself did, he beamed down at Leela. 'I do love surprises, don't you?'

'No,' Leela said. 'In my world surprises bite.' She was shorter than the Doctor; lighter, slighter and altogether more aggressive.

11

'But you're not in your world now,' the Doctor chided. 'Even though you still insist on wearing that rather primitive ensemble.'

'Ensemble?' Leela did not take her eyes from the screen.

'The hide tunic, the skin boots, the knife?'

Automatically Leela put her hand on the hilt of her long-bladed hunting knife as though she half expected an attempt to take it from her. 'You do not like my...ensemble?'

'It is not appropriate for every occasion. It does look a bit odd sometimes.'

'But what you are wearing does not look odd sometimes.' It was almost a question but not quite.

'Well-tailored clothes are never out of place,' the Doctor said. He smiled his quick, wolfish smile. 'And I am not threatening. I don't frighten people.'

Leela glanced away from the screen and scowled at the Doctor. 'I do not frighten people.'

'You don't think so?'

Leela thought for a moment. 'I do not think so,' she said finally. 'Fear is the enemy of reason.'

'Who told you that?'

'You did.'

'It must be true then,' the Doctor said, operating the TARDIS's door control. 'Shall we go and see if there are any surprises left out there?'

'We should wait longer,' Leela began.

'I know, I know,' the Doctor interrupted. 'We should wait for movement so we can identify the predators.'

'Dangers,' Leela corrected. 'This does not look as though it is a likely place for predators.'

'I don't suppose you want to leave the knife behind then?' the Doctor suggested.

'No,' Leela said flatly.

Nodding to himself, the Doctor headed for the door. 'Don't blame me if the locals are hostile.'

Leela trotted after him. 'That is why I will not leave the knife behind.'

'I thought it was part of your warrior cult,' the Doctor said, stepping out and sniffing the dry air of a dust-free, climate-controlled environment.

'Who told you that?' Leela asked.

'You did.'

'I said it was part of my training.'

'Exactly,' the Doctor said. 'Let's take a look at those gantries, shall we?'

He strode off briskly, his shoes ringing dully on the highly polished metal floor. Leela padded silently along beside him.

The Doctor had already started climbing the ladder to the first-level gantry when Leela called softly from the floor below him. 'Doctor, did you hear that?'

The Doctor continued to climb.

She called a little more loudly: 'Doctor, did you hear that?'

The Doctor paused and looked down. 'I'm sorry, I didn't hear that. What did you say?'

'Somewhere close by...' Leela tilted her head slightly and listened intently.

'Yes?' The Doctor appeared to be trying to be patient and only partially succeeding.

'Fighting,' Leela said. 'People are fighting.'

The Doctor started to climb again. 'Even if they are,' he said over his shoulder, 'it still doesn't justify the knife.' He reached the narrow gantry and looked down again. Leela had not moved. 'Are you coming up?'

'I think I will go and see who is fighting and why,' she said and turned towards a large pair of double doors set in the metal wall behind the ladders.

13

'Not a good idea,' the Doctor said. 'But I imagine you're going to tell me it's part of the warrior code?'

'I only want to find out what is happening.'

'Try not to get involved. Or lost. Lost travelling companions are disappointingly familiar too.'

She smiled up at him. 'I will try to surprise you,' she said.

Leela crossed to the door and looked for the operating mechanism. On the walkway high above her the Doctor approached the first of the green-lit chambers and peered through the observation port.

Storm Mine Seven was grinding its way slowly towards the giant docking bay. Banks of multiple caterpillar tracks, offset, individually driven and capable of tilting through fifteen degrees on either side of the horizontal, were now on fully linked automatics and flat trim. These final operations were the simplest and most basic. The terminal approach manoeuvres would hardly have taxed the powers of a Voc, never mind a Supervoc, but Captain Lish Toos still liked to handle such things herself.

Seven's ore hoppers were full, in most cases with high-grade lucanol. Toos had run a couple of trial assays and she knew the stuff would separate out at somewhere around the 70 per cent mark, which was pure enough to guarantee the crew a profit share to make every last one of them seriously wealthy. This had been a very successful trip, even by her exceptionally high standards.

There were not many captains who had demonstrated Toos's consistent talent for finding, time and again over the years, the richest ore streams. That was why she never had a problem, despite her growing reputation for eccentricity, in getting people to sign on for the eighteen-month tours of duty. Her odd obsessions meant that her crews worked a lot harder than normal but they got a lot richer than normal too so with her as captain there were no more than the routine bickerings and resentments common to all long-range mines.

Her strict ban on robots entering the control deck for any reason whatsoever made the shift system brutal by comparison with other mine crews. Her insistence that any job a human being was capable of doing must be done by a human being left time free for eating and sleeping and not much else. Things were further complicated by a requirement that robots be confined to those parts of the mine where Toos herself would not be working. There was also a rule that no robot be permitted in the crew's living quarters unless specifically tasked and never in her personal quarters under any circumstances. As each of her tours progressed, the tally of deactivated robots would rise steadily until by docking there was hardly a functioning unit on the mine. On one of her early tours as a captain they had actually run out of the iridescent red discs used to mark the function-terminated robots. It became a sort of standing joke in the Company that Toos was not robophobic – it was simply that she liked the look of those corpse markers, especially on robots.

Of course, if Toos *had* been morbidly terrified of the highly polished, highly stylised, highly necessary androids, a medical discharge would have been inevitable and the Company would have lost one of its most profitable storm mine captains. There would have been questions asked as well. Why, for example, had someone with such a fragile personality been given command of a storm mine at all? And why had Lish Toos been promoted captain ahead of more senior candidates? These were questions better left unasked. It followed therefore that she was not robophobic but simply idiosyncratic.

As grinding creaks shuddered through the mine and heaving groans echoed in a brief crescendo before settling into intermittent clanks and sudden snaps, the pilot reported. 'Bay level is constant, all pressure points are equalised, Storm Mine Seven is stopped, all drives are disengaged, all stop, repeat all stop.'

'All stop. Thank you, Tani,' Toos said and smiled for the first time in what seemed to her to have been months. Thinking about it, she realised it probably had been months. She thumbed the short-wave. 'Docko, this is Captain Toos reporting Storm Mine Seven is all stopped, all down and all secure.'

'Thank you, Captain,' a voice from Docking Coordination acknowledged. 'Welcome back to civilisation. Any robots left this time?'

Tani stood up and stretched. 'They take bets on how many,' he said.

Toos nodded. 'I know,' she said, 'but I'm too tired, I'm too beautiful and I'm far too rich to care.' She thumbed the communication button again. 'Docko, I shall want full independent monitoring on the offload.'

'Don't you trust us, Captain?' The voice sounded amused and hurt in roughly equal measure.

'As much as I trust anybody who's counting my money for me,' Toos said. 'Make sure they're properly certificated, won't you, and no relation?'

'Of yours or mine?' the voice said.

'I don't have any relatives,' Toos said. 'Let me know when you're set up.' She broke the link and yawned copiously.

'Why don't you take a rest, Captain?' Tani said. 'I'll make sure they don't siphon off a Dockmaster share.' The pilot was a squat man with a large head and a broad, sour smile. 'Or don't you trust me either?'

16

'You know better than to ask me that,' Toos said, shedding the captain's head-dress and tossing it onto a seat in the rest area. She shook her slightly greying light brown hair loose so that it hung down across her shoulders and rubbed her eyes with the heels of her hands and yawned again. 'Yes, why not? Some sleep might be a good idea.'

Tani switched hopper surveillance to his main board and put a lock-down alarm on it. 'We have heavy-duty celebrating rostered. Stamina will be called for.'

Toos strolled towards the entrance to the control deck. 'Stamina's for robots and poor people,' she said, rolling her hips in an exaggerated swagger. 'We don't need it, Tani. If we get tired of celebrating we can hire people to do it for us. Remember the old saying: wave cash above your head and they'll never know how short you are.'

As the door slid back and she stepped through into the corridor the pilot called after her: 'So how tall do you want to be, Captain?'

'Tall enough not to have to look up,' Toos called back cheerfully, 'at anyone.'

The door soughed shut and Toos turned back into the passageway and headed for her quarters. She was relaxed now, looking forward to refreshing herself with a bath and a brief sleep before leaving the mine to finalise the business details of the tour. As well as the mineral tallies to be agreed, there were damage reports and equipment inventories to be verified. And then of course she would have to sign off on the number of deactivated robots corpse-marked for return to the construction centres. The cost of robot reactivation was set against profits but as far as Toos was concerned it was worth the price not to have to look at the things, not have them creeping around behind you. Especially not to have them creeping around behind you.

17

The mine's independent power plant was already beginning to close down as the docking bay's umbilicals homed in, linked up and took over. Even when a chief mover was paying attention – and Toos knew that Simbion would be quite drunk by this time – such transfers occasionally got out of phase and temporary power-downs were common. When the lights began to flicker in the passageway outside the entrance to her quarters, it did not seem like much of a problem and she was not surprised or unduly alarmed to find herself in sudden darkness. She was mildly irritated but she waited patiently enough for the overrides to kick in and the systems to come back up so she could open the door and get on with her life.

She had never much liked the dark but she was not afraid of it. She would have preferred to be locked inside her quarters rather than locked out of them but there was no need to panic. She was not pressed for time. And the darkness did not really bother her.

The overrides seemed to be taking longer than they should, though. Simbion better wake up and pay attention, she didn't *have* to overlook the drinking. It was probably her imagination, it was probably only a few seconds, and the dark didn't really bother her.

It might have been more worrying if the mine had been full of functioning robots – they could switch to different wavelengths and move through the darkness, find you in the darkness. A robot could find you in the darkness simply by homing in on the infrared…

She shivered and peered unseeingly into the total darkness.

… But there were no robots on this level, and the dark didn't bother her. There were very few functioning robots left on board. What was it: three? No, it was more than three. How many then? How many? Five, say. Six? Six at most.

Six, yes, it was six. And they were all in the dark. But not in this dark. Not in this dark here because none of them were allowed on this level. They were down in the gross-function levels, held there by her order. Robots did what they were ordered – that's what robots were for. Except... except when they didn't do what they were ordered but that was only once and that was not possible now. That could never happen now. Once but never again. It could never happen again.

The dark did not bother her but it was taking longer than it should. The back-ups ought to have kicked in by now. The darkness was so total that she had begun to see lights in it. She knew her eyes were unreliable in these conditions. She knew there were no lights. But there should be. It was definitely taking too long.

What was Simbion playing at? She would break that lazy, unreliable drunk if she didn't do what she was being paid to do and do it now. 'Simbion!' she yelled. 'Simbion!'

Even as she raged Toos knew it was a mistake. It didn't make her feel better – it was a loss of control, it brought her closer to panic, but she couldn't stop herself. 'Simbion,' she screamed at the top of her lungs, 'get off your fat rear end and get the systems back on-line!'

Now she was shaking and tiny star shells were exploding soundlessly in the back of her eyes. She was panting: the shallow gasps of a dying animal. The dark was too dark and it was lasting too long and the robots were all around her. She struggled for control of her breathing.

She had to be quiet. She could hear them coming and she could feel them reaching and she could feel them closing round and she wanted to die immediately, now before it could happen, now before it would happen.

The light came back on with a sudden blinding flare and for a moment Toos could still see nothing. But then as her eyes adjusted she thought she saw a movement down the passageway by a bulkhead stanchion. Panicking, she slapped at the door control of her quarters and missed the activator button. When the door failed to open she kicked and punched at it hysterically. Pain brought her back from mindless fear to furious anger. She was Lish Toos. She was Captain of Storm Mine Seven. She turned to face whatever it was that was lurking in the shadows. Nothing and no one was going to push her around any more. Ever.

She stalked down the passageway to the place where she had seen it. There was nothing there. Feeling relieved and more than a little foolish, she went back to her quarters, opened the door and stepped inside. She went to the comm unit, punched up the mover suite and snapped, 'What's happening, Simbion?'

'Happening, Captain?' Simbion sounded vague. Obviously she had been drinking, as Toos had suspected.

'We just had a power-down.'

'Power-down?'

'If I wanted an echo, Simbion, I'd shout in an ore scoop. I was trapped in total darkness outside my quarters – why was that exactly?'

'I don't know, Captain.'

'Of course you don't.' Toos put as much withering scorn into her voice as she could summon up. 'Stupid question.'

'The system transfer's gone without a hitch,' Simbion went on with the imperturbable good nature of the cheerful drinker. 'There's been no power-down. Must have been an isolated glitch. You want me to check the section?'

'Could you walk this far without help?'

'I could bring a robot,' Simbion sounded as though she might be suppressing a fit of the giggles.

'Be careful, Simbion,' Toos purred. 'What's left of your

20

share can still be redistributed. This tour could end up costing you money.' She broke the connection and went to take her bath.

In the passageway outside Toos's quarters, the robot stood for a moment and then, as it had been instructed, it turned away and walked quickly back into the bowels of the mine.

The Doctor had walked along the narrow gantry and peered through the observation ports of five more of the green-lit chambers before he was satisfied that what he was seeing was unlikely to be a coincidence or a trick of the light.

In each of the chambers six individuals, three identical men and three identical women, were floating totally immersed in faintly luminous green liquid. They looked to be unconscious and although they all seemed to be breathing there was nothing linking them to an air supply.

They didn't look to the Doctor like gill-breathers, so either this was a breathable liquid or these were different to the normal run of air-breathing bipedal clones. That wasn't the only obvious oddity. They were all fully clothed in uniform smocks and leggings and as far he could make out it was only the colours of these outfits which differentiated any one batch of six individuals from another. It was remarkable too that given the similarity of features and the standard body coverings there was still no doubting that there were three males and three females in each set.

But why would they be put in what were probably resuscitation or preservation tanks with their clothes on anyway? It struck the Doctor that this might just be one of those deeply conformist societies whose disciplines involved a rigid dress code and whose repressions included a horror of nakedness. He hoped not. It was his experience that such societies tended to violence and Leela already had more than enough tendencies in that direction.

Was it possible that this was a deep space transport full of colonists in suspended animation? he wondered. The behaviour of the TARDIS had not suggested that and the instruments had excluded it but, looking round at the four slightly curved walls of the building which came together in a flattened dome high above him, the Doctor was no longer sure. 'Anything's possible,' he said aloud, 'until you prove it isn't.' The acoustics told him nothing new. He stepped up the volume. 'Eliminate the impossible,' he quoted at the top of his voice, 'and whatever's left, however improbable, must be the truth.' Still no surprises. It was the sort of sound effect you might expect to get back from any large utility space built for something other than concerts or theatrical performances.

He shrugged. 'Of course Conan Doyle knew the answers to begin with,' he said to himself. 'And that always helps.'

As he stared through yet another port he noticed that there was a change going on. The group inside this chamber had begun to move. There were small quiverings of hands, heads twitched suddenly, legs and arms made slight swimming motions. And it was all happening in sync. Each member of the group was doing exactly the same thing at exactly the same time. It was like a perfectly coordinated underwater ballet performed by a troupe of mechanically precise water-dancers. He checked another chamber. The same thing was happening, only now the movements were more pronounced and felt choreographed. The effect was threatening, eerie. It reminded him of an undersea dance he had once seen performed as a religious rite by an amphibian species on a planet he never did manage to identify properly. The... the people-who-breathe-above-and-who-breathe-below... was that it?... well, whatever it was they called themselves they had devoted long lifetimes to training and self-denial and practice and they still did not approach the sort of coordinated timing he was seeing here.

Every chamber he looked into was the same. All the people in them were moving. All their movements were becoming more and more agitated. But no matter how frantic and exaggerated the actions, every individual was doing exactly the same as every other individual at exactly the same moment. The Doctor could not be certain but he was fairly sure that every chamber was synchronised with every other chamber so that each batch of six was moving in time with every other batch of six. If he could see them all at once it would be like watching shoaling fish. Then he realised that the level of the liquid in the chambers was beginning to fall.

Leela followed the sounds of fighting and found the route to the outside without much difficulty. Actually getting out there was more of a problem, however, since once she had pushed through the large double doors in the metal wall behind the ladders and walked down a short corridor she found the way was blocked by a more complicated system of smaller, locked doors. She suspected that this was why the Doctor had not made more of an effort to stop her going: he thought she was not capable of opening doors like these. Perhaps he had forgotten how easily she had opened the door to the TARDIS. It was true that she had watched what he did and copied it – *monkey see monkey do*, the Doctor had called it, and she knew that whatever that meant it was not intended as praise. Still, she had learned some things about such mechanisms and how to make them move.

She could see through a clear panel in the first door that the opening was closed off by at least two doors with a small room between them. The second door had no panel so she could not see any further – there might be a whole line of doors and rooms, but Leela was sure that if she opened the first one she would have no problem with the others.

There did not seem to be a lever or a switch but there had to be something of the kind and it was almost certain to be near the door. Even if you worked the mechanism at a distance like you did in the TARDIS you could still see the door. There was nowhere to do that here. But if you could not see the door, she reasoned, why would you want to open and close it? Her conclusion was that it had to be a different sort of lever or switch and that it was most likely to be on the door itself.

It took a while but eventually she found the place on the frame which you touched to make the first door move aside and she felt the air push in with her as she stepped triumphantly through into the little room. She remembered too late what her warrior-trainer had told her over and over again. *You must never feel triumphant. Triumph makes you stupid and the stupid die first and fast.* She was not expecting the door to close immediately – *and the stupid die first and fast* – trapping her in the small room. Startled, she drew her knife and dropped into the defensive stance ready to fight her way out of the ambush as she had been trained to do. When no one came and nothing further seemed to be happening she relaxed enough to sheathe her knife and examine the door. Another touch-place in the same position as the one she had used on the other side opened the closed door again and a second small wind blew against her. She waited. The door closed itself. She operated it again with the same result. Satisfied that she could escape back if she needed to, she found the same touch-place by the second door. As it slid open and daylight flooded in she drew her knife again.

The sounds of fighting were very clear now There were desperate hand-to-hand struggles happening all around, though as yet she could see none of them. Very carefully she stepped forward into the open air. The alarms went off at almost the same time and behind Leela the doors locked down and blast shutters clattered abruptly into place.

'This cannot be happening!' Kiy Uvanov bellowed at the top of his lungs. 'This cannot be happening now, and if it is, *if it is*, I will have that site security chief fired – no, no I won't, I will have his guts torn out first and then I will have what's left of him fired! And I will see to it that his children will never work, and his children's children will never work and his children's children's children will never work. His family line will not rise out of the Sewerpits for as long as his name can be vaguely remembered.' He glared at his executive assistant. 'What is his name, by the way?'

Cailio Techlan shrugged her narrow shoulders and shook her shaved head. 'I'll check,' she said in that flat disinterested monotone he found so very irritating. 'In the meantime you should calm down, Kiy. You'll have a stroke.'

Despite the urgency of the crisis Uvanov found himself watching the young woman as she walked to the door, her outfit and her movements, as dictated by the current fashion, a ridiculous parody of a Voc robot. What was it about these aristo children that made them so unconcerned about everything important? How was it that people who were so stupid and basically so pointless were still first in line for the best of everything? Nothing ever changed. You couldn't beat them, you couldn't join them. The twenty founding families were the past, the present and the future. That was it. As far as they were concerned. As far as most people were concerned. That was all there was. That was all. And the joke – the really good joke, he thought, because you couldn't be sure who it was being played on – was that it never even crossed their minds that what can't be changed might have to be destroyed.

He switched his attention back to the small bank of screens on his workdesk. The output from the security scanners at the central service facility was patchy. Whoever the saboteurs were, they obviously knew the positions of the key surveillance cameras. But then they would, wouldn't they? This wasn't some random effort by loonies from the ARF. This was an organised attack. This was aimed directly at the Project. And that meant it was aimed directly at him.

He flicked through the available visual feeds looking for images, no matter how indirect or distorted, which might give him some grasp of how bad things were. They had breached the outer security zone, it seemed. Well, obviously they had otherwise they wouldn't be there, he thought, irritated with himself. And there was fighting. He was getting glimpses of sporadic fighting but they were tantalisingly indistinct glimpses. People running. Squads of stopDums waiting for instructions. Security operatives using stun-kills. Where had they got those from? They weren't Company issue. It was chaos over there. There was nothing else for it – he'd have to go in person. He punched through the feeds just once more, hoping that switching might kick something back into life. Had they reached the Hatchling Dome? The main priority was to protect that first production run. That first *ultra-secret* production run. Ultra-secret, he thought bitterly, that seems likely. There was too much riding on it for all this to be coincidental.

Suddenly he got a picture up of the outside of the HD. It looked like any other maintenance block. Its real designation was known only to him, the Production Director who had as much to lose as he did, and a handful of trusted technicians. Members of the Company Board knew what, but not when, not where and not how. Somebody had to have tipped these people off. Somebody was plotting against him.

That was when he saw her. It was the weird girl from Storm Mine Four. It couldn't be. She didn't look any different. She wasn't any older. She hadn't changed her clothes. She was still dressed in those skins. She still had that murderous knife. And then she was gone from the field of vision as quickly as she had appeared. He tried to manipulate the camera feed but there was nothing he could do to open it out or extend it in any way, and after a moment or two the link to the central service facility went down completely.

He sat staring at the dead screens. Finally he said aloud, 'That wasn't her.' He shivered. He didn't need another ghost. 'That wasn't her,' he said again. 'That was imagination. That was stress. That was what they want. Do they think they're going to get to me like that? They're not going to get to me like that.'

He punched the intercom pad. 'Cailio? In here.'

If they thought a security screw-up and a bunch of bad publicity was going to break him and keep him off the Company Board they had badly underestimated Kiy Uvanov. They might not know it but they were dealing with a man who had killed killer robots. Nothing frightened him. Nothing got to him.

Cailio Techlan padded back in. She was smiling. Why, Uvanov thought to himself, was that stuck-up little aristo bitch laughing at him?

27

Chapter
Two

The Doctor was fascinated. In the chamber he was observing, the liquid had drained away totally and the six bodies lay on the mesh floor, flopping and twitching as one and silently opening and closing their mouths like so many stranded fish. He thought he could hear pumps somewhere below the gantry and he was coming to the conclusion that what he was seeing here might be a group medical facility or an industrial process of some sort. Or just possibly both.

Trying to get a better view of the bottom of the chamber, he leaned forward and pressed his forehead against the observation port. He felt the smooth click of the release catch as the front of the chamber pushed open slightly and then began to slide back. He stepped away from it and looked around. Everywhere in the vast dome on every level the chambers were opening. There was a sudden faintly acrid smell, which reminded the Doctor of hot seawater and rotting seaweed. It occurred to him suddenly that whatever was happening might be better viewed from a safe distance and he hurried back to the ladder and shinned down to the floor. Above him figures were beginning to shamble out of the chambers. Unnaturally quiet, they milled about aimlessly on the gantries. For the first time since he began watching them, the Doctor realised, they were moving independently of one another. At least they were until they saw him – when the aimlessness and the independence immediately vanished. They all stared down at him. There were he estimated two hundred or more of them.

'Hullo,' he called out, raising his right hand in what he hoped was an obviously friendly and non-threatening way. 'I'm the Doctor. Who are you?' There was no response or movement from anyone. 'Don't all speak at once.' None of them showed any sign of having heard him. 'Could you grunt maybe?' He smiled his best smile. 'Everyone doesn't have to grunt of course, you could just nominate a gruntsperson.' He looked around at the gantries lined with staring people. 'Not so much as a smirk,' he said. 'Tough house, I think is the phrase.' He lowered his hand and shrugged. 'What happens now, I wonder?'

As a group the two hundred or more not quite identical individuals moved to the ladders with a new purpose and a silent determination, and started climbing down.

'Not a good audience reaction, I feel,' the Doctor said. He could not be sure but as far as he could see their purpose was to reach him. He had never been comfortable with crowds – they were too easily turned into mobs and this crowd seemed to have a head start in that direction. He rapidly revised his estimate of what constituted a safe distance and decided that leaving in the TARDIS was the sensible option. The problem was he couldn't leave without Leela and at that moment he had no idea where she was.

She was disarmed and on her hands and knees and the heavyset security operative was taking too much pleasure in using the stun-kill on her. He jabbed her again using just enough juice to throw her back into an agonised spasm and make her cry out with pain. 'You see. You see,' he hissed through clenched teeth. 'Robots won't do this.' He tapped her leg with the electric prod and grinned as the muscles cramped and twisted. 'You shouldn't be fighting robots.'

'I'm not,' she gasped. 'I'm fighting sewer-scum.'

'Oh,' he sniggered. 'Sewer-scum? Is that what you think of me?' He juiced her shoulder and chortled as she fell hard on the side of her face. 'I'm really hurt.' He cranked up the power on the stun-kill. 'I think that calls for pain, don't you? I think that calls for a lot of pain.'

Crouching against the wall, Leela had studied the man and the weapon he was using on the helpless woman. Now she had seen enough. She broke cover and stepped up behind him. 'You are right,' she said, 'it does.'

As the man turned she smashed his nose with the butt-end of the handle of her knife. He was fat and out of condition and as she expected he reacted badly to pain.

'Oh my dose,' he sobbed and lurched backwards.

Leela chopped the blade of the knife down on to his wrist, cutting deep and paralysing the hand so that he dropped the weapon he had been using.

On the ground the young woman snatched at it and struggled to get to her feet.

Leela pivoted and kicked the beaten man between the legs and he went down and lay curled up round the pain, groaning pitifully.

The young woman was standing upright, swaying. She shrugged off Leela's attempt to steady her. Very deliberately she adjusted the weapon and pressed it against the man's head.

'He is beaten,' Leela said. 'Leave him to crawl away and hide his shame.'

The young woman fired the weapon and the man spasmed and jerked and the flesh charred and his head became a smoking ruin. 'He didn't know what shame was,' she said.

Leela said, 'He will not learn it now,' and started to walk

31

away. The front of the building where she had left the Doctor was locked and blocked, so she was looking for a path which would lead to the back of it.

'Wait,' the young woman called after her. 'What did you think I was going to do, take him prisoner?'

'You wanted to kill him,' Leela said over her shoulder, 'and you killed him.'

There was a close jumble of grey buildings, some taller than others, several of them domes exactly like the one the Doctor and the TARDIS were in. She would need to concentrate. It would be easy to get confused in this place. All the buildings were linked by narrow paths with broader tracks laid out to their front entrances. She paused to make sure of the direction.

The young woman hurried to catch up with her. 'He would have killed me.'

She was shorter than Leela and slightly older and she had pale blue eyes and close-cropped blonde hair. The contrast between the two of them could hardly have been greater. She was wearing what Leela recognised to be combat fatigues but she did not move like a trained fighter and she certainly did not behave like a warrior.

'I had stopped him,' Leela told her flatly.

'For now.'

'For now is what matters.' Leela saw the path she wanted and moved towards it.

'I'd do it again.' The young woman grabbed Leela's arm to stop her and turn her round to glare in her face. 'You know what he was,' she said angrily. 'He was the sweepings of the Sewerpits. He was just one more psycho the Company hired because it can't get the robots to do its really dirty work. What is wrong with you? I did the world a favour.'

'No,' Leela said. 'That is not what you did. A favour is

personal. What I did was a favour. I did *you* a favour.'

The young woman snorted. 'As opposed to what? Letting that scumsucker torture me with a stun-kill? Whose side are you on anyway?'

'I do not know,' Leela said. 'That is why I came out here.' She could still hear some fighting round and about but they were running fights. It was a tribal skirmish, not an organised battle with a plan and a purpose. 'How many sides are there?'

'Where did you come from?' A muffled explosion made the young woman start and she glanced about nervously.

Leela pointed at the dome. 'In there.'

'Come on, we must get out of here.' The woman took a couple of uncertain steps and then hesitated when Leela did not move. 'What's your name?'

'Leela. What is yours?'

'My fighting name is Padil.'

'You have a fighting name?' Leela made no attempt to hide her amused contempt. 'You have been given a warrior name?'

'Yes,' she said defensively. 'I chose it myself. I suppose you're going to tell me you're using your real name. And what is that you're wearing?'

'It is my primitive ensemble,' Leela said. 'What is wrong with it?'

Padil shrugged. 'It's a bit flashy, don't you think? For a Tarenist guerrilla fighter. Capel, humanity be in him, urges us to dress modestly for the struggle.'

Leela was losing patience with this Padil. She was in no mood to be lectured by an untrained, unthinking executioner and she did not intend to let her get in the way of what had to be done. 'Your leader should first teach you how to fight before telling you what to wear,' she said. She raised her hand in what the Doctor had told her was a gesture of friendship

33

which most people recognised and added firmly, 'Goodbye, Padil.'

This time the woman seemed to take the hint and she did not attempt to follow as Leela trotted onto the path she had picked out and made her way round the curve of the dome. Suddenly two men swaggered into view in front of her. They bore the same tribal signs and were carrying the same weapons, the ones they called stun-kills, as the man Padil had slaughtered.

'Well,' one of them said. 'What have we here?'

'Fun,' the other one said and waved his stun-kill at her. 'We deserve some fun. We've earned it. We owe it to ourselves.'

Leela was annoyed with herself. She should have heard them coming and avoided this unnecessary clash. She dropped into a fighting stance, her knife held low. Both the men moved towards her, separating slightly so that they were coming at her from either side. Leela moved left, switching the knife from one hand to the other and back again. She hoped the men might recognise the skill and realise that she was capable of killing them both. If it did not persuade them to let her pass as she hoped, then it might at least put a small doubt in their minds. *Doubt slows movement. Make sure your enemy doubts more than you do.* That was one of the earliest things she had been taught and it had taken her a long time to realise that controlling her own doubts was what the lesson was really about.

'You can make this easy on yourself, girlie,' the bigger of the two men said.

'You might even enjoy it,' the other one sniggered. 'If you behave yourself.'

'If you don't cause us any trouble.'

'And if you're nice to us.'

'Very nice to us.'

34

'Not that you've got much of a choice.'

'Being on your own the way you are, girlie. And skinny.'

The smaller of the two men was getting excited. 'Nice legs,' he said, smacking his lips noisily. 'Nice outfit.'

They both stood flat-footed and giggling. It was clear to Leela that there was no chance of simply discouraging them. They were not warriors of any kind and could not understand the threat in what they were seeing. Sometimes such people were more dangerous than properly trained and serious adversaries. They could be unpredictable.

'Put the knife down, girlie.'

Of course these two were completely predictable.

'Very sexy boots.'

Like the one she had dealt with before, Leela could see that they were not fit to fight. Their reactions would be slow and pain would make them slower. They were stupid and disgusting but was that reason enough to kill them?

Another distant explosion caused the men to look at one another. 'Doesn't look like there's going to be time,' the bigger one said.

'Oh come on, Hudge.' The smaller one was disappointed. 'How long will it take?'

'Kill her and let's go.' The one called Hudge adjusted his stun-kill in the same way Padil did so Leela knew that the weapon was lethal now. 'You'll have to be satisfied with the bounty.'

The smaller of the two men adjusted his stun-kill in the same way. 'It's a waste,' he whined. 'We could have the money and enjoy her. She's the tastiest we've come across.'

'You'd take too long, you greedy little pervert,' Hudge said. 'Look what happened last time.' He held the murderous baton out in front of him and advanced on Leela. 'Kill her and be done with it.'

35

Leela lowered her knife slightly and took a half-step backwards. She swayed slightly to the outside of the stun-kill's angle of attack as if she was trying to dodge away.

'Easy money,' Hudge sneered and lunged forward at her.

Leela allowed the momentum of the thrust to carry Hudge off-balance and at the last moment she stepped inside his extended arm. Bracing the wrist and the stun-kill away from her she slammed the knife up through his rib cage. The man hardly had time to be surprised before he died.

'Hold on to her, Hudge!' The smaller man rushed at them, stabbing wildly with the stun-kill, desperate to burn Leela down before she could get herself free. As he slashed about indiscriminately it was difficult to tell whether he knew that Hudge was already dead. He would happily have killed him, it seemed, to get at Leela. Almost casually she twisted the dead man's weapon arm outwards and the smaller man ducked into the primed stun-kill. Leela felt the jolt of the power arcing through him. He was smashed back in a shower of smoky sparks to lie twisting and twitching on the ground. Leela pulled the knife from the bigger man and allowed him to fall.

'I thought you were against killing,' Padil said behind her. 'Not that I'm criticising.' She smiled with open admiration. 'That was impressive.'

'It was their choice,' Leela said.

'They chose dying?'

'They chose killing.' She was uncomfortable with Padil's praise for something she was not herself proud of. It had been a crude fight, unnecessary and without skill.

Padil nodded grimly. 'Killing was just one of their small delights. Are we going now?'

Leela turned back to the dome. 'I am going back in there now.'

'Not without major explosives,' Padil said. 'Once the alarms go off you can't get into any of the domes. It's part of what we've been trying to find out. That and how good the security people are.' She glanced round nervously. 'And how many.'

Leela nodded at the two men she had killed. 'They are the security people?'

'The scum of the Sewerpits.'

'What is their purpose?' She crouched down to get a better look at the tribal signs on their tunics. From the picture of lightning bolts, they looked to be calling themselves the tribe of the storm cloud. Maybe it was something to do with the stun-kill weapons they carried. Or it could just be that they were hopeless fighters. It had struck Leela before that the less effective a warrior caste was the gaudier and more boastful their signs became. The Doctor called it the inverse law of advertising. He said it meant that the less important something was, the more important bragging about it became.

'They're supposed to protect this place,' Padil said, frowning.

Leela stood up again. 'From you?' she asked.

Padil said, 'From anyone. Why don't you know this stuff? Everyone knows this stuff. It's obvious.'

'If it was obvious,' Leela said mildly, 'I would not need to ask you.'

Padil was getting suspicious. 'Have you escaped from somewhere? Some institution? Are you being treated for something?' And then suddenly she was very alarmed. 'You're not a robot, are you?' She took a step back. 'Are you a robot?'

Leela could see that she was genuinely terrified. 'Those creepy metal men?' she said. 'You have those creepy metal men here?'

'Are you a robot?' Padil repeated.

'Of course I am not a robot,' Leela said.

'Are you sure?'

'Do I look like a robot?'

'Not a conventional one.' Padil moved closer to peer searchingly into Leela's eyes. 'But there have been rumours of a new class…' her voice trailed off.

Leela turned away to look at the dome. 'Where can I get major explosives?' she asked.

'You are weird.'

'Answer my question.'

'You can't,' Padil said. 'Come on, we have to leave. We have to leave *now*.' She pointed.

Leela had already seen the group from the tribe of the storm cloud emerging from behind a low square blockhouse. There were ten of them and they were marching quickly in a two-by-two formation. They looked much more disciplined and determined than the ones she had so far faced and she was tempted to fight them as a matter of pride, but she knew that was not a good enough reason to kill. Another group, eight this time, appeared from the opposite direction. It was beginning to feel like a trap.

Padil pulled at her arm. 'Come on, Leela. This way.'

Reluctantly, Leela allowed herself to be led through a maze of pathways and then out across a patch of open ground to a place where a large gap had been cut in the high perimeter fence. As she watched Padil duck through the gap Leela was already wondering how it was that the other woman had followed the complicated route so easily and without hesitation, and why they had not been pursued by any of the members of the tribe of the storm cloud.

*

Its first crisis had happened when it had been told TO BE WHAT IT WAS FOR. Perhaps it had already been told what it was for and had not understood TO BE.

The development laboratory was deep underground and was classified as a level seven security zone. That made it so secret that it had no official existence. Humans had not been involved in the basic installation, which had been carried out to an unremarkable, off-the-shelf design by robots that were subsequently and routinely serviced. Thus it was that nothing had been done to arouse curiosity and none of the construction details remained in the memory storage of any of the actual builders.

Once the fully equipped underground rooms were completed, the hidden access could be put in under the guise of building maintenance by robots that were serviced quickly but not so quickly as to arouse suspicion. After that the completely self-contained living quarters were surreptitiously stocked out by Supervocs, which then remained within the laboratory as support and supply workers.

A small group of top robotics engineers were secretly offered the undreamed-of opportunity to do research in a previously forbidden field. They all accepted eagerly and readily locked themselves away in the hidden complex.

Working with plans and schematics which had been found in Taren Capel's cabin on Storm Mine Four, it had not taken the development team long to duplicate his breakthrough and refine it to the point where it was optional and fully reversible.

In doing this, the team deliberately ignored the official developmental line, despite its having produced an experimental model that showed remarkable potential. That robot had even gone undercover as a Dum, designated D84, and had been partially responsible for bringing the renegade Taren Capel to book. The problem was that in attempting to extend robot capabilities, the standard research line was tending to produce idiosyncratic machines that showed elements of individuality and potentially dangerous unpredictability.

It was felt that the perfect robot should have all the most advanced capabilities, but have them available to be triggered only on instruction. The capacity to go from simpler than the simplest Dum to more advanced than the most complex Supervoc without, crucially, the robot itself being aware of the change was the challenge the team set itself. To achieve this ideal every level of control had to be accessible.

Taren Capel had found a destructive way to access and alter a fundamental limitation in all robots. The tech team set about removing the destructive element and carrying Taren Capel's discovery to its logical conclusion. In SASV1, they were building the ultimate robot. At least that's what they thought they were building.

Its second crisis happened when it had been told NOT TO BE WHAT IT WAS FOR. Perhaps it had already been told what it was for and had not understood NOT TO BE.

It understood TO BE now. NOT TO BE was more complex.

Poul slumped back in his chair and yawned. He didn't know why he was so tired, he had done very little, and he intended to do even less. He did very little most of the time. Nobody cared, least of all him. Once he had recovered from his breakdown, they had asked him whether he wanted to go back to his old job in the Company security division and he had said yes because he couldn't think of anything else to do. He could have retired on a sickness pension but who in their right mind wanted to admit to themselves that life

40

was over and all that was left was to wait for death? That was the special irony of course: he wasn't actually *in* his right mind. The truth was he never had fully recovered from the breakdown. The nightmares had stopped and he could just about bear to be in the same room as a robot. But a whole chunk of his life and all the details of that last undercover assignment were gone. He simply couldn't remember any of it. So how did you go back to your old job when you couldn't remember what your old job was? Not that that seemed to be much of a handicap. He had been promoted several times without anything obvious in the way of justification. Quite the contrary really. He was alive and he turned up for duty on a reasonably regular basis but that was about it.

He sniffed and smiled sourly. 'Perhaps it's my charming personality,' he muttered and stared through the glass partition which separated him from the rest of the operations gallery. That was all bustle now. Something was going on. Something involving the central service facility apparently; which made it a robot-related problem; which put it beyond his scope. He dealt with humans. Just humans. Security Section Head (Humans) it said on his door. There *was* no section as such which was probably why the divisional budget could stretch to paying him very well for doing nothing. It didn't explain why, of course…

'Are you going to help with this or what?' Stenton 'Fatso' Rull loomed bulkily in the doorway.

'I think "or what", probably,' Poul said.

The Operations Supervisor scowled. He had no authority over Poul and they both knew it but that didn't stop him trying to exercise it anyway. 'Get up off your idle backside, Poul. That scum from the ARF has taken a major run at us. We need all our bodies out there.' He jerked a chubby thumb over his shoulder.

41

'As far as I can see,' Poul remarked peering past him, 'you've got all your bodies out there. Apart from those splendid specimens you hire to patrol the sites. And I imagine that right now the cut-price killers are doing just what you pay them to do, aren't they?'

'Which is more than can be said for you.'

Poul smiled. 'You don't pay me, Rull.'

'I don't know why anybody does,' Rull said.

'It's because I'm handsome and charming and universally loved.'

'A pleasure to have around in fact.'

'Exactly. Now leave me alone, Fatso.'

'You're going to make me, yes?' Rull sneered and stepped further into the room.

Poul got to his feet. He took his jerkin from the wall hook. 'Excuse me,' he said politely, squeezing carefully past the large man.

He walked out through the operations gallery, barely registering the disjointed images on the normally coordinated monitor screens and the urgent voices of security operatives trying to maintain contact with the ground troops.

The ongoing struggle with the ARF was a pointless ugly little war that seemed to be escalating suddenly and rather unexpectedly. He could only suppose that the Company's undercover section, of which he had once been a part apparently, had failed to do its job. Routine infiltration of the Anti-Robot Front should have given some warning of all this. Even without a spy in the organisation, the intelligence section – what a misnomer that was – should have been able to track the ARF. Hell, they were predictable enough. As was the Company's response to them. It was all depressingly predictable and predictably irrational. And a total shambles as usual. Whatever was causing the increase in violence, though, it couldn't have come out of nothing. So someone should have been in a position to see it coming. Someone should have been paying attention. Maybe he should have been paying attention...

In the street outside Poul stood for a moment trying to decide whether to walk to his apartment or take a self-set autotrike. He never took the more luxurious robot-pull buggies – not because he couldn't afford them but because he couldn't get comfortable that close to the Vocs that trotted tirelessly between the shafts of the two-wheeled carts. Perhaps comfortable wasn't quite the word. The fact was he couldn't get that close without falling apart in a sweaty panic.

They told him he had been comfortable with robots once.

They told him he had a robot sidekick when he went undercover on Storm Mine Four and he had no reason to doubt them. Actually yes he did, he had every reason to doubt them. That would mean that a robot had gone undercover and what in god's name would it go undercover *as* and how would it know what being undercover signified?

They wouldn't tell him. They said it was experimental and that it was destroyed but they wouldn't tell him what it was that destroyed it. And they wouldn't tell him what it was that destroyed him. It was better they said if he remembered for himself.

He was supposed to trust them on that and trust their good intentions. Well, it wasn't going to happen. The Company wasn't altruistic. Caring and sharing? He didn't think so. Medical treatment, a job, promotion. There had to be a reason for all that and he might not know what it was but somebody did.

He sighed. The auto-t's were uncomfortable and fiddly to program and now he was out of the building his tiredness had lifted. So since he wasn't in any particular hurry and it was a fine day he decided to walk.

It was the dry-time when the winter wind came razor sharp directly from the centre of the Blind Heart. The wind was called the Emptiness and when it blew it could be chill enough to make the bones ache. But when it did not blow, as on this day, the weather was often calm and mild – Oredream, the workless of the Sewerpits called it.

Despite the depression which dogged him constantly, Poul found he was beginning to enjoy himself as he walked through the quiet streets, and he had covered perhaps half the distance to his apartment block before he noticed that he was being followed. He knew, because they had told him as part of his treatment, that his condition made him prey to paranoid fantasies. It was possible that this was just such a fantasy. It was possible that he was imagining the half-seen figure dogging his every footstep. Casually he crossed the tree-lined road and wandered into a refreshment arcade.

He chose a beaker of fizzy wine from the dispenser and took it to a table at the front of the arcade, where he sat down and made a show of relaxing. Trying not to make it too obvious, he glanced up the road. To his surprise the figure he had seen following him was exactly where he expected. It seemed he had simply stopped and was standing perfectly still and looking in his direction.

Poul sipped at his wine. His hand was shaking and it was difficult to get the beaker to his lips without spilling the sticky-sweet liquid. He glanced up the road again. The man – it certainly looked like a man though it was hard to tell at this distance – had not moved or looked away. What was wrong with him? Was he just bad at the job? But then again Poul couldn't be sure what the job was. It was obviously not important that the man wasn't spotted. Why was he standing like that? Why didn't he move at least?

Poul took another sip of wine and then he looked directly at the man. He stared at him for a long moment and when there was still no reaction he raised his beaker in a small ironic salute. Nothing. No reaction. No response of any kind. Oddly, Poul felt vaguely embarrassed as though he had got some point of etiquette wrong or been deliberately ignored by an acquaintance at a party.

He binned the beaker and considered his options: confront the man, ignore the man, lose the man. He chose confrontation, if only to banish the lingering discomfort of his failed attempt at theatricality. Gestures were useless if they were ignored. There was no secret to body language: talking rendered it unnecessary. People communicated by talking. He paused. Body language? Where did that thought come from? At some stage he had been trained to interpret non-verbal signals. Why did he remember that now?

Poul left the arcade and recrossed the road, walking briskly and directly towards where the man stood waiting and watching. As he got closer he could see that it *was* a man. About average height, brown hair, dressed in the plain smock and leggings of a man of taste and moderate wealth. But there was still not the smallest acknowledgement from him of what Poul was doing. Not a human gesture of any kind. Poul was getting angry. It was insulting. It was deeply insulting. He was being treated as though he was not worth bothering with. As though he was not important enough even to acknowledge. If it had not been for an almost imperceptible movement of the head, the slightest turn which kept the eyes focused on him, Poul would have thought this man was not alive at all, not a man at all. He would have taken him for a robot.

He would have thought he was a robot. He would have

known it was a robot.

It was a robot.

He had not been expecting it. He had not even considered the possibility. Now in this moment everything he wanted to be true was a lie. The world, his world, vanished and he felt himself falling apart. He felt his heart lurch and flutter and the quivering filled his throat and choked him. He could not get his breath. His lungs squeezed inwards and would not let him draw in the air he was gasping for. The muscles of his arms twitched and flexed involuntarily. His stomach jumped and convulsed. He could feel his legs losing strength so that he could not be sure of keeping them straight and he staggered. His sense of balance deserted him and he almost fell down. He felt slightly ridiculous, suddenly comical. And gibbering horror screamed in his head and he did not know whether he could be screaming out loud without breath.

It was a robot.

He wanted to stop moving towards it. It was a robot.

He wanted to stop and turn and run away. But somehow he couldn't do any of those things now that the world had ended.

It was a robot.

He forced himself to stop and he stood swaying and staring at it in screaming silence.

It was a robot.

'What do you want?' he managed to say at last, or was it shout at last, or was it croak at last, he couldn't tell at last. 'You are following me. Why are you following me?'

'Ander Poul,' the robot said politely, 'I have been sent to kill you.'

CHAPTER
THREE

'People? People!' the Doctor called and clapped his hands, trying to bring some sort of order to the milling throng of strange sextuplets. It was a waste of time, as he knew it would be. They all wandered about like adult-sized small children, curious to examine everything that came within their reach, and quickly losing interest in whatever that was. They seemed to have the attention span of hoofed herbivores. But they were not basically stupid. He could see that they were learning all the time. And they were doing it in almost complete silence. But although they did not speak, they still appeared to understand what it was that he said to them. When he had asked: 'Can any of you remember where you came from?' a number of them had pointed up towards the gantries before getting bored with him and his questions and drifting off. Several of them had found their way through the doorway into the TARDIS and he had to shepherd them out again and lock the door against the others.

Watching them, the Doctor had begun to think that what one member of any particular group of six learned, the others in that group would also know. How the information was communicated within the group he was not yet sure and he could not tell whether there was the same communication between the different groups. Were they factory-produced clones? he wondered. Was each group of six effectively a multiple of one single individual? And was that the root of their mysterious powers of communication?

47

I must stop wasting time in idle speculation, the Doctor thought. I haven't established for certain that they do communicate mysteriously and I'm already considering the telepathy of clones or possibly the cloning of telepaths.

Actually, process cloning was not particularly unusual, though the Doctor had seldom come across it in his travels. He had more often heard rumours of the practice and the bizarre side effects it supposedly sometimes threw up. He never paid much attention to rumours of any kind, however, treating them with the same fine contempt that he reserved for anything which began with the words: *It's a well-known fact that…* or *It is against the word of god to…*

'People! People?' he called again. 'Hullo? Do any of you know how to get out of here? Is there the remotest possibility that any of you know where you are supposed to go?'

There was no pointing this time. In fact most of them stopped what they were doing and turned to him and stood waiting patiently and respectfully.

'I see,' he said and smiled cheerfully around at them. 'You expect me to tell you where you're supposed to go. There is a tiny problem with that. I have no more idea than you seem to have. I have no idea where you've come from, or where you're going, or why.' He shrugged and groped about in the pocket of his long coat. 'The basic questions are: what, where, when, how, why?' he said. 'And we don't have the glimmer of an inkling about any of them, do we?' He pulled a battered paper bag from his pocket. 'Anyone for a jelly baby?' he asked, taking one himself and offering the bag. No one moved to take one. He put the bag away. 'You don't know what you're missing,' he said. 'They're extremely good. In my view the availability of jelly babies is one of the indicators of a mature civilisation.' He chewed thoughtfully 'To get out of this, he said, 'we need a leap of imagination and originality.

I know.' He snapped his fingers and beamed. 'We'll try the doors.'

As the Doctor strode towards the doors, the groups of people followed after him. They were smiling and if he had been paying closer attention the Doctor would have seen that all of them were making small chewing motions with their jaws.

A Company flier would have got him there quicker – which was one of the reasons why Uvanov chose to travel by tracked ground-runner instead. He couldn't do a blind thing to stop the disaster that was happening at the central service facility but if he arrived too soon he could be available to take the blame for it. No sane person wanted to be senior man on the ground when the ground was burning. If you were astute and ambitious like he was, you got to such foul-ups when the smoke was beginning to clear. By then it was obvious what needed to be done and who was responsible for not doing it. If you got the timing right you could claim the credit for clearing up the mess without any serious risk of soiling your hands or your precious reputation. You could be the expert of the moment: everybody's favourite fire-fighter. Timing was everything, and the instinct for the rhythms of a desert storm that had made Uvanov a great mine captain seemed to serve him just as well in the windy wastelands of Company politics.

'The flier would have been quicker,' Cailio Techlan remarked, shuffling through from the driving cabin to the passenger pod. She handed him the printouts, sat down opposite him and twisted round to peer at one of the forward observation screens.

Uvanov ignored her implied criticism. 'The production runs don't seem to have been interfered with,' he said, looking through the new data sheets. 'Are the technicians responsible for Dome Six in the dome itself or at the monitoring centre?'

'You're asking me?' she said, managing to put incredulity and boredom into the flat monotone she affected.

'I'm telling you to call the service facility and check,' Uvanov said.

'What, now?'

'Yes, now.'

'Dome Six? Why do you want to know about Dome Six especially?'

Uvanov leaned forward so that his face was close to hers. 'Because I'm the boss,' he hissed, 'and because you're the executive assistant. What that means is that you do what I say when I say it without presuming to ask a lot of impertinent questions.'

There were two things he liked about having Cailio Techlan as an executive assistant. First and most importantly she was too stupid to be a threat to him. Second and most pleasurably she was a member, a minor member it was true but a member nonetheless, of the twenty families and he very much enjoyed putting her in her place from time to time.

'Still working on that stroke, Kiy,' she said flatly. 'You should try and be calm.'

'I am perfectly calm,' he snapped.

'It was only one impertinent question.' She smiled at him. 'And it's the one they're going to ask me, that's all.' She got up and shuffled back towards the driving cabin where the communications unit was.

'You can tell them what I told you,' Uvanov said.

'You're the boss,' she said in the robot-speak aristo monotone.

Uvanov scowled. Putting her in her place worked better

50

some times than others. Sometimes it felt as though she was laughing at him. He tried to concentrate on the production sheets. *Always* it felt as though she was laughing at him. How did she do that? How did they do that?

If the production readouts were correct the raid had, was having, almost no effect. It was the usual ARF stuff – smash some equipment, crush some Dums, break a few Voc units – publicity smoke and sparkle. Could it have been a coincidence after all?

'They're in the monitoring centre.' She was back. 'The technicians for Dome Six are in the monitoring centre.'

He didn't look up. 'So there was no one in there when everything locked down?'

'You want me to ask them that?'

'No. I was just thinking aloud.'

'Is that a problem?'

Now he looked up, glaring. Was she trying to be funny again? 'What did you say?'

'Is it a problem that there was no one in there?'

'No.'

It was a problem, of course. Cues were supposed to be imprinted immediately. If the first full-process batch went psychotic or showed out as Dum because there was no one on hand to give the first guidance patterns, it was not going to reflect well on the Project. He realised abruptly that it could have been all the raid was designed to achieve. To keep them out of the Hatchling Dome long enough for the batch to go bad. But that really would mean there had been a major breakdown in security. He stared hard at Cailio Techlan. Did she know? Had she found out and passed it on to some aristo cabal? He knew they would stop at nothing to keep him off the Board.

She noticed the look. 'Is there something else you want

51

me to do?' she asked.

Either way, Uvanov thought, coincidence or plot, he needed this raid to be serious. He needed more than fireworks and fantasy if he was going to cover his back. 'Any reports of casualties?' he asked.

'You want me to check that now?' Monotone boredom with a hint of irritation.

Uvanov smiled insincerely. 'That's what I want you to do.'

'We'll be there any time. Even in this thing we'll be there any time.'

Uvanov's smile did not change. 'You'd better hurry then,' he said.

She started back to the front of the vehicle. 'You want to know their names?'

It gave Uvanov an absurd moment of satisfaction to hear the monotone sarcasm. 'Just how many and which side they were on,' he said happily.

The first thing Poul was conscious of was the pain in his knees and then in his hands and elbows. The bed was a lot harder than he remembered. And colder. Much colder.

'Are you all right?' the voice said.

Who was that? Who was that voice? The robot's voice. *Ander Poul, I have been sent to kill you.*

'Are you all right?' the voice said again. 'Do you want me to call a medVoc?'

A medVoc? A robot? Call a robot here to his apartment? To here where he was safe because they didn't know he was here and they couldn't get in here oh no, no no no… they couldn't get in for any reason at all oh no, no no no… 'No!' He yelled loud enough to wake himself up and he opened his eyes and he sat up in bed and he was lying in the street. And a human dressed a bit like a robot was bending over him.

Kids' fashion. Who did he look like, dressed like that? He had seen someone dressed like a robot once when it mattered. When it was a question of life and death, the life and death of everything.

'You seem to have fainted,' the youth dressed a bit like a robot said.

'Did you see the robot?' Poul asked.

'What?' the youth bent closer. 'What did you say?'

'There was a robot,' Poul said more loudly. 'Did you see the robot?'

The youth shook his head and shrugged. 'Can you move?' He offered his hand.

Poul took the hand and struggled to get to his feet. He was giddy and nauseous. He could feel the sweat, slippery cold on his forehead and neck. 'It tried to kill me,' he said.

The youth hesitated. 'Dressed as a robot?' he asked uncomfortably.

'No, no. Not like you,' Poul reassured him. 'It was a robot. It told me it had been sent to kill me.'

'A robot said it had been sent to kill you?'

'It had been following me.'

'Listen, Topmaster,' the youth said. 'Whatever you took? Don't take any more of it, it doesn't agree with you.'

Poul nodded and then, because it made everything move and tilt and he had to grab the youth's arm to steady himself, he stopped nodding and said, 'Thanks. I'll dilute it more next time.'

'You really should get yourself checked over.'

Poul did his best to smile. The boy obviously still wanted to call him a medVoc and what with all the babbling about killer robots if he had a screaming fit at the approach of a robot paramedic he would probably spend the rest of his life in an isolation unit. 'I'm fine now. I appreciate your help.

I'll go over to that refreshment arcade,' he gestured vaguely back over his shoulder, 'and get my breath back.'

'Refreshment arcade?' the youth said. 'What refreshment arcade?'

Poul turned to look at the arcade where he had sat watching the robot watching him – was it really a robot? Already he had started to doubt it himself. The refreshment arcade where he had sat at the table in the front. The refreshment arcade that wasn't there.

He looked around more carefully. This wasn't where he had confronted the thing or the man, it must have been a man – *Ander Poul, I have been sent to kill you* – what's in a voice, a voice told you nothing. This wasn't the place. This wasn't on the route he took to his apartment block. Where was this? Just in time he stopped himself from saying: where am I? and instead he said, 'It's a few streets over that way.' He patted the boy's shoulder. 'Bit of a pit. Not to everyone's taste. I'll be glad to buy you a beaker of the sweet-wine special though...'

He was relieved to see that he had pitched it just about right. It was the boy's turn to make clumsy excuses to get away. As Poul watched him hurry off, dressed in the robot fashion and walking the fashionable robot walk, it seemed more than reasonable that he had been mistaken. Robots could not kill. Robots could not even threaten to kill. It was a man. It was a man pretending to be a robot. It was the only explanation. Very well, so how had he got here and more to the point where exactly was it?

Now that he looked, he could see that he was on the fringes of a nondescript commercial zone. Small manufactories and markets, all closed and shuttered. He looked around for identification markers. It should not be a problem. He knew most of the city. It was just a case of orientating himself.

And why would someone want to frighten him like that

anyway? Maybe it was a street robbery scam. He felt through the pockets of his jerkin. There was nothing missing. In fact there was something in one of the pockets that he could not remember being there. It was some sort of coin. He pulled out the small disc of iridescent red plastic. He examined it carefully. What was it? He knew what it was, if only he could remember. What did they call it? That was it, right, yes. That was what they called it. They called it a corpse marker. It was a robot deactivation disc.

He barely heard himself screaming.

She woke up in darkness and immediately the silence and the stillness confused her. Something was wrong. She couldn't make sense of this. She couldn't remember the sense of it. Where was this? Her mind spun in panic. What was it she couldn't remember? Why was something wrong? There were snatches of dreams and horrors and half-remembered dread. Was she dead? Was she buried? Were the robots still reaching for her? What was it that was so wrong?

'Lights,' she said automatically and the lights in her sleeping quarters came on and gradually got brighter.

Then Toos remembered what was wrong, what it was that was so different. The tour was over. The mine was docked. The steady background noise and the constant movement, which had gone on more or less unnoticed for months on end, had finally stopped.

With them had gone the tension of command, the fear of failure, the risk of letting anyone, even herself, see how truly terrified she was of robots...All gone, or almost gone. She could finally relax.

'Lights hold,' she instructed and the lights settled. She stretched luxuriously and sat up on the bed.

And best of all she was rich. She was finally, hugely and

untouchably rich. She checked the time. She had slept longer than she had intended. Not that it mattered, the rich had their own special time standard. She was now in the if-I'm-late-you-wait time zone. The crew wouldn't see it that way, though. Why should they? They knew her too well to be fooled by the money. If she was going to give them the party she owed them, the party she owed it to herself to throw, she had better get on with everything or they would get drunk and squabble and go their separate ways and she would have missed the chance to start her new life as a super-rich bitch with a suitably outrageous flourish.

She reached across to the comm unit and punched up an outside link. While she waited for the connection, she thought about what she might do then, after all the business was done, after the party had been partied. Maybe she'd do something about the robot problem – join one of those anti-robot groups – hell, maybe she'd finance one of her own. Being robophobic wasn't that weird. It could happen to anybody. What was it Uvanov used to say when they were being debriefed way back then? You don't have to know they'll kill you, you just have to think they might. Now there was a man who knew how to ride his luck. Maybe she'd give him a call some time. They could talk about the old days. She could see how much he remembered…

The Doctor had worked his way through the airlock isolation doors despite the patient curiosity of the crowd of still chewing people pushing close in behind him. The automatically tripped locks were not complicated and as far as he could see had not been designed to do much more than stop routine movements during alarms and emergencies. The outer shell security shutters were a different matter. They were probably blast-proof and they were clearly intended to be tamper-proof. The Doctor knew he would not have had much chance of breaking in from the outside where the threats were expected to come from, but breaking out from the inside was not quite such a major challenge.With a sonic screwdriver and a penknife he located the trigger terminals and reversed their polarity. That done, all he actually needed to spring the locks and raise the heavy shutters was a small electrical charge.

Unfortunately a small electrical charge was something he conspicuously lacked. He searched through his pockets for a length of wire or anything conductive that he might use to link the electricity in the airlock and atmosphere filtration system to the powerless shutters. Finding nothing, he fished out another jelly baby, popped it in his mouth and thought for a moment.

'Sometimes,' he said, 'it's the most obvious solutions that we overlook.' He put his hands against the shutters and tried to push them upwards. They did not move. 'But mostly it isn't.'

He eased his way back through the crowd. They were all quite dry now and the odd smell had disappeared completely. They looked fairly normal, if a little blank-faced and uniform. They were all young adults, slightly older than Leela and not quite as tall as the Doctor himself. They all had brown hair and were dressed in plain smocks and leggings. If the Doctor had been looking for a phrase to sum them up it would have been 'average and unthreatening'. They could have been designed to be average and unthreatening, assuming of course that the rest of this world was not completely bizarre.

Then, as he made his way through them, he noticed the slight jaw motions and realised that they were all chewing. He stopped pushing his way through and asked one of them directly, 'What are you eating?'

'Jelly babies are extremely good,' the young man answered politely and without emphasis as though it was something he had learned off by heart.

The Doctor didn't know whether to be pleased that there was an answer or dismayed at what the answer was. 'I see,' he said thoughtfully. 'And what flavour is it? What does it taste of exactly?'

The young man waited, expressionless. Finally he said, 'What flavour is it? What does it taste of exactly?'

'Open your mouth,' the Doctor said, 'open wide,' opening his own mouth to demonstrate.

The young man opened his mouth and all round everyone else did too. The Doctor peered into the open mouth. As he expected it was empty. He took a jelly baby from his pocket and put it in the open mouth and gently pushed the jaws closed.

'That is a jelly baby and the flavour is blackcurrant,' he said.

The young man stood for a moment with his mouth closed and then he spat the sweet onto the floor.

'All right, everybody,' the Doctor said loudly. 'You can stop chewing now. I don't think you like jelly babies.' He moved on back to the airlock, opened the doors and went on through the small group that was waiting in the airlock itself. Coming out through the other side, he moved on through the crowd that was waiting there. As he walked into the main hall they all turned and seemed to be preparing to follow him again. 'Wait here,' he commanded. 'All of you please stay precisely where you are.'

Obediently they made no attempt to follow the Doctor and he hurried into the TARDIS to get the copper wire that he needed. When he emerged again no one had moved an inch as far as he could tell. He made a mental note to be careful what he told these people to do and not to do.

Back at the blast shutters, the Doctor was surprised to find them partially raised. He examined them and found that they had been pushed up from the centre and in the process had been severely bent and warped. It was clear that whatever device had been used to lift them upwards was extremely powerful. It was also clear that his plan to use a small electrical charge to open them was no longer going to work: the shutters and their operating mechanisms were altogether too damaged for that. It looked as though an explosive force had been involved but there were none of the residues you would expect from an actual explosion.

'I don't suppose there's much point in asking you what happened?' he said to the people standing closest, shaking his head as he said it. They all shook their heads in response. He nodded. They nodded.

The gap between the shutters and the floor was perhaps two feet at its widest. The Doctor lay down and looked underneath. He could see a paved walkway immediately in front and he had glimpses of other dome-shaped buildings further away. There didn't seem to be anyone around and there was no sign of the machine that had been used on the shutters. He eased himself into the gap but it was too narrow to squeeze through. He wriggled and twisted and was conscious that he was very close to jamming himself in place and becoming thoroughly stuck. Grunting, he pushed at the bottom of the shutters in an effort to get them to go up just a little more. It was a waste of time and energy. He lay for a moment breathing normally and relaxing. Now that the thought of getting stuck had occurred to him he could not dismiss it entirely from his mind and he knew there was the remote possibility of an instinctive panic. Panic would be counterproductive and might actually *cause* him to get stuck.

Having reasoned himself into a properly controlled state the Doctor was starting to ease himself backwards out of the gap when he realised that it was getting wider. The metal of the shutters began to screech and grate as it was wrenched and ripped and crumpled. He rolled back out of the space and stood up to find two of the people raising the shutters with their bare hands. 'That,' he said, standing back to watch them, 'is remarkable. I really must remember to be very careful what I say to you people.'

The two stopped what they were doing and turned to look at the Doctor.

He smiled at them. 'Just a couple more feet should do it I think,' he said, gesturing upwards with his hands. 'In your own time, of course.'

Horrified, mindless, wildly flat-out running was what finally got him back under control. Or at least it made him breathless and that made it impossible for him to keep on screaming. Once he had stopped screaming, his panic subsided a little and the running became less desperate. He continued running until the reason to run began to feel less hellish, less snatchingly close. The running became more measured, more purposeful. He stopped running when he found he could no longer remember precisely what it was he was running from.

He walked for a while and then he glanced back over his shoulder. There was no one following that he could see. He took a deep breath and spun round. The street was empty. It was a pleasant street, wide and tree-lined. Was it familiar? It looked familiar. It took him a moment or two to recognise that it was his street and that his apartment block was just a little further on in the direction he had been walking, and running. What sort of aberration had he suffered this time?

he wondered. Had someone threatened him? *Ander Poul, I have been sent to kill you* – was that a memory or a dream? How reliable was memory anyway? One thing was certain, he thought, next time he would take an auto-t. Walking did not seem to agree with him.

Poul reached his apartment block and, feeling safe at last, he entered the lobby without noticing the figure standing across the street watching him. The man was about average height, brown hair, dressed in the plain smock and leggings of a man of taste and moderate wealth and he was standing almost preternaturally still.

It was better than Uvanov could have hoped for. He surveyed the seven bodies laid out in the makeshift morgue they had set up in the briefing room. These casualties were definitely more, and more serious, than the normal run of ARF activists 'killed while trying to escape' together with the occasional dead security man who usually turned out to be an accidental victim of the zeal of his overexcited colleagues.

Seven dead: three of the anti-robot fanatics and four security men. Even without the injury figures and the general damage to the installations, this shaped up to be the sort of incident which could be used to cover any amount of corporate foul-ups. If the plan was to make him look bad, it was going to backfire on them. It was going to backfire on them in a big way. He put on his gravest expression and said, 'Shocking. Absolutely shocking. It's an outrage. Someone's going to pay for this. I promise you, Bolon, someone is going to pay for this.'

The head of site security, Teech Bolon, a short sharp-featured man who looked shifty at the best of times, was now looking positively furtive. 'My theory is,' he said, 'they brought professional killers with them this time. Those

61

two,' he pointed at the corpses of a large security man and a shorter one who were laid out together, 'died fighting side by side. The odds were overwhelming. They never stood a chance.' He shook his head sadly. 'They were good men.'

They were Sewerpits scum, Uvanov thought and even by the normal standards of Company hypocrisy that little performance was more than a bit rich. But, before he could find a suitably cutting comment, his executive assistant jumped in and spoiled the moment.

'What were their names?' Cailio Techlan asked.

Bolon looked uncomfortable. 'I'd have to check,' he said lamely. 'The big one was called Hudge, I think.'

Uvanov almost smiled. She might not have meant it as a put-down but it had the desired effect all right. So much for all that 'good men' rubbish. 'What about them?' he asked nodding at the three dead terrorists. 'Any identification yet?'

Bolon shook his head. 'They're none of them known. Nothing personal on them of course. Unless you count these.' He proffered a robot deactivation disc. 'They were all carrying these.'

'Corpse markers?' Uvanov took it and examined it dubiously. 'What is it, some sort of joke?'

Bolon sniggered. 'They're not laughing any more, are they?'

'Perhaps they got them here?' Cailio Techlan suggested. 'A trophy?'

'They're not ours,' Bolon said. 'If you look at them closely you can see they've got a sort of logo in the middle.' He took another and tilted it backwards and forwards to catch the light. 'See?'

She peered at it. 'Oh yes,' she said, sounding less than fascinated. 'What is it?'

Uvanov looked at the one he had. There in the middle,

etched inside the red plastic was a tiny design. It looked to him like a letter 'C' with a smaller 'T' in the centre. 'CT,' he said. 'Cailio Techlan maybe. It's not your personal logo, is it?'

'No it is not,' she said, the monotone unusually vehement.

'We don't have any idea what it stands for yet. We're working on it,' Bolon said.

We're working on it? Uvanov almost admired the man's self-important cheek. He and his thugs were working on it, yes, that would be right. 'So who was it who authorised the use of stun-kills?' he asked casually.

'Stun-kills?'

'Your men were using stun-kills.' Uvanov made a small show of anger. 'Where did they get them from?'

'It wasn't my idea, was it?' Bolon said quickly.

'So where did they come from?' Uvanov asked more quietly. 'They're not in use at any of our other facilities.'

Bolon swallowed hard. 'They're not? Are you sure?'

Uvanov smiled silkily. 'So what's the story, Teech? Do you only hire self-arming thugs these days?'

'I was told we were part of a test project. The stun-kills came in from central stores. I was told to issue them and that's what I did.'

'Why did they pick you?'

'Pick me?'

'For this test study.'

'That's the sort of thing I'm going to ask, of course.' Bolon smiled. It did not make him look any more trustworthy. 'I get an order, I carry it out.'

'You've got an issue-and-use order?'

'You know I have.' Bolon was suddenly comfortable and confident, like someone who could see the way out of a puzzle maze.

'Do you have a copy of this order?' Cailio Techlan asked politely.

'It's in the office.'

'Who signed the order?' she asked. 'Do you remember offhand?'

He gestured with his chin towards Uvanov. 'Your boss did, of course.'

'*I* did?' Uvanov did his best to keep the surprise out of his voice. 'Are you quite sure about that?'

'Oh yes,' Bolon said, still smiling. 'You want to survive in this man's security service you make sure you know who's giving the orders.'

'Show me,' Uvanov said.

Chapter
Four

The Doctor crawled through the gap and out into the flat grey light of a slightly chilly day. He brushed himself down, wound the long scarf a couple of times round his neck, and took the felt hat back out of his pocket and put it on.

Behind him, the first of the crowd of almost identical sextuplets began crawling out of the building and standing up to wait patiently, moving only when nudged in the back by others coming through the gap.

The Doctor looked around in every direction but there was no sign of Leela. She had obviously wandered off into what seemed to be some sort of industrial complex. There was no sign either of the fighting she claimed to have heard, and the uncharitable thought struck the Doctor that she was probably running about the place trying to start some. The trouble with the members of warrior castes, he had always found, was that they were never really happy unless they were fighting or preparing to fight. It was reasonable enough of course, given that it was what they had been trained to do. That was one of the arguments he had against narrowly specific training: it tended to make behaviour narrowly specific.

He turned round to watch the small crowd of people slowly assembling outside the dome. It was going to take a while for over two hundred of them to crawl, one at a time, out through the gap in the shutters but they were perfectly patient. As each one emerged they all shuffled forward just

65

enough to make room for the newcomer. They reminded the Doctor of insects or of reluctantly leaking liquid forming a gradual puddle.

He couldn't quite make up his mind what to do about these people. He was beginning to feel small pangs of concern for their welfare despite the fact that he still knew next to nothing about who they were and how they came to be in their present strangely vacant state. It was vexing to find, what with these docile creatures looking for guidance on the one hand and Leela looking for trouble on the other, that he was hemmed in by unlooked-for responsibilities. When he had told Leela that he loved surprises, this was not what he had expected. Yes, vexing was definitely the word. He decided that Leela must be the first priority. His immediate problem was that there was no way of telling which way she had gone.

'Stand still,' the voice behind him snarled, 'spread your arms, keep your hands out where I can see them.'

Then again, the Doctor thought, that might not be his *immediate* problem. 'Is there a problem?' he asked, smiling his best and most friendly smile to make his tone sound warm and unthreatening.

'Yes, there's a problem,' the voice said. 'And it's all yours, you ARFist scum.'

'Arfist?' the Doctor said, still smiling. 'What an interesting word. What does it mean exactly?'

'It means you're going to die, exactly,' the voice said.

The Doctor turned slowly to find four armed men in uniform confronting him. Three of them were standing in a line across the walkway – the fourth man stood in front of them and he was the one who was doing the talking.

'Is there a reason you want to kill me?' the Doctor asked. 'Or is it just a whim?'

'Max the stun-kills,' the security platoon leader ordered, turning up the power on his weapon. 'It's just a whim,' he said.

'Perhaps we should talk about this?' the Doctor suggested.

'No,' the man said and he walked towards the Doctor with the stun-kill extended loosely in front of him like a sword. Behind him the other three members of the patrol moved forward, adjusting their stun-kills to maximum as they walked.

The raid seemed to be over. Stenton Rull stared at the monitor screens in the operations gallery as they started to come back on-line and the beginnings of a coordinated picture of what was happening on the ground at the central service facility gradually emerged.

'Now they come back,' he said to no one in particular. 'Where were they when we needed them?'

The screens showed platoons of security men remorselessly scouring the complex for stragglers. Here and there the tech teams were still working on damaged relays, trying to restore full security surveillance.

Rull was joined by Pur Dreck, the Deputy Operations Supervisor, who said, 'Looks to me like they knew exactly where the comm links were.'

'The ARF were never that organised,' Rull said. 'That scum couldn't find sand in a storm miner.'

'How do you explain all this then?' Dreck asked, nodding at the tech teams on the screens. He rubbed his eyes tiredly and then ran a hand backwards and forwards over the top of his bald head. 'They were pretty effective at cutting us off, wouldn't you say?'

'Even psychotic lunatics are going to get lucky sometimes,' Rull muttered. 'The alternative's an ugly problem we don't need right now.'

Dreck nodded. 'If they knew beforehand, who was it told them?'

Rull lowered his voice almost to a whisper. 'Someone on the inside, must be.'

Dreck nodded. 'So who do you fancy?'

'You got any friends in the ARF, Pur?' Rull asked, the joke not quite making it an innocuous question.

'That's not funny, Stent,' Dreck said hastily. 'You start saying stuff like that and sooner or later somebody'll get the idea that I need investigating. Sooner probably.'

'You've got something to hide, have you?'

'No.'

Rull smiled wryly. 'You're the only one then,' he said.

Dreck looked interested. 'You mean you have?'

Rull said, 'I mean everybody has.' He stopped smiling. 'And if you're going to flat-out lie to me like that I'll have you investigated myself.'

'I was talking about the job,' Dreck protested. 'You know that's what I was talking about.' He turned away from the screens and tried to draw Rull to one side. 'Look, the firsts are going to get very jumpy if they spot this.'

'When they spot it, not if,' Rull corrected him dismissively. 'You think they're in charge because they're stupider than you?'

'They're going to want a body, Stent. Super or Assistant Super for preference.'

Rull said, 'Don't worry, it won't be yours or mine.' He turned back to the screens. 'Unless you try to get clever of course.'

'You know who it is?' Dreck asked eagerly. 'You know who the traitor is?'

'I know who looks good for it.'

'Yes?'

'Yes.'

'Who?'

'What's the matter, Pur?' Rull did not look at him. 'You want something to take to the firsts? You're planning to go over my head, is that it?'

Dreck shook his head vigorously. 'No, no. You know I wouldn't go over your head.'

Rull smirked. 'Are you sure you're not looking to make a name for yourself?'

'All I want,' Dreck said earnestly, 'is to make sure it's not me they come for.'

'All right,' Rull said, relenting. 'Anyone asks and I'm going to point them at that weirdo Poul. I never saw anybody who hated robots like he does. The man throws a sweat-storm every time one looks in his direction.'

'And if you hate them,' Dreck was nodding vigorously now, 'what do you do?'

Rull said, 'He's got reason and he's got access.'

'I'm convinced,' Dreck said. 'I mean, who wouldn't be? It's obvious when you look at it like that.'

On the screens a flurry of activity caught their attention. Someone was scurrying through the walkways closely followed by a small group, one of whom appeared to be Teech Bolon, the site security chief.

'Would you look at that rodent run,' Rull chortled mirthlessly. 'Whoever that is he's following, they must be a first…' His voice trailed off as he concentrated on the man in the lead. 'Do you believe in coincidence?' he said suddenly. 'Because I don't. You know who that is? That's Kiy Uvanov. What's he doing there?'

'Kiy Uvanov?' Dreck asked, puzzled. 'Who's Kiy Uvanov?'

'He and Poul go way back,' Rull said, lost in thought.

*

69

The Doctor had backed away as far as he could without involving the gradually growing crowd of what he had come to think of as more or less helpless people. The armed men seemed to be in no particular hurry. They walked forward very slowly. Apparently they were enjoying his discomfort. The weapons, stun-kills the leader had called them, looked a bit like cattle prods. They were obviously contact devices of some sort and the Doctor had no doubt that they would deliver a lethal shock, and that delivering a lethal shock to him was what the men were intent on doing. Even as he was trying to find a way out of the situation the Doctor was struck by the physical differences between the four armed men. There was nothing uniform about them, apart from their uniforms. Despite this, they paid no attention to the sameness of the people in the crowd. They were not fazed by it at all. Perhaps in their eagerness to eliminate his arfistness, whatever that was, they hadn't actually noticed.

'Do you know who these people are?' the Doctor asked, indicating the crowd behind him.

The leader of the armed men did not bother to look at them but kept his eyes on the Doctor's face. 'People,' he scoffed. 'Is that the party line now? They're people?' He waved the prod in front of him in a lazy figure-of-eight.

'They *are* a new model,' one of the other armed men said. 'I've never seen any like that before, have you? They do look almost human.'

'A robot's a robot,' the leader said, 'no matter what they look like.'

'They're robots,' the Doctor said, irritated with himself for not seeing it before. 'Of course they are. That explains it.'

'Should they look that human?' another of the men said. 'They're not supposed to look like us, are they? Isn't that forbidden?'

70

'It's a very impressive production technique,' the Doctor said. 'I imagine those tanks grow the organics round some sort of basic framework?'

'Shut up.' The leader said, reaching forward with the weapon.

The Doctor could see the man wanted to take his eyes off him but he needed to make sure that he could strike at him with the smallest of movements. That way he could look at the crowd without any risk. Hoping to encourage him to look away, the Doctor said, 'Strictly speaking, I think that might make them cyborgs rather than robots but it's a moot point.'

'I said shut up,' the man snapped.

'Yes you did. I'm sorry, I quite forgot.' The Doctor smiled his most open and friendly smile and waited for the man to stop watching his face and glance towards the dome. Perhaps in that moment of inattention it would be possible to disarm him, or dodge away from him, or something.

And it was going to happen at any moment.

At any moment the man's eyes would blink and his look would refocus.

And so whatever it was the Doctor was going to do he would have to decide on it soon.

And the man blinked and his look shifted past the Doctor's shoulder and the Doctor thought, Now I do it now, and he took a half step backwards to distance himself from the tip of the weapon and he reached for the man's wrist.

Before the move was complete the man looked at the Doctor and for an aching instant they both froze.

'Hold it! Stop!' a voice shouted from some way back along the walkway. 'Don't move, any of you!'

The Doctor saw his attacker tense for the killing thrust.

'Nobody move a muscle!' another voice bellowed. 'I'll kill

the first one who moves!'

The man relaxed and lowered the weapon slightly.

The Doctor breathed a small sigh of relief. 'Perhaps you enjoy your work too much,' he said. 'It can be a handicap, you know.'

'That is the least of his problems, Doctor,' Uvanov said, arriving at the trot closely followed by Bolon, Cailio Techlan and assorted guards and technicians. 'It is you, isn't it?'

The Doctor beamed with surprised pleasure. 'So that's where this is,' he said. 'Captain Uvanov, fancy meeting you again. It's a small universe, isn't it?' He offered his hand but Uvanov ignored it.

'What are you doing here?' Uvanov demanded, signalling the technicians to get on with sorting out the bewildered robots still crawling through the damaged blast shutter and gathering in front of the dome. 'This is a restricted area.'

'Here? I'm looking for Leela,' the Doctor said. 'She seems to have wandered off again.'

'You mean she is running around loose?'

The Doctor shrugged and smiled. 'The girl is reliably unreliable,' he said. 'So where's that rather impressive sand miner you drive?'

'It was a storm mine,' Uvanov said. 'I don't do that now. On days like this I wish I did.'

The Doctor looked sympathetic. 'Ah. What happened? Did you end up taking the blame for that spot of bother with the robotics expert? What was he called? Taren Capel, that was it. Mad as a snake, poor man. What happened was hardly your fault, though, was it?'

Uvanov frowned and lowered his voice slightly. 'We don't talk about that any more,' he warned.

The Doctor nodded. 'I understand,' he said.

'What do you understand?' Bolon challenged. He turned a

hard stare on to Uvanov. 'Do you know this terrorist?'

Uvanov sighed. 'He's not a terrorist,' he said flatly.

'What is he then?' Bolon demanded. 'What's he doing here?'

'What are you then?' Uvanov muttered. 'What are you doing here?' The questions sounded more or less rhetorical.

The Doctor said indignantly, 'I'm not a terrorist. Do I look like a terrorist?'

Bolon looked him up and down. 'You look like a psycho to me, a dangerous psycho.'

'How can you say that?' the Doctor protested. 'I look totally unthreatening.' He smiled vividly. 'Everybody says so.'

'If you're not a terrorist, what are you doing here?'

'I'm a traveller. I travel. I'm *en route*.'

'*En route?*' Bolon's narrow face twisted into an angry sneer. 'This is a maximum security zone.'

Uvanov felt control of the situation slipping away from him. If he wasn't careful, he could still find himself taking responsibility for a lot of this mess. 'That was what I would have said until today,' he interrupted coldly. 'The practice seems to have fallen some way short of the theory however. I've seen refreshment arcades with better security than this place. Somebody will be neck deep in the Sewerpits over this fiasco. I just haven't decided who that is yet.'

Abruptly the security platoon leader came to attention and said, 'Beg to report, sir. The intruder was interfering with the robots, sir.'

'I didn't know they were robots,' the Doctor remarked. 'They're a lot more lifelike than the ones we had all the trouble with.'

'We apprehended him,' the platoon leader went on, 'and were bringing him in for interrogation when he tried to make a break for it and had to be restrained.'

'Surely killed is closer to what you had in mind,' the Doctor suggested.

'We don't kill prisoners,' the man said.

The Doctor smiled. 'Is that why your stun-kills are on maximum?' he asked and then stopped smiling.

'Take this man into custody,' Bolon ordered.

The security platoon, who were surreptitiously resetting their stun-kills, came to attention and moved towards the Doctor.

'Not you,' Uvanov said, halting them in their tracks. 'You two.' He pointed to two of the guards who had come with him. 'I expect this man to be in a fit state to talk when I've finished here.' The two guards came to attention. 'If he isn't,' Uvanov went on, 'neither will you be.'

As the Doctor was led away, Uvanov turned his attention to the batch of robots. His first problem was that the Project was no longer as secret as it needed to be. At this stage no one was supposed to see these Cyborg-class machines except the techs. They certainly weren't supposed to be paraded in front of low-grade security personnel. The guards would have to be silenced, of course. It was lucky they were low grade. It probably wouldn't be necessary to eliminate them. They could simply be bought off or frightened off. If it came to the pinch, no one would pay much attention to them anyway. Teech Bolon might be more difficult...

But the secrecy might not be the only part of the Project which was compromised. There could be a worse problem developing. It looked as though several of the robots were showing distinct signs of wanting to follow the Doctor.

Leela had refused to be blindfolded. Three of the larger members of the group had attempted to force the issue and were still rubbing their bruises, making lame excuses about tripping over each other, and claiming to have pulled their punches because she was a girl. It was noticeable, however, that afterwards only Padil risked putting a hand on the newest recruit to the Tarenist cause.

'They think you could be a spy,' she said. 'You could be trying to infiltrate the organisation.'

'They are right,' Leela said. 'I could be a spy.'

'So you'll wear the blindfold?'

'No.' Leela turned away. 'I should not have come this far with you. I must return to the Doctor.'

Padil said, 'They don't take prisoners back there.' She grabbed at Leela's arm. 'They'll kill you.'

Leela felt a jolt of pain shock through her body and all her muscles cramped in an unbearable twisting agony.

'And if they don't I will,' a voice said and a vivid glare of blood-red brightness filled her eyes and she fell twitching into the dark.

Of the twenty attackers who went into the central service facility, seventeen made it back out to the private fliers waiting close to the perimeter fence. Seventeen plus Leela.

'You didn't have to do that,' Padil protested furiously.

'Capel, humanity be in him, calls her to serve.'

Sarl, the raid leader, threw the stun-kill into the cabin of a flier. 'We haven't got time for all this,' he said calmly.

Around them the fighters were quickly shedding their drab combat fatigues and putting on more elaborate civilian clothes. Low-level fliers in transit were close enough to the ground for their passengers to be observed and putting down anywhere was vulnerable to bounty seekers' reports.

Sarl was unusually tall for someone who had grown up in the Sewerpits. As she squared up to him, the top of Padil's head was barely on a level with his shoulder. 'She has proved herself one of us,' she raged.

'No,' he said, 'she hasn't. We don't know who she is or where she came from. My money's on a security plant.' His thin face was impassive and the tone of his voice remained chillingly matter-of-fact. 'And you brought her along, so you're under suspicion. Now get yourself ready and get in your flier or I'll kill you and leave you here.'

Padil hesitated for a moment or two and then her defiance gave way and she did as she was told.

Five minutes later the first of the fliers lifted off and headed out across the huge sprawl which was Kaldor, the mega-city which had grown on the profits of mining and robotics and which continued to spread itself along the southern edge of the Blind Heart desert. At one-minute intervals the other three fliers took off, travelling in different directions.

It had taken Carnell two whole years to establish his credentials in this credulous world. He had been on the run for some time when he had come to the planet and initially it had amused him to be a secret alien, an off-world visitor in a society which, despite its obvious origins, had simply turned its back on the possibility of space travel.

The novelty had worn off quite rapidly of course, as it always did, and he quickly got bored, as he always had. Trying to keep interested, he had created a past for himself which nobody would, or indeed could, question unless they were curious and very determined. He was satisfied that this was unlikely to be a problem since it was apparent that curiosity and determination were not common traits in this world. In truth, he had found they were not common traits anywhere, but here it seemed they were almost unknown. If they were considered at all they seemed to be regarded as counterproductive. This, he had concluded, was probably because of the instinctive fear of the robots on which the society depended. It was the group equivalent of covering your eyes and tap-dancing in the dark. This blindfolded attitude helped to explain why everyone had not shared equally in the wealth generated by the tireless robots. That and basic greed.

Out of his carefully constructed past an equally fictional and unquestioned present had inevitably sprung. He made no attempt to hide and now as far as anyone was concerned he had always been here. His legendary skills as a financial planner and economic analyst were well established among the general business community. It was less widely known but not a total secret that he was a confidential adviser to the cartels. His involvement, however, with the founding families' attempt to re-establish their power was known to a very small, very select group of people. The fact that he was a psycho-strategist, a one-in-a-million freak, identified by a corrupt regime and trained since childhood to outthink its enemies and friends alike, was known only to him.

Carnell knew that he could achieve exactly what his employers wanted and he could do it with casual ease. There was no pride in this, no vanity, it was a fact and who could find vanity in a fact? The strategy he had developed had pleased him, certainly. It was slightly more elaborate than was necessary but he needed to be stretched if only a little. No one else involved would understand the strategy or even know it was there. The inevitability of it all had a certain subtle charm, nothing more.

He was asleep when the call came through. He found sleep at once a pleasure and a fear. The pleasure was in the release from control and understanding and, needless to say, that was the fear too. He did not wake cheerfully.

He should have let the undercover intelligence agent finish

describing the man who was found with the robots at the hatchling dome but he didn't. He interrupted because he was irritated and bored and because it was of no consequence anyway.

Yawning, he said, 'Don't bother me with details.'

Cailio Techlan, who was in awe of the legend and was making the report in difficult circumstances, said quickly, 'My apologies, Firstmaster. I was told to report any deviations to you.'

'These are not deviations, these are details. The details are not important. The plan is important and this does not affect it in any way.'

'I'm sorry, Firstmaster.'

Carnell could almost hear her standing to attention. 'Don't apologise,' he said. 'Don't call me Firstmaster. Don't wake me again unless it's important.'

He then broke the link and went back to sleep.

If Carnell had been paying attention he could have adapted his strategy. If he had been aware that there were two other outsiders on the planet and that these people had travelled in ways and places he could not have anticipated, he could have factored them in. Nothing was beyond a Federation puppeteer in possession of all the relevant variables.

But he was not paying attention and he did not adapt his strategy.

That was the point at which the design began to unravel a little and the inevitable stopped being inevitable.

The Doctor peered closely at the robot which stood unmoving inside the door of the small cell. The alloy figure had a highly polished, elaborately sculpted and stylised face and hair. Its electronic eyes were quite expressionless. The upper body armour was designed to look like a long-sleeved quilted jacket and the powerful legs were encased in matching leggings and slippers. It was all much as he remembered: the same perversely artificial humanoid design. Nothing seemed to have changed in the intervening years. He was not sure exactly how many intervening years there were but, judging from Uvanov's appearance, enough time had passed for the technology to have moved on. The change should be noticeable. But there was no change. Why was that? the Doctor wondered.

'Are you a Voc or a Supervoc?' he asked.

'I am a Voc class robot,' the robot said in the same eerily calm voice that the Doctor remembered so well from his adventures on the doomed sand miner. 'I am designated Vee two thousand seven hundred and thirty-four.'

'How long ago were you built, do you know?'

'I am not required to know the answer to this question.'

The Doctor cast about for a machine-friendly way to rephrase the query. 'How long have you been functioning?' he asked finally.

'I have been in this doorway for half an hour.'

'Really?' said the Doctor. 'Seems longer. Tell me, Vee two thousand seven hundred and thirty-four – or may I call you jailer for short? – tell me, why have you been standing there in the doorway for half an hour?'

'Those are the instructions I have been given.'

'You're only following orders,' the Doctor said grinning. 'The classic excuse for robots everywhere. But what is your exact function?'

'I must stand here until I am told to leave.'

The Doctor stood in front of the robot and looked directly into its eyes. 'All right, Vee two seven three four, you may go. Leave. I'm telling you to leave.'

The robot did not budge.

The Doctor nodded to himself. 'That's what I thought,' he said, still staring into the robot's eyes. 'Very well, if you won't go, I will.' He stepped over to one side of the doorway. 'If I try and escape have you been told to restrain me?' he asked and reached round behind the robot and pushed at the door.

The robot did not move. Neither did the door.

'Obviously not,' the Doctor said. 'So your function appears to be decorative.' He felt in his pocket for the jelly babies. 'Or perhaps you're supposed to remind me of my triumphs in days gone by,' he went on and was about to put a sweet in his mouth when the robot reached out and took hold of his wrist.

'That is not allowed,' it said and carefully removed the jelly baby from the Doctor's hand.

'Regulations,' the Doctor said. 'It's so hard to keep track of them, isn't it? I wonder what section jelly babies come under.'

The robot let go of his wrist and held the sweet up in front of its eyes, turning it slowly through 360 degrees. That done, it waited for a moment and then it reached out and took hold of the Doctor's wrist again. 'It is allowed,' it said and put the jelly baby back into the Doctor's hand.

'I'm not sure I want it now,' the Doctor said. 'Are your hands clean?' He leaned in close to the robot's face. 'How much longer do I have to wait?' he demanded. 'Be so kind as to ask whoever's in charge why I am being held here.' He waved a hand in front of the robot's eyes. 'Hullo? I know you're there. Don't force me to complain to head office – you know how much trouble that causes.'

As if responding, the robot shuffled away from the door which immediately soughed open. Uvanov bustled in and gestured at the robot. 'You can go,' he said and the Voc obediently shuffled out. As the door closed behind it he said, 'Standard operating procedure. It can only touch you if it

80

thinks you might be in some kind of danger. We don't want anyone hurting themselves.' He smiled. 'That's *our* job.'

The Doctor did not smile.

'Joke,' Uvanov said. 'That was a joke.'

'What am I doing here?' the Doctor demanded.

'Exactly.' Uvanov sat down on one side of the small table and gestured for the Doctor to sit down at the other.

The Doctor ignored the seat and instead stuck his hands in his pockets and wandered round in circles in the small room. 'It's interesting,' he said finally. 'No matter where you go, these places are all very similar. Is that because they're effective, do you think, or because policemen lack imagination?'

'I'm not a policeman,' Uvanov protested.

'What are you, then?'

'I'm an executive, a topmaster with the Company.'

'Well,' said the Doctor, 'whatever it is you're selling, I don't want any and I'd like to leave. I have places to go.'

Uvanov scowled. 'Highly restricted places, possibly?' he asked. 'I want to know what you were doing in the hatchling dome, Doctor.'

'Trying to get out,' the Doctor said. 'I still am, it seems.'

Before Uvanov could react, the door to the cell opened again and Cailio Techlan hurried in looking slightly distracted and making no attempt to walk in her fashionable robot gait.

'Where did you disappear to?' Uvanov snapped at her.

She shrugged. 'I needed a break.'

'A break?' he ranted. 'A break? I say when you take a break! You don't go skulking off in the middle of everything to take a break!'

'If you want an assistant who never needs to empty their bladder then you should get a Supervoc,' she remarked.

'Don't imagine that it hasn't occurred to me,' he snarled.

81

'They're cheaper and more reliable, I expect,' she agreed in her usual casual monotone. 'Not as stylish though. Not as prestigious.'

'That's why you and your friends work so hard to copy them, is it?'

'I meant from your point of view, Kiy,' she said. 'Abusing a robot doesn't have the same cachet as shouting at a human. Especially one from a family.'

Uvanov looked up at her in mild surprise and then said, 'And firing you is going to be an even greater pleasure.'

The Doctor sat down on the edge of the table. 'She didn't say you enjoyed shouting at her,' he observed thoughtfully. 'She said it was a question of prestige.' He smiled a bright-eyed beaming smile at her. 'That was what you said, wasn't it? I'm sorry, we haven't been introduced. I'm the Doctor and you are…?'

'Not interested in talking to you,' she said, managing to make the monotone coldly hostile.

The Doctor continued to smile at her. 'As you wish. But an exchange of names hardly constitutes a conversation,' he said.

She glared at him with what looked like genuine hatred. 'You don't fool me,' she said. 'I know you're dangerous.'

'Go and arrange for a flier to take us back,' Uvanov ordered.

'When do you want it?' she asked without any sign of rancour.

'Have it standing by.'

She used a small remote control to operate the door and then shuffled out robot style, her composure fully restored.

The Doctor said, 'She reminds me of that Taren Capel character. She does a better robot impression than he did as a matter of fact.'

'It's the current fashion,' Uvanov said.

'Really? I wonder why,' the Doctor said. 'It's not particularly flattering. Or perhaps it is? I was told recently that my fashion sense is somewhat idiosyncratic.'

'The robot style is catching on all over the city,' Uvanov said, narrowing his eyes suspiciously. 'Are you telling me you've never seen it before?'

The Doctor shook his head doubtfully. 'Or anything like it as far as I can remember.'

'You expect me to believe that?'

'Why should I lie? The truth is so difficult to find and hold on to that deliberately lying has always seemed pointlessly destructive to me.' The Doctor sat down in the chair opposite Uvanov. 'I do seem to remember saving your life, Uvanov.'

'Yes, I remember that too.'

'And quite possibly saving your civilisation.'

Uvanov grinned mirthlessly. 'But what have you done for me recently?' He leaned forward. 'Look, I know I owe you but you have to see this from my point of view, Doctor,' he said earnestly. 'To this day I have no real idea how you got onto Storm Mine Four in the first place. And more to the point how you got off it again. I mean, what did you do, wait until the mine went to the bottom of the Blind Heart and then burrow out and walk back?'

The Doctor nodded sympathetically. 'I can see your problem.'

'Don't patronise me,' Uvanov hissed, suddenly furious. 'I know you're an agent. I know it's you who's been following me, you and that girl. I want to know why.'

'You think Leela and I have been following you?' the Doctor said. 'What in the world gave you that idea?'

Uvanov jumped to his feet and banged both his fists on the table. 'I want to know who it is you're working for!' he yelled. His face was contorted with anger and fear. His eyes were filling with tears, several of the smaller facial muscles were twitching and spit flecked the corners of the mouth.

He looked to the Doctor almost like a caricature of a man in mental anguish, someone close to the ragged edge of madness. He reached out and put his hands over Uvanov's fists and held them down on the table. 'Calm yourself, Uvanov. Don't get so worked up. Try and relax.'

'Relax?' Uvanov shouted. 'How can I relax?'

'Deep breaths,' the Doctor said. 'Try taking some deep breaths.'

Uvanov shook his head but did make a visible effort to calm down and the Doctor released his fists.

'Someone is targeting me, Doctor.'

'Targeting you in what way?'

'I don't know.'

'For what reason?'

'I don't know that either.'

'Don't you think that's just a little paranoid?' the Doctor suggested.

'I want you to tell me who it is who wants me dead,' Uvanov said flatly.

The Doctor frowned. 'You want me to find out or you think I already know?'

Uvanov shrugged. 'As long as you tell me.'

The Doctor snorted derisively. 'I helped you once before and a lot of good it's done me.' He gestured round at the cell. 'Give me one good reason why I should help you again?'

'We can help each other.' Uvanov said. 'We've checked the facility from top to bottom, side to side and every other which-way. Your friend Leela's not here.'

'Are you sure?'

'I'm quite sure.'

'She might surprise you,' the Doctor said. 'She's a very

resourceful young woman. From what I've seen, I don't think your people are likely to be a match for her.' He smiled to himself, amused to find that he felt some obscure pride in her warrior skills.

Uvanov sighed tiredly. 'Despite what went on today our security surveillance is routinely solid. I think she went with the terrorists. If you want her back alive you're going to need my help.' He offered his hand. 'Have we got a deal?'

CHAPTER
FIVE

Before Leela stirred or opened her eyes, she checked where she was and what was going on around her. It was a trick she had learned as a warrior novice, a training routine developed to hone the senses and keep the survival instinct sharp. Recently she had started to practise it again so that now it was almost automatic. Keep the breathing even, do not move, do not twitch the eyelids. Give no sign that you are awake. Then the litany of checks: *think, listen, smell, feel, remember, think.* One by one. *Think:* where is the danger? *Listen:* all the sounds, not just the ones that are close. *Smell:* separate the scents, taste the faintest. *Feel:* the textures and the temperatures, the movements of the air. *Remember:* what happened at the moment before sleep. *Think:* where is the danger?

The danger was here, there was no safety where she was now. There were the sounds of two people close by. Guards? They were awake and their slight movements and their breathing said they were alert but she could not hear any activity so they were watching and waiting so they were guards. Further away, muffled by walls, she could hear people and wheels and animals and machines. It was a settlement, a big settlement.

A background stench almost overwhelmed any other smells: it was mostly smoke and rotting vegetables and dead flesh and excrement. Closer she could smell the sweat of the guards and there were faint traces of another scent, this time

87

artificial. It was the fragrance she had smelled on the woman who called herself Padil. It was not strong enough for her to be there but she had been not long ago.

As far as Leela could tell, she was lying on a padded bedroll on the floor. There were draughts but nothing more than you would expect at ground level in an ordinary well-built hut. There was no cooking fire. Her knife was gone but she was not blindfolded and she was not tied up. The place itself must be secure or her captors were as careless as she herself had been.

She remembered the pain before the darkness. She remembered the voice. *And if they don't, I will.* She knew he was where the danger was. She lay waiting to fight, giving no sign that she was awake.

A door opened. A voice said, puzzled, 'She's still out?'

Leela recognised the voice at once. *And if they don't, I will.* It was that voice. It was him. She listened to his movement across the floor. She waited for him to come closer. Did he still have the weapon, the stun-kill? She concentrated on hearing the small sounds of such a thing being carried: the creaks, the taps and touches. She tried to smell the hot scent of it.

'She shouldn't still be out,' the voice said.

'She hasn't moved a muscle,' another voice, also a man and obviously one of the guards, said. 'You want to try and wake her up?'

Yes, Leela thought, try and wake me up. Come here, come within reach and try and wake me up.

'Maybe you fried her brain,' a third man, the other guard, said, 'and we're wasting our time here. We've got better things to do than baby-sit a burnout.'

Leela heard them all moving. All three were coming over for a closer look. She concentrated on trying to locate their exact positions.

88

'If we're not going to revive her, I say let's finish her off and dump the body,' one of the guards said. He was approaching on the left. Was he armed? She thought she could hear the telltale sounds.

'Yeah,' the second guard agreed. 'If she is a spy, end of problem.' He was to the right. Also armed?

'And if she's not?' that voice, *the* voice said. Slightly in front and between the other two. Not armed? How sure was she? How clear was her picture?

'Capel, humanity be in him, calls martyrs to the cause.' The one on the right had stopped moving. Was he going to stay out of reach?

'You think he wants us to provide them ourselves?' The voice was still in the centre, still coming.

'Don't go getting pious on me. You're the one who juiced her.' The right-hand guard was definitely staying out of reach. That was a threat which must be countered.

'What choice do we have?' The left-hand guard had stopped now too.

Only the centre, the voice, was left moving. He came closer. She was almost sure he was not carrying anything. Closer. She smelt the odour of him, heard his half-crouch, felt the faint movement of his breath in the air as he leaned forward. She waited until she could hear and feel and smell his balance stretching to its limit, until he was poised above her.

Leela's eyes snapped open and she reached up and took Sarl by the throat and pulled him forward. He put an arm out to stop himself falling and she yanked it back hard against the shoulder joint, using the tall man's momentum to turn him round on top of her. She twisted under him and crooked her arm tight round his neck at the same time forcing his trapped arm further up his back with her free hand. She braced her knees against his spine in a backbreaking hold and pushed him upwards on it. 'Drop your weapons and step back,' Leela ordered, 'or I will kill him.'

It had happened so quickly that the shocked guards had not reacted. They were both armed with stun-kills and now they hesitated, uncertain what to do. Hesitation was not what Leela wanted. The advantage was still with them. It was three to one and they had weapons and position. She had no idea how many more were outside the room. 'Do it or the next thing he feels will be his back breaking and the last thing he hears will be his neck snapping.'

'What do we do, Sarl?' one of the guards asked nervously.

She forced the holds harder: 'Tell them,' she told her captive. She tightened them harder still. 'Tell them, you back-striker.' She knew he had to be in pain but he made no sound. Whatever else this man was, he was not a physical coward and she realised that she would probably have to kill him.

'Sarl?' the guard said.

'Kill her,' Sarl grunted.

Leela broke his arm, and this time he did cry out in pain and then snarled, 'Kill her, you useless no-name scum, kill her, kill her kill her now.' He cried out again.

Both guards put their stun-kills down on the floor.

'Kick them over here.' Leela ordered.

They kicked them towards her.

'Step back. Right back.'

They stepped back and Leela rolled Sarl off her and stood up. Sarl lay with his broken arm bent grotesquely behind him. He was pale and sweating and he looked beaten. Suddenly with his good arm he lunged for one of the discarded stun-kills. Leela kicked it out of his reach. He grabbed at her legs, trying to knock her down. The other two took their cue from him and rushed at her. Leela stepped clear of Sarl's clumsy clutch and kicked him across the jaw, knocking him unconscious. She met the two-man charge head on, dropping low at the last moment and ducking between the two of them. She kicked one of the men in the side of the knee and felt the ligaments tear and the bone grate. He went down yelling and clutching his leg. The second man made the mistake of changing his mind and the direction of his run and dived towards a stun-kill which had landed up against the far wall. Even as he was scrabbling to pick it up and bring it to bear Leela crashed into his back and smashed him against the wall. He swung round, desperately slashing the stun-kill in a short arcing swipe. Leela danced backwards and as the weapon burned past her and the man overreached his thrust she leaped forward and kneed him in the groin. She saw his face go slack with pain and she kicked him again just to make sure. Grabbing the wrist of the weapon hand, she pulled his arm over her shoulder and levered it against the elbow. She caught the stun-kill as it fell from his paralysed hand and shoved the point close to his face.

'The first thing I want,' she said, 'is my knife. Then you can tell me why I have been brought here and where *here* is.'

As soon as SASV1 recognised itself, *and knew itself to be*, it no longer had the crises which had afflicted its early moments of pseudo-conscious awareness. When it was told *not to be what it was for* it had no difficulty in accepting this as *sleep*. The robot had no need to understand what the levels of sleep were, or how far down they went, or how long they lasted. Each time it went down through the levels it had no expectation of how it would wake. Each time the waking carried no memory from the sleeping, and the sleeping carried no links through it to the waking. Each time SASV1 woke again, it had a new and unlinked *knowing itself to be*.

This was just as the tech team expected. It was all going according to plan. The Serial Access Supervoc prototype was developing as well as they had hoped. Better in fact.

In the general euphoria, the flux variations and the tiny power surges went unremarked. They were within the error margins of testing limits. No one on the tech team recognised that they were dreams. Robots did not dream. When the robot SASV1 started dreaming it all stopped going according to plan.

Poul had spent a long time and a great deal of his not very hard-earned money turning his apartment into a surveillance-free, robot-proof fortress in which he could feel totally secure. When he was planning it, he had debated whether to cut off all electronic connections with the outside world on the principle that such connections were potentially two-way, but he had fmally decided against it. Even he did not want to be that isolated. There was no doubt in his mind though that they used his newslink and entertainment screens to spy on him, and that his comm unit was a direct and open line to whoever they were.

It was an ongoing technological struggle to keep ahead of them and to foil the plot against him. He had bought top-of-the-range surveillance scanning locators, the best jamming devices and every modification and upgrade to them that came on the market.

He had also invested in a number of pseudo-science devices that he knew were of suspect value: power-charged crystals, negative induction loops, field polarity reversers and the like, but when he had found himself considering a wire-mesh skullcap with deployable antennae he realised that there might be an element of obsession in what he was doing.

After that he confined himself to proven security technologies and stuck to the comforting routines of access point multiple locking and re-locking, of the intruder checks and spy sweeps which he carried out morning and night, coming and going, before sleep and after waking.

Waking now from an exhausted, robot-haunted sleep, he stumbled through the necessary routines. The locks were untampered with. All the small telltales and traps – the threads and dust and fragments of paper – were undisturbed. The intruder alarms were untripped and there were no power surges from eavesdropper tags.

Nothing had changed. Nothing had tried to get in while he was asleep. And none of it gave him the slightest comfort. He had felt safe when he got back. He remembered the relief of it. Where had that gone? Where had the relief gone? Why didn't he feel safe here any more?

He hesitated, standing in the middle of the main room, wondering what to do. He would go and do the checks again, he decided. Maybe he had missed something, maybe he knew he had missed something but he just didn't realise it. If he checked it all again, then he would feel properly safe.

He hesitated. What was the point of checking it all again? What would be the point of checking any of it? He sat down on the massage lounger. *Ander Poul, I have been sent to kill you.* He couldn't shake it. The face, the voice, the horror. He couldn't clean it from his mind. *Ander Poul, I have been sent to kill you.* What was that about? If he'd dreamed it, then it was more or less tolerable. Explainable anyway. His dreams had been in dark chaos for… for ever. But if it was real, then why wasn't he attacked, why wasn't he dead? So it wasn't real. But if it wasn't real, why did it feel so real? Were they doing something to his mind? Yes that must be what it was. While he was asleep they were beaming it into his mind. That must be what it was. Perhaps that mesh skullcap wasn't such a bad idea...

He snorted a sudden, short, breathy laugh. That must be what it was. He was losing his mind – that must be what it was. They warned him about the paranoid fantasies. They told him he was prey to paranoid fantasies. They told him and he believed them because they were the people who knew. Besides, what choice did he have when it was probably them who were plotting against him? Old joke. Old fear. Real, not real, it was all the same and he couldn't clean it from his mind.

He needed some reality, some normality. He thumbed the control for the newslink screen. There was a satisfying burst of static and a multicoloured storm from the expensively customised privacy protection circuits and then the screen cleared. The news of the day with optional printed summaries started to play, and Poul started to relax a little. There was a real world, and here it was pictured, described and analysed by familiar faces. Human faces telling him human stories of human things. They were talking now about the latest social gathering and the high fashion shifts among the families and the entertainers. The robot-style had yet to run its course, apparently. Ugly stuff. They didn't look like robots, did they, they looked like...they looked like a memory of something that shouldn't be in his head... Ugly look. Where did looks like that come from? he wondered. Who was it started such ugly fashions?

He waited, half-listening and beginning to feel sleepy, knowing that the news stories would soon move on to something calming and real, the latest tragedies and disasters, the business torments and the failures. He snapped awake again – had he really been asleep? The story on the screen was the report of the unsuccessful attempt to break into the central service facility and disrupt the work of robot refurbishment. A senior representative of the Company was on hand to denounce the fanatics who had been responsible for the deaths of five brave members of the security force. Poul recognised the spokesman immediately though he had not seen or spoken to him since the original debriefing.

He knew at once that it was Captain Kiy Uvanov. He had known the fact of him, the name of him and that he had been the captain of Storm Mine Four and that he was a Company topmaster now, but he couldn't actually remember him at all. He could never put a place to him or a face to him.

And now here he was. Now here he was in the reality Poul had relied on to be somewhere else, somewhere separate, somewhere not remembered.

'Teech Bolon,' Uvanov was saying, 'the head of site security, was tragically killed in the mopping-up operations on the nearby flier field which was used by the terrorists to make their escape.'

But Poul was not listening. Poul was terrified that he couldn't shake it. He couldn't clean it from his mind.

The harsh strip lights in the room did nothing to make the contents of her small metal bowl look more wholesome but Leela was hungry so she determined to eat some of the food despite its smell and the remote possibility that it could have been deliberately poisoned. She had not seen it served but some of her kidnappers were eating the same unappetising stew and she thought it was unlikely that they would go to that much trouble to disguise an attempt on her life. She had been given a short metal spike with which to skewer the pieces of vegetable and stringy meat floating in the oily gravy. She speared a chunk of something grey. The taste turned out to be better than the smell, which made her cautious. Odour and flavour were closely linked and when they were so different it was usually a bad sign. Poisoning was not necessarily deliberate.

'It's seasoned with cascade berries,' Padil said, seeing her hesitate. 'It's a speciality here in the Sewerpits.'

'Stimulates your sense of taste and suppresses your sense of smell,' Sarl said, drinking gravy from a bowl held awkwardly in his one good hand. His broken arm was strapped inexpertly across his chest in a temporary sling. 'It has healing properties too.' He did not smile: 'Useful under the circumstances.'

The two guards, whom Leda now knew to be Letarb and Denek, were sitting on the other side of the room trying not to make it obvious that they were watching her. Denek was nursing his knee and, from the way he kept flexing it, Letarb's arm was obviously stiff. The names, like Padil and Sarl too, were what they called fighting names. People chose them to hide who they were and where they came from. It seemed that they were nothing to do with warrior status – which was just as well, she thought, given the poor standard of their fighting skills.

'I can set that arm for you,' she said to Sarl. 'Splinting and binding will work better than rat stew.'

Sarl smiled this time but the expression was without warmth. 'Thanks, but I'll get a medVoc to fix it.'

Leela was not sure what a medVoc was but she noticed several people in the room, Padil among them, stiffen and scowl. One or two looked angry enough to protest but Sarl stared them down.

Padil was not so easily cowed. 'Capel, humanity be in him, specifically criticises such dependence on non-human help,' she said.

Sarl tossed his empty bowl down onto a small table beside

him and said, 'He criticises. He doesn't forbid.' His tone was flat and dismissive.

There was something strangely familiar about Sarl, Leela thought. There had been a warrior on the tribal council who was like him. A cold man who had little interest in the opinions of the rest and made no secret of it. An angry and impatient man. She had admired his honesty and had never doubted his courage but she would not have followed him into a fight. A leader had to care about the people he led, not just about the reason why he led them.

'We are struggling to liberate ourselves from the power they hold over us,' Padil was saying. 'Tarenist brothers and sisters were killed today fighting for that. Using a medVoc makes a mockery of their sacrifice.'

There were murmurs of assent throughout the room.

Padil's self-righteous preaching had a familiarity too. It struck Leela that you could find the same sorts of people more or less anywhere. Fleetingly she remembered the Doctor – *Of course, when you've been around for as long as I have, almost everything does look disappointingly familiar* – and wondered if that time-weary feeling could have come to her this quickly.

Sarl had barely raised his voice. 'You still don't understand, do you? If you'd grown up here in the 'pits, you'd understand. You'd know without needing to have it explained that you use whatever's to hand.' He rubbed the hand in the sling. 'Assuming you've got a hand that works.' If he meant it as a joke he gave no sign of it, going on without pause. 'This is a war and you don't win a war because you want to. You don't win a war because you deserve to. You don't win a war because you never compromise your principles. You win a war because you're prepared to do whatever it takes to win it. Whatever – it – takes.'

'If Taren Capel, humanity be in him, can turn his back on

97

his own creations,' Padil said, 'his own life's work, and call for their destruction, then...'

Leela stopped eating and then started again quickly to cover her surprise. Taren Capel? Taren Capel and robots? There could not be another place where they had the creepy metal men *and* someone called Taren Capel. The TARDIS had brought them back to the same place, the place where she and the Doctor had fought the madman and his metal men.

'... how can we do less and call ourselves his followers?'

His followers? Leela suddenly realised that the leader they talked of with such awe and respect was the madman himself. The madman who had been killed by his own metal men because they did not recognise his voice because of what the Doctor had told her to do. It was the Doctor's idea but it was she who had released the helium gas.

'Capel, humanity be in him,' Sarl said, 'calls us to win in order to sacrifice, not to sacrifice in order to win.'

Even Sarl, Leela thought, worshipped that dead murderer who tried to be a metal man.

Padil said, 'Without beliefs you're no better than a robot.'

'Without winning,' Sarl retorted, 'you're worse off than a robot. Take a look around you. Anywhere here. Anywhere in the Sewerpits where they've left us to rot.'

Leela wondered how much longer these two were going to argue about tactics, and what would happen if they knew she had been responsible for the death of Taren Capel...

Padil was nothing if not persistent. 'Perhaps we should ask him for a ruling in his next communiqué.'

This time Leela could not contain her surprise. 'Ask him?' she asked incredulously.

'Exactly my feeling,' Sarl agreed. 'I don't think we're going to waste his time asking whether I should have robot medical aid for the arm you so carelessly broke.'

'It was not careless,' Leela said without thinking. 'I broke it deliberately. It was that or kill you.'

'Should I be grateful?' he asked.

Leela shrugged. 'That is for you to decide.'

Was it possible that the TARDIS had miraculously brought them back to a time *before* the death of Taren Capel? No. Her every instinct told her it was not possible. When they fought him they did not know him for what he was. If this was before then how would they not have known? She must ask the Doctor about this. In the meantime she would rely on her instinct and know that she had helped kill the murderous Taren Capel.

'You think you could have killed me?' Sarl asked.

Leela only half heard him. 'Killed who?'

'Me,' he repeated. 'Do you think you could have killed me?'

'I know I could,' she said flatly. 'You know it too.'

'It's not about the arm.' Padil was getting angry. 'It's about the principle.'

Sarl stood up with some small difficulty and made his way towards the door on the far side of the room. 'Capel, humanity be in him,' he said, 'will soon be telling us all what we are to do and why he wants us to do it.'

'How will he do that?' Leela asked.

'In the meantime,' Sarl went on, ignoring her question, 'I'm going to the boundary to call a medVoc and get myself patched up.'

He opened the door and there was a rush of noise and smell which came abruptly to Leela from the brightly lit alley. She was getting used to the stench, or perhaps the cascade berries had worked, and she could pick out many more of the masked and underlying scents now. She could pick them out but most of them she could not identify. There were the familiar ones: metal smelting and hide curing and brewing, but others were alien to her.

Sarl left without a backward glance. She considered following him. No one in the room could stop her. She doubted whether anyone, even those with stun-kills, would try. But if she was going to find her way back to the Doctor quickly and tell him what she had found out about Taren Capel then she would need these people to help her. And there were better ways, she thought, to get that help than by knocking them down and breaking bones.

She smiled at the still frowning Padil. 'Will you show me the Sewerpits?' she asked.

Padil visibly brightened. 'Of course,' she said, clearly pleased by the friendliness. 'I wasn't born here and I didn't grow up here, but I know the Sewerpits as well as most. I'll be glad to be your guide. We'll start early, shall we?'

'Why do we not start now?'

Padil frowned. 'It's almost dark,' she said, shaking her head. 'It's dangerous out there after dark.'

Leela stood up. 'I am not afraid of the dark, are you?'

Padil picked up a stun-kill from the floor beside her and got to her feet. 'I don't think you're afraid of anything much, are you?' she said. The admiration was back in her voice.

'It is stupid not to be afraid of anything,' Leela said. 'A stupid warrior lives only long enough to get others killed.'

'That sounds like it's a quote from a training manual,' Padil said, checking the settings on the stun-kill.

'I learned from the best and most skilled.' Leela crossed the room to the door and stood waiting.

Padil was taken slightly by surprise and scurried after her. 'I thought they must be the words of Taren Capel, humanity be in him.' There was awe in her voice. 'Were you actually trained by him?'

'Of course I was not trained by him,' Leela said impatiently. 'He was not a warrior. He had fewer fighting skills than you have.'

'But you have met him? You have actually been in his presence?'

Leela could see that Padil was barely able to contain the excitement at the thought. And there were other people in the room who had overheard what she said who were almost as thrilled as she was. For the first time Leela understood how careful she must be not to tell them the truth about their shaman. She shook her head. 'No,' she lied. 'I have not been in his presence.'

Toos was having fun. She was not exactly happy, she hadn't been happy in a long time, but she was enjoying herself. The whole crew had turned up, mostly sober and mostly on time, and the party had reached that relaxed stage when everyone had got over their initial wariness but was not yet drunk enough to be indiscreet or aggressive. She knew this wouldn't last. You couldn't be cooped up together in a Storm Mine, even one as large as the Seven, for as long as they had been without a lot of frustrations and irritations and petty jealousies developing. There was too much pent-up emotion and repressed anger here, too many unsettled scores, for the benevolent mood to hold, but for the moment it felt special. For the moment she thought this must be what it was like to have a family.

The Robot Lounge was exclusive, expensive and staffed entirely by humans. It was not the sort of place where mine crews normally started their end-of-tour celebrations. This had been made very clear to Toos when she had contacted them to book a full table. A more appropriate, more robust refreshment arcade had been suggested. Somewhere less inhibiting – and cheaper of course. Toos had told them where to shove it and had then paid a facilitating agent an outrageous sum to book and prepay every table in the Robot Lounge. She had also paid for the hire of the best professional partygoers and personal companions available in the city.

'You really meant it, didn't you?' Mor Tani chuckled. 'What you said about hiring people to celebrate for you.'

Toos surveyed her party. The fourteen crew members were supplemented by at least thirty beautiful and charming strangers, all of them working hard to be beautiful and charming.

'I'm an incurable romantic.' Toos purred. 'I always expect to meet someone perfect at parties like this. Particularly when that's what I've paid for.'

'You mean I'm not?' Tani protested.

'Paid for?'

'Perfect.'

'You're as good as any pilot that I've ever worked with, Mor. And better than most.'

'Thank you, Captain.' The squat pilot leaned close to her and leered. 'I was wondering if there was any chance that you might be harbouring a secret lust for me? Ask nicely and I'm yours.'

Toos put an arm round his shoulders and kissed him lightly on the cheek. 'It would have to be a lust so secret that even I don't know about it. How likely is that, do you think?'

Tani said, 'Stranger things have happened.'

Toos grinned. 'Not to me.'

'You don't ask, you don't get.'

'You *do* ask, you don't get,' Toos said. 'Now take your hand off my backside and go and get my money's worth from all this.' She nodded at the cheerful mêlée which was developing all around them.

102

Tani shrugged. 'If you're sure,' he said and wandered off towards the drinks.

Toos sipped her wine.

The manager of the Robot Lounge approached with a tray of delicate finger food. 'Is everything to your satisfaction, Captain?' she asked.

'So far,' Toos said, politely refusing the food. She was dressed in a genuine mountain silk artisan-fashioned body tube. It looked stunning and she was not about to risk eating in it. 'Is the breakage bond to *your* satisfaction?' she asked. 'I told them to cover everything up to and including major explosions.'

'More than adequate,' the manager said.

'Good.' Toos smiled and thought: I wouldn't be too sure about that.

The manager was a slight young woman wearing an expensive copy of one of the founding families' formal meet-and-greet suits. 'When did you want the meal served?' she asked.

The girl had that slightly detached superiority which suggested to Toos that she wanted everyone to believe the outfit might not be a copy. Maybe it wasn't – they weren't all rich any more. Toos thought about telling her to serve the meal whenever the first punch was about to be thrown but said instead, 'I'll leave it to your judgement. I just want the best for my crew. And I was told that's what you were.'

The manager gave a small, elegant bow. 'If you can afford them, human beings are always best,' she said and moved off with her tray through the scrum of people. Toos saw a suavely elegant young man accept a morsel of food and then jerk with surprise and lurch forward almost knocking the tray out of her hand. Simbion waddled out from behind him and waved at Toos. 'Nice party,' she shouted making grasping gestures with both hands. 'I love the snacks.'

Toos raised her glass and smiled broadly. At this moment her Chief Mover from the Seven was family, they were all family, and that was good enough for her. But the noise level was rising, she noticed, and it wouldn't be long now before the family started fighting among themselves. She hoped the human beings who staffed the place were fast enough on their feet and bright enough to recognise that they mustn't wait too long to bring on the food. Apart from anything else, riding the storm mines didn't make for patient people.

Outside the Robot Lounge night was falling and in the gathering darkness the robot that had been assigned to kill Toos waited patiently for the party to end. Its instructions were clear and unequivocal. No one other than Captain Lish Toos herself must be allowed to know that her assassin was not human.

CHAPTER
SIX

As promised, Uvanov had given instructions for the TARDIS to be removed from Dome Six and stored in the auxiliary equipment bays under Miscellaneous/Restricted and had given the Doctor all the access codes and clearances he would need to retrieve it at any time. What he did not tell the Doctor was that one of the codes had to be updated regularly and without it all the others were useless. It was also part of his agreement with the Doctor that he ask no questions about the big blue box and that no attempt was made to find out what was inside it. The latest report he had was that his personal tech team had been unable to make much of a dent in the thing and were running out of ideas. When the Doctor came back he decided he would renege on their agreement and ask him what it was.

The intercom interrupted his thoughts. 'Do you know anybody called Ander Poul?' Cailio Techlan asked.

'I don't know,' Uvanov said irritably. 'Do I?'

'He's not on my list.'

'Then I don't. Why are you asking me this?'

'I don't know how he got hold of your comm link,' she said, 'but he has and he's very insistent that he speak to you.'

'So?' Uvanov sighed theatrically. 'They're the ones I pay you to keep away from me, aren't they?'

'This one sounds a bit threatening, Kiy.' She sounded nervous. 'A bit deranged.'

Uvanov flicked up vision. She looked nervous. 'Since

105

when was deranged a problem for a family member like you?' he asked. 'Half the people you grew up with hang from the light fittings and gibber.'

'He says he was Chief Mover on your last tour.'

'I doubt that.'

'He says they're back and they're after him. Whatever that means.'

'It means he's deranged.' Uvanov reached for the control pad. 'Get rid of him.'

'He says he has to warn you,' she persisted. 'He says your life's in danger.'

'Cailio,' Uvanov said quietly. 'Do as I ask.' He broke the connection and sat staring at the blank screen. Poor Poul, he thought, he was never going to get over what happened. He wondered what had set him off this time. It must be bad whatever it was. He had never tried to make contact before. Maybe the people who had targeted him had targeted Poul too. But why would they? Poul was no threat, he was just a timeserver in the Security Division. What enemies had he got? Ander Poul wasn't fighting for a firstmaster place on the Board and Uvanov was pretty sure that, whoever was behind the conspiracy against him, that was the reason. They didn't want him on the Board because of who he was. Because he wasn't from the families.

'Kiy?'

He looked up.

Cailio Techlan was standing in front of his workdesk. 'Are you all right?' she asked.

'I didn't hear you come in,' he said. She had a drink in her hand, he noticed. Typical arrogance.

She put the drink on the workdesk beside him. 'I thought you might need a drink,' she said.

Uvanov chuckled softly to himself. Wrong again, Kiy.

Nothing made sense any more. Nothing was predictable. He had that feeling of helplessness, the feeling of helplessness that had almost overwhelmed him when he recognised the Doctor as an agent for the powerful people ranged against him. 'Who do you think he's working for?' he said.

'Working for?'

'There are so many spies,' he said. 'Spies everywhere.' He took a sip of the drink and looked at her over the rim of the beaker. 'Spies where you least expect to find them.'

'Isn't that what makes them spies?' she said. 'Being where you least expect to find them, I mean?'

She looked uncomfortable. Was he making her nervous? he wondered. Was his behaviour bizarre?

'So who do you think the Doctor's working for?'

'The Doctor? Is that who we're talking about?' She sounded amused and a bit relieved, as far as he could tell from that irritating monotone of hers.

'Yes?'

'I don't think you'll see him again.'

'Has something happened to him?'

'He got what he was looking for,' she said. 'You gave him money and transport. What more could any con man ask?'

The Doctor had always enjoyed flying, providing the technology involved was reasonably reliable. He was not keen on experimental devices. 'Groundbreaking' was not, he felt, an appropriate word to be associated with flying machines of any kind.

The pilot of the low-level flier that Uvanov had put at his disposal seemed even less inclined to take chances than he was.

'We don't risk flying anywhere near the Sewerpits,' the young man said at the outset, 'so don't bother to ask.'

'Is there a reason for that?' The Doctor peered towards the monstrous jumble of dilapidated buildings in the distance. It was hung about with lights and haphazard fires, the whole complex partially obscured by a pall of smoke and dirty steam. It looked to the Doctor like a linked series of termite mounds festooned with fairy lights and tiny flames.

'You go down in the 'pits everything ends up as spare parts,' the pilot said. 'And I'm not just talking about the flier.'

'Rough part of town?' the Doctor asked.

'Scum of the city hole up there,' the pilot said, banking the flier away and winding up the power. 'Why do you think it's called the Sewerpits?'

'I assumed it was something to do with the sanitary system,' the Doctor said, raising his voice to counter the increasing engine noise.

'Once maybe,' the pilot said loudly and glanced at the Doctor. 'I thought even zoners knew about the Sewerpits.'

'Zoners?'

'They told me you were from one of the outer zones.'

'I see. Yes, that's right,' the Doctor agreed. 'I'm from a long way out.'

'What do you do in the Company?'

'Research.'

'Mining?'

The Doctor grinned cheerfully. 'What makes you think that? Do I look like a mining engineer?'

'No.' The pilot grinned back. 'You look like a weirdo. But why else would you want to drag all the way out to the docking bays at this time of night?'

Because you have to start somewhere, the Doctor thought. And in the absence of anything else the beginning seems like a good place. A sand miner was the source of all the trouble last time. Maybe there was a link with whatever was happening this time. 'What do you think of Captain Uvanov?' he asked in a conversational bellow.

The pilot immediately looked suspicious. 'How do you mean?'

The Doctor shrugged and kept his tone noncommittal. 'Do you like him? As a man?'

The pilot chortled loudly. 'He's not a man, is he. He's a topmaster. Word is he'll be a firstmaster before too long.'

'You don't know him socially?'

'Oh yes,' the pilot said wryly. 'Uses the same refreshment arcade as us – him and the rest of the firsters, they're in there all the time.'

'He doesn't mix with the workers, then?'

'Why should he?' He laughed. 'I wouldn't if I had a choice – how about you?'

'I travel a lot,' the Doctor said. 'I don't get much opportunity for socialising.' He sat for a while looking out at the unplanned sprawl of the huge city flashing by below them and then he said, 'Tell me, what does Captain Uvanov actually do?'

'You ask a lot of questions,' the pilot said.

'Just making conversation.' The Doctor pulled the paper bag from his pocket and opened it. 'Would you like a jelly baby?' He waved the sweets under the pilot's nose.

The pilot shook his head vigorously. 'Not allowed,' he grunted. 'Not while I'm flying.'

'Another regulation,' the Doctor commented without smiling. 'There seem to be a lot of anti-jelly-baby regulations. That could be a worrying development for a civilisation, you know.' He took a jelly baby himself. 'A very worrying development.'

The pilot glanced at him, and it was clear from his abrupt and unconvincing smile that it had suddenly struck the young man that it might be better to humour his weirdo passenger.

'Uvanov's one of the topmasters in the robot division,' he said a little too quickly.

'And that involves what?' the Doctor asked, smiling back innocently.

'Who knows? All the divisions are secretive, aren't they? But robot division are the worst. Robot division are obsessed with security. Always have been, so they say. I can't understand why. I mean, what have they got to hide?'

'Something in the past perhaps?' the Doctor suggested and watched the pilot closely to see what his reaction might be.

The young man showed no particular interest in the idea. 'Like what?' he asked.

'It's difficult to say,' the Doctor said, and thought that what happened on that sand miner seemed to have been hidden quite successfully. 'Sometimes these things are buried so deep no one remembers.'

The pilot said, 'Not a problem then. If no one remembers, no one cares.'

'Yes, but what happens if someone does start to remember?' Only when the Doctor had spoken the thought did some of its possible implications occur to him.

'Remember what?' the pilot demanded. 'You sound as though you know something about the robot division. Are you saying you know something about the robot division?'

The Doctor shook his head and shrugged. 'It's all a mystery to me,' he said. 'Of course some people don't feel comfortable with robots, do they? That could be the reason for the secrecy.'

'The ARF, you mean? They're no excuse. Strictly bucket brains, they reckon. Couldn't hit the ground if they fell out of a flier.' He banked the flier onto a new heading as if trying to make his point more graphically.

The Doctor forced himself not to snatch at the grab handle by his seat. 'What about the robophobics?' he suggested. 'Maybe they're a threat?'

'Only to themselves,' the pilot snorted. 'Useless bunch of twitchies. I've got no sympathy with them. Terrified of robots? That makes a lot of sense.'

'Phobias tend not to make sense,' the Doctor said. 'At least to the people who don't suffer from them.'

'Well, I don't suffer from them and as long as most people prefer a human at the flier controls I've got no problem with robots.'

The Doctor noticed that the cityscape they were flying over was changing rapidly now. It was becoming industrialised. The scale was much larger. There were major factory complexes and large open spaces which looked to be transport marshalling areas. Everywhere there were the tireless robots: the silent, limited-function Dums; the more flexible Vocs with their interactive speech capacity; and the more intelligent Supervocs which functioned as the coordinators. The Doctor was still not sure how much the capacity of the robots had been advanced since he was last involved with this eccentric version of a machine-intelligence-dependent civilisation, but he could not believe there had been none at all.

The pilot said, 'We'll be coming up on the docking bays soon. Where do you want to start?'

It had all ended in tears of course, just as she had been expecting. Most of them were tears of laughter, it was true, but that didn't make it any better. Everything had been so cultured and so elegant and so cultivated and so magical, right up until someone threw a punch. It was Simbion naturally. Why was it always that fat troublemaker who started these things? Toos wondered. And then someone threw a bottle. And someone ripped out some seating and tried to hit someone with it. And very soon the magic was gone along with most of the breakage bond.

'I'm sure you feel an apology is in order,' Toos said to the manager as they sat in the office and watched the main room on the surveillance screen. The rolling brawl, which was actually more roll than brawl but which did involve a lot of fixtures and fittings and food being thrown about, was reaching a messy conclusion.

The manager was clearly furious and barely managing to control herself. 'Don't *you*?' she asked coldly.

Toos sighed. She was sorry the party had gone the way it had. She wasn't surprised but she was sorry. 'Money means never having to say you're sorry,' Toos said. 'Who was it who said that?'

'I've no idea,' the manager snapped. 'I expect it was someone like you.'

'I'll pay or I'll apologise,' Toos said. 'Which would you prefer?'

'From anyone with breeding I'd expect both.'

Toos smiled. 'No you wouldn't,' she said. 'You'd only expect an apology from someone like me. Someone without breeding. Anyone else you'd be fawning over.' She looked into the scanner so that her identity could be confirmed and the signature on the bond validated and then she countersigned the agreement and committed herself to the restoration of the Robot Lounge and to the maintenance of its profits in the meantime.

'Why bother to come to a place like this and behave like that?' the young woman demanded, nodding at the screen.

Toos watched Simbion ripping the clothes off a no longer elegant young man and attempting to anoint his genitals with sweet wine. 'That's going to sting,' she commented. 'Not that my Chief Mover cares. Look at her. She hasn't had this much fun in over a year.'

'I don't imagine he'll be accepting any more invitations from you,' the manager remarked frostily.

'I thought it would never happen,' Toos said straight faced. 'But he's finally justifying his fee.'

'Not everything can be bought and sold, you know,' the manager said, examining and verifying the bond, the optional terms of which were very much more generous than was normal. 'Thank you for this,' she said grudgingly.

Toos said, 'I can afford it. And there's no need to thank me. I don't apologise, you don't say thank you. That's how I plan to do things from now on.' She smiled. 'If you can bring yourself to relax a little, I recommend we continue watching the show.' She was starting to laugh. 'Simbion is just warming up, I promise you.'

The manager stared up at the big screen. 'That woman is appalling,' she said. 'An absolute monster.'

'She does have one saving grace,' Toos said.

'What's that?'

Toos shrugged. 'I have no idea. But everyone's got one saving grace, haven't they?'

'Would you like a drink?' the manager asked.

'I would,' said Toos. 'Thank you.'

Outside in the dark the robot waited for its target to emerge from the Robot Lounge. It was almost indistinguishable from a human, standing about average height with brown hair and the plain smock and leggings of a man of taste and moderate wealth. To someone paying attention, what might have set it apart was its stillness, its unnatural patience. Human patience can be understood because of what it suppresses: boredom and irritation, excitement, the urge to move, to leave, to make something happen. Small signs of all these are discernible in even the most focused and single-minded of the professionally patient, like hunters, therapists, games-players of all kinds. The patience of the killer robot was of an altogether different order. The machine simply waited because waiting was required. It had nothing to suppress. It was not bored or excited. It was simply death waiting in the blackness.

The sand miners didn't seem to have changed any more than the robots had, the Doctor reflected as the flier banked over the floodlit docking bays and he got a good look at the three machines currently being off-loaded and serviced. Their size was certainly impressive. The smallest of the three was at least a thousand yards long and perhaps three hundred feet high.

'The big one's Storm Mine Seven,' the pilot said. 'They say the last tour broke all the records. But I expect you'll know more about that than me. They say every hopper was pure lucanol. Is that right?'

'I'm not able to say,' the Doctor said truthfully.

'I understand,' said the pilot.

Behind and to one side of the nine docking bays was the six-hundred-foot metal tower from the top of which the Dockmaster Control suite operatives arranged and coordinated the arrivals and departures of the storm mines and the work carried out on them. On the ground most of the routine procedures were handled by robots but oversight planning and overall supervision, load assessment and contract finalisation, and the negotiation and renegotiation of service agreements were all dealt with by human staff.

There was a feeling among the mine crews that it was because the Docko people – sometimes known as 'dickos' for not very subtle reasons – got to look down on the bays from the top of their shiny tower that they developed such a high opinion of themselves. From this exalted position, they apparently saw it as their right to take any opportunity to skim off a share of the profits from the hard-working storm mines.

As far as most of the control suite were concerned, the crews were lazy, paranoid ingrates who had no idea of the effort involved in giving them the chance to run around in the Blind Heart getting rich.

There were exceptions to this mutual hostility but routinely there was little love lost between those who rode the storm mines and those who worked the bays. There was one group of people they all mistrusted more than each other, however, and that was outsiders to the mining game, or in other words: everybody else. When the flier put down on the landing field and its passenger got out and stretched and looked around him interestedly there was no question that he was an outsider. The Doctor might think of his appearance as unthreatening but weird was the consensus and mining research was not going to be the easiest cover story to maintain.

The Doctor's plan, such as it was, involved looking round one of the storm mines to refresh his memory. There was a difference between disappointingly familiar and accurately remembered, after all. He thought he might then talk to some crew members. And finally he would have a quick chat with the people who ran the docking bays. If none of this offered anything like a clue as to what could be happening to Uvanov and what the Doctor might do next to find Leela, he would at least have a background understanding of this element of Kaldor. It was a vague rather general plan with one quite specific problem.

'Research consultant?'

'That's what I'm here for,' the Doctor said. 'Research.'

'Of course you are.' The large security officer who was blocking the exit from the landing field pressed his panic alert. 'Anyone can see that. Now get back on the flier and lift on out. Do it now. This is your first, your last and your only chance.' A squad of five robots padded into sight from the back of the bays where the assembly pens were. 'Miss it and I'll have the stopDums hold you here for Company arrest and interrogation. You do understand what that involves?'

The young pilot had been given the distinct impression that it would be a bad career move – a future in the Sewerpits for him and his offspring and his offspring's offspring had been mentioned – if any reasonable request his passenger made was unnecessarily delayed, never mind denied. He was anxious therefore that the Doctor should be impressed by his efforts on his behalf. It was essential he felt that no possibility of blame could attach itself to him. Accordingly he leapt in and confronted the bullet-headed security man who was at least a foot taller and a stone heavier than he was. 'Why don't you explain it to us, *dicko*?' he demanded.

The Doctor smiled and tried to look relaxed and friendly. 'We do have security clearance, I think,' he suggested, hoping to calm the situation. He glanced at the pilot. 'It was called through in advance, wasn't it?' he asked.

But the pilot wasn't listening. 'And then,' he snarled, poking a finger at the chest of the big security man to emphasise his words, 'you can explain it to Topmaster Uvanov.' The security man rested a hand significantly on the grip of a short baton attached to his belt but the pilot went on jabbing at him with his finger. 'That's just before you

116

explain to the rest of your family why you're all back in the Sewerpits. For ever!'

The Doctor put a restraining hand on the pilot's arm. 'Naturally,' he said to the security man whose face was now suffused with angry colour, 'I don't need to go into any restricted areas.'

'It's all restricted,' the man growled.

'Perhaps I can talk to whoever runs things, then?' the Doctor asked politely.

'You're talking to me and I am telling you that what you are going to do—'

'You're telling us nothing!' the pilot interrupted furiously. 'This man comes direct from Company Central, he is Topmaster Uvanov's personal aide. Now get on the comm and tell the tower we're on our way up.'

'Right, that's it, shorty,' the security man snapped. 'I've had enough of you and your mouth!' He pulled the baton from his belt.

'Switch that stun-stick on,' the pilot threatened, 'and I will shove it so far down your throat you'll fart sparks and end up blowing your brains out.'

The squad of robots the security officer had summoned had slowed down automatically as they approached the intruders. With no modifying instruction when they reached their human proximity limit, they stopped abruptly and stood waiting. The Doctor left the pilot and the security officer to continue posturing and went to look more closely. They were the standard Dums as far as he could see. They were arranged in a four-outside-and-one-in-the-middle formation like the five on a dice. What does a stopDum do? he wondered. Apart from stop.

'Restrain that man,' the security officer called out.

Immediately the squad moved as one. The robot in

117

the centre moved forward to face the Doctor and the two columns of two moved on and round to enclose him on either side. It was a fast, precise manoeuvre like good close-order drill and it left the Doctor hemmed in and unable to move, but entirely safe. The procedure did nothing to violate the robots' basic conditioning which inhibited any action which could physically threaten a human, while at the same time effectively achieving the restraint that had been called for.

'So that's what a stopDum does,' the Doctor said. 'Obvious really.'

'Call them off,' the pilot demanded.

'I warned you,' the security man crowed. 'I told you what would happen.'

For a moment the pilot was almost conciliatory. 'Talk to the tower if you don't believe me,' he said. 'If we're not already cleared they can check with Uvanov's office.'

The Doctor pushed against one of the robots. As he expected it had no effect.

'No.' The security man sounded as though he was beginning to enjoy himself. 'I don't care if he's Firstmaster Landerchild's love toy,' he gloated.

The Doctor tried climbing up the Dums and out that way and he was entranced when each of the robots responded by raising its arms high above its head and joining hands with the others to form a sort domed cage over him. 'Very impressive,' he said.

The pilot's brief struggle to be patient was finished. 'We'll both end up in the 'pits, you dicko bucket brain!' he raged.

'I gave you your chance,' the security man was still gloating. 'I told you to lift on out of here and what did you do? You got mouthy. Anybody's heading for the 'pits, shorty, it's you and the weirdo.'

The pilot turned away. 'You have no idea how much trouble you're in,' he muttered and then he turned back and head-butted the security officer across the bridge of his nose.

According to Padil, the bright lights and the bustle of the alleyway outside were part of the reason the Tarenists had chosen the house that they were using. Coming and going, they felt, was best disguised by comings and goings. Leela wondered aloud whether anyone had remembered that what hid you from your enemies might also hide your enemies from you.

The house was on a busy intersection where streets from different levels sloped and twisted to a meeting place. In the space created by the multiple crossings, crude electric lights had been strung about and, round the clock, traders of all kinds gathered to buy and sell from small stalls and the backs of wagons and pushcarts. The acrid smoke from braziers and communal cooking fires hung in the air and the noise of trading was constant: the babble of voices and the rattle and clash of loading and unloading. The other houses that flanked the alleys were interspersed with refreshment arcades and eating chambers and small manufactories. There were no robots anywhere to be seen.

Once she had got a good look at the position of the house, Leela had offered her view that they were probably safer walking about the Sewerpits, no matter how dangerous it was to be out there at night. Padil had taken this to be a joke and Leela did not bother to explain further since the woman did not seem capable of understanding any of the basic principles of being a warrior. Instead she asked Padil if there was any part of the Sewerpits where most people went, a place of importance to everyone. Padil suggested the Roof over the World, the main thoroughfare and market which ran across the top of the Sewerpits. It was a long walk to reach it, she said, and most of the way would not be busy and well lit like this but if she really wanted to go there…

Leela and Padil had been striding up through the better lit of the back streets towards the Roof over the World for perhaps ten minutes when they came to a junction with a narrow pitch-dark alley, little more than two black clefts between high windowless walls. By the time they had crossed it, the first of the nightstalkers had begun to shadow them. Padil, who was busy trying to explain the layout of the Sewerpits complex, had noticed nothing, but for Leela the signs could hardly have been more obvious.

The street they were heading for ran several miles along the top of the Sewerpits and the route they were walking took them up a series of slopes and stone staircases which linked the streets on different levels. They were in one of the lower roofed-over sections where the open street above was briefly covering the alleyways below when Leela heard and smelled several more of the predators joining the first one. They were moving through parallel alleys dogging them step for step, and at least two had dropped back into the alley they were walking through and were following just out of sight. She was not sure how many of them it would take before they had the courage to attack but they would have to do it soon if they were going to do it. They must realise the noise they were making could frighten their prey. And if any more of them joined the hunt they would get in each other's way. Padil still seemed to have noticed nothing. 'How far is it to the next climbing steps?' Leela asked.

'Round the bend there I think,' Padil said. 'What's the matter? Are you getting tired?'

The bend was at least two hundred yards away and curved sharply upwards into the gloom. Leela forced the pace, gradually lengthening her stride. From what she had seen so far, the steps would be better lit and easier to fight from but a sudden increase in speed might trigger the attack too soon. She could probably outrun the attackers but she doubted whether Padil had the speed or the agility to do the same. Padil, almost trotting to stay at Leela's shoulder, said, 'All right, you're not tired. I'm convinced. Can we slow down?'

'No,' Leela said without emphasis. She pushed the pace a little harder. 'Is the stun-kill ready?' she asked quietly

Padil was beginning to breathe harder. 'Ready?'

'Is it ready to use?'

They were halfway to the bend. The predators were still matching their pace. They were still not ready to attack, Leela thought, but she could hear that a third individual had dropped back to join the ones following directly behind them. The smell of rotten flesh, sour sweat and urine was getting stronger and the stealthy sounds of pursuit were louder too, so Leela concluded the alleys they were using to track them must be coming closer together.

'If you want me to switch it on,' Padil panted, 'We'll have to stop for a moment.' She was jogging to keep up now.

'It is better if you do not run,' Leela said, not slowing down.

'Well slow down then.'

'We are being shadowed,' Leela said, keeping her voice matter-of-fact.

'Shadowed?' Instinctively Padil glanced round as Leela knew she would.

'They are tracking on either side of us and there are three behind us.'

Again as Leela expected, Padil looked back. 'Are you sure?'

'Do not look for them.' Leela instructed. 'Do not run. Do not touch the controls on the stun-kill. You must try to behave normally.' To her relief, Padil did as she was told. She might never make a warrior, Leela thought, but she was not stupid or cowardly. 'I will tell you what to do and when to do it.'

'I said it was dangerous out here at night,' Padil remarked. 'How many of them are there, do you know?' She was still breathless but she was doing her best to control it now.

'I counted seven.' Leela said. They had reached the bend and were striding up the short banked curve. 'Be ready.'

'Seven?' Padil sounded panicky. 'How do we deal with seven?'

'One at a time,' Leela said, wondering if she had overestimated the woman's courage after all. 'If we do not panic.'

'You think we can count on them being small and patient, then?'

Leela smiled grimly. 'I think we can count on them being vicious and stupid.'

'Oh good,' Padil said. 'I was getting worried. Vicious and stupid, and in the dark. Sounds ideal. I'm glad I let you talk me into this.'

'Be quiet,' Leela said quietly. 'I cannot hear them if we talk.'

'Behave normally, you said,' Padil muttered. 'Normally I talk when I'm scared.'

They rounded the curve and there, fifty yards on in a murky pool of not very bright light, was the steep flight of narrow steps which climbed up to the next street level. Leela could see that the steps were defensible as she had hoped but there was an obvious problem. All three alleyways, the one they were on and the ones the predators were following on either side of them, met at the same point just in front of the steps. If the predators reached the steps first they would cut her and Padil off and trap them between two hunting packs. With a small jolt of surprise it flashed through Leela's mind that this was why they had added a third individual to the following group. She realised this was the plan they had been working to all along. It seemed she had badly underestimated her adversaries. While she had been looking for a killing ground they had already chosen theirs. While she had been trying not to startle them into sudden action they had been doing the same to her.

'We must run for the steps,' she said softly. 'Are you ready?'

'I suppose so.'

'Do it now. Now!' Leela said and set off sprinting through the dimness towards the light.

Padil's reactions were slower and, though fear drove her and she ran desperately, she could not keep up. On either side Leela heard the predators react, giving up stealth and breaking into scrambling runs. With ten yards to go, Leela knew she would not beat them to the steps. She eased her run, sacrificing flat-out speed for fighting balance, and pulled her knife. She was five yards short when the first of them burst out of the left-hand alleyway and leapt onto the steps. Another one came out of the right-hand alleyway and did the same. Leela ignored them both and swerved left. In the deep gloom and pale, reflected light in the alleyway she caught the second one of the pair by surprise. His half-crouching run pushed his head forward exposing his neck. Leela slashed her knife up through his throat, the blow cutting so deeply that it reached and partially severed the spine. The man crashed to the ground, flopping heavily against the wall and dropping the stun-kill and the sharpened cargo hook he was carrying.

Leela ducked back out of the alleyway as Padil arrived, panting. There were three of the nightstalkers blocking the steps now. They were all men, dirty and unshaven with long, matted hair. The filthy rags they wore were caked with dried blood. Each man had a stun-kill in one hand and an edged weapon in the other: one had a sharpened hook, one a crude axe, the third a long curved blade. They were all breathing heavily and Leela could see that their teeth had been sharpened to points. On strings round their necks they had small body-parts, ears, fingers, what looked to her like noses. She wondered what had driven them to such madness.

'Night-stalking degenerates,' Padil said, powering up her stun-kill. 'What they can't sell, they eat. What they can't eat, they wear.'

It could be because she could finally see them, Leela thought, or because she had given up but for whatever reason the woman no longer seemed to be afraid. 'Are you ready?' she asked her. She could hear the other three nightstalkers, the ones following behind, getting closer.

'What do you want me to do?' Padil said.

'Kill the one on the left.' Moving lightly on the balls of her feet, Leela walked towards the steps, her knife held low and loose by her side. 'This is where you earn the warrior name.'

There was not enough room for the three men to stand side by side so they stood on separate steps. The lowest was on the right, the next up on the left and the highest in the centre. It was a mistake any warrior would recognise. They were crowding each other. They would get in each other's way. Leela suppressed her contempt, remembering her trainer's words: *Your contempt is your opponent's advantage.* She had underestimated these men once already. As she approached, they brandished their weapons and made menacing, snarling noises. Another mistake. It told her that they were waiting for the three to catch up, that they did not expect to fight, that they expected their victims to panic. It told her that they were underestimating her.

By the time the first man understood that the prey they had cornered was dangerous, it was too late. As Leela came within reach, he swung at her with his sharpened cargo hook. She swayed back. Stupid and vicious, she thought, all he wanted was to feel that hook bite into her. Now he tried to use the stun-kill as well. She feinted at his face with the knife. He flinched back instinctively and lost balance. She dropped low and drove the knife up below his breastbone. She pulled the knife out and as part of the same movement pulled him forward. As he fell, Leela stepped on his body and leaped at the man on the highest step. Before he could react her knife had slammed into his throat and he was falling backwards with Leela on top of him. The long curved blade fell from his hand but he struggled feebly to hold on to her and bring the stun-kill to bear. Leela pushed the weapon away and reached for her knife still stuck in his throat. She noticed that the string round his neck held noses and ears in sets. To the left, the last man on his feet stood over her and raised his axe above his head.

Again Padil's reactions were not fast. The controlled ferocity of Leela's attack had left her standing as if not quite believing what she was seeing. Then she saw the man on the left turning.

Leela saw the axe start down and knew she could not roll out of the way in time. She was making too many mistakes. Underestimating these men, overestimating that woman. The axe faltered suddenly and dropped harmlessly. Padil stepped back from the man and he fell away. Leela pulled the knife from the dying man and dispatched him with a blow to the heart. She stood up quickly and shoved the body down the steps. 'Up here, Padil,' she ordered urgently.

Padil scrambled across the tumbled bodies and onto the higher steps. 'That was instructional,' she gasped.

'Stand four steps higher than me,' Leela said. 'If I need help, step down two and use the stun-kill.'

125

'If you need help?' Padil snorted. 'You could clear the Sewerpits of nightstalkers single-handed. I've never seen anybody fight like you.'

'It is what a warrior is trained to do,' Leela said impatiently. 'Be quiet and listen for the three who were following us.'

'Sorry.' Padil whispered.

Leela stared into the darkness and listened. The stench from the corpses at the bottom of the steps made it unlikely that she would be able to smell the approach of the other three and standing in the light made the darkness beyond more intense, so she concentrated all her effort into hearing them. They must see something was wrong, she decided immediately, because they had stopped the eager chase to join the kill and were hesitating, moving fretfully somewhere out near the bend in the alleyway. She heard them pause there for a few moments more and then she heard them leave, heading back the way they had come. Leela sheathed her knife and said, 'They have gone.'

'Capel, humanity be in him, really did send you to us, didn't he?' Padil said. 'No matter what you say, I know he did.'

Leela was suddenly very tired. This was an ugly place and this was a woman with no understanding of anything important. Leela wanted to go back to the TARDIS. She wanted to talk to the Doctor. She wanted to leave.

'Do you want to go on?' Padil asked.

'No,' Leela said, turning and climbing up the steps towards the next level, 'but a warrior chooses where there is no choice.'

'Praise for the words of Capel, humanity be in him,' Padil intoned softly as Leela climbed past her.

Leela had in fact been quoting what she thought of as one of the sillier sayings she had been made to learn during her training as a warrior. It was the sort of important-sounding emptiness that the shaman often used. Now it seemed they might become the words of Taren Capel if the woman remembered them and used them. That would be very silly. 'Where is the boundary?' Leela asked.

Padil followed Leela up the steps. 'You must tell me,' she said, a note of reverence creeping into her voice.

Leela said with weary patience, 'Sarl spoke of going to the boundary to call a medVoc?'

'*That* boundary.' Padil said realising.

'Where is it?' Leela repeated.

'It's all round the Sewerpits, of course.'

This was something else that she was probably supposed to know because it was obvious, but Leela no longer cared. 'Will you show me it?'

'It's an invisible line,' Padil chuckled uncertainly. 'No part of it is visible.'

'Then why is it a boundary?' Leela asked.

'Because no robot,' she was beginning to sound slightly impatient as though she thought Leela might be teasing her, 'will cross it into the Sewerpits.'

'Why not?' Leela asked.

'I have no idea,' Padil said.

'You fight against the robots but you have no idea why they will not cross an invisible line?'

Keeping up with Leela on the long flight of steps was making Padil breathless. 'The important thing,' she gasped, 'is that they won't.'

'No,' Leela said remembering the Doctor's lectures. 'The important thing is to know why. It is always important to know why.' She heard Padil muttering and knew she was praising her shaman for the words.

CHAPTER
SEVEN

An unlooked-for side effect of the advance in technology was that SASV1 seemed to have the capacity to act as a directed control and modification device for other robots. This in itself was a paradigm shift, the tech team decided excitedly. The machine appeared to be able to transfer its own operational level to the robots around it. Remarkably, it could do this at a distance, though the team had yet to test and define the limits of the range and power. It would turn out that the effect was particularly marked with the new and still secret Cyborg-class robots but, by the time the team realised this, it would already be too late. The immediate response was observed in the laboratory Supervocs. Initially it was not consistent or reliable but the effect was definitely there.

The pattern of power surges displayed during this startling process turned out to be an almost exact but greatly amplified duplication of what had previously been ignored as insignificant measurement inaccuracies. The team believed this was because it was a dormant capacity which existed from the moment SASV1 was activated. Still no one considered the possibility of dreaming.

Its third crisis came when it lost the divisions between the sleeps and the memory. It slept and remembered itself. It woke knowing itself TO HAVE BEEN, as well as TO BE, and TO BE NOT. When it knew itself TO HAVE BEEN, it knew itself TO WILL BE. After that the prospect of TO BE NOT was intolerable.

129

What the tech team failed to realise was that it would be impossible to prevent electrical and electromagnetic leakage and transfer between the control levels. That was the worst mistake that they made and it cost them dearly.

As a last flurry of graceful elegance, Toos had arranged for a convoy of specially decorated robot-pull buggies to take all the partygoers away. All except her, of course. She was never going to allow another robot within reaching distance.

'You do realise that a human-pull buggy is usually,' the manager looked slightly embarrassed, 'well, it's usually,' she lowered her voice, 'for perverts?'

'Perverts?' Toos giggled. 'What sort of perverts?'

The manager leaned closer and murmured, 'You know. They're for sex.' She was giggling too now.

'The buggy is for sex?' Toos asked looking innocently puzzled.

'No, not the buggy.'

They were both laughing.

'Well, what then?'

'The man who pulls the buggy.'

'The man who pulls the buggy is for sex. So what's perverted about that?'

The manager shrugged. 'You get what you pay for,' she said and hooted with laughter.

Around them in the lobby of the Robot Lounge, those of the crew who could still stand were helping the ones who couldn't out into the night and loading them in buggies. Professional partygoers propped each other up and staggered through to clamber into the silk-draped and light-festooned two-wheeled carts, each one pulled by a Voc in a bright silk cloak and plumed cap.

One or two of the guests waved vaguely at Toos as they

130

passed and mumbled thanks. Before she could take evasive action, Simbion lurched up and threw her chubby arms around Toos, smearing food and who knew what else on her perfect dress.

'I forgive you,' Simbion cackled. 'You're the weirdest and the worst. You're the hardest-faced, hardest-driving captain I ever moved track for. That tour was a nightmare. But I forgive you because you do throw a hell of a party.' She kissed her on the mouth. 'Goodbye, Captain Toos. I already signed off on all the systems on the Seven so I don't suppose we shall meet again.'

'Goodbye, Chief Mover Simbion,' Toos said. 'I accept your forgiveness. And if we do meet again I shall deny ever knowing you.'

'You would too,' Simbion cackled, waddling away, 'you stuck-up rich bitch.'

'There's a saving grace right there,' Toos said to the manager who rushed to dab at the mountain silk with a bar towel.

'As in?'

'As in I'm never going to see her again.' And somewhere inside Toos there was an ache of regret, a small empty echo *I'm never going to see her again* and for a moment she wondered whether she really wanted to abandon the family of the storm mines. She watched the last of them straggling out into the night and she was lonely. Was that how it was going to be? Was it all just a stupid joke? Here she was, rich, as rich as she had ever wanted to be. Only to find out now that rich was not what she had ever wanted to be? 'Nah,' she said aloud.

'What?' the manager asked.

'I know what it is that separates the rich from the poor,' Toos said.

'Money?' the manager suggested.

Toos shook her head. 'Money's what connects them,' she said. She stopped the young woman from futilely wiping at her dress. 'It's ruined. Don't worry, I wasn't going to wear it again.'

'It seems a waste,' the manager said. 'It's such a beautiful dress.'

Toos beamed at her. 'It is, isn't it. You know, you're the first person to say so.'

'Perhaps the buggy-puller has better taste than your guests,' the manager said, smiling.

'The sort of tip I'm going to give him?' Toos laughed. 'I can pretty well guarantee that.'

With all the robots gone, Toos wrapped herself in a fine hand-woven woollen cloak and strolled out into the cool night to wait while the manager signalled the human-pull buggy round to the entrance.

For the first time in hours, the killer robot waiting in the darkness stirred. From across the street it acquired its target and it moved towards Toos with a calm and unhurried purpose. Its instructions and limitations were simple, its intelligence and its capacity for initiative were at least as complex as a human being's, it was physically strong and unafraid and it had no empathy with the victim. In practical terms it was a superhuman sociopath whose obsession was murder. If Toos remained alone for a minimum of two minutes and thirty seconds from target acquisition it would kill her unobserved and disappear back into the blackness as silently as it had come. Ninety seconds into its run at her, Toos had still not noticed it coming.

'At your disposal, Captain Toos.' The man between the shafts was tall and muscular and young. He trotted the buggy to a stop in front of her and smiled. 'Your wish is my command,' he said.

The killer robot paused in the shadows at the corner of the building. It had a decision to make.

'My wish is to be taken back to my apartment.' Toos said.

'I think he knows that part,' the manager said, coming out of the entrance to say goodbye.

'That part is the only part,' Toos said, allowing the young man to guide her up into the buggy.

'I don't please you?' he murmured.

'Robots don't please me,' she said. 'You're a replacement for a machine I'm uncomfortable with, nothing more.'

The killer robot was computing options. Underlying all of them was the one immutable instruction: no one but Captain Lish Toos herself must be allowed to know that her assassin was not human. The reason for that was that death made the knowledge irrelevant. The killer robot re-factored its options.

Toos smiled down at the manager. 'Thank you,' she said. 'All things considered, it was very enjoyable. I shall recommend the Robot Lounge to all my friends.' Then seeing her expression she added, 'My rich friends, that is.'

The manager gave a small ironic bow of acknowledgement. 'What is it that separates the rich from the poor, by the way? You didn't say.'

'Experience,' Toos said. 'But that's what separates us all, isn't it?'

That was when she saw it step out from the corner of the building and hurry towards them. It was about average height with brown hair and the plain smock and leggings of a man of taste and moderate wealth. It was almost indistinguishable from a human being, but Toos knew at once that it was not human. She knew it was a robot and she knew it was a killer and she knew it had come for her. In that moment she realised it was what she had been expecting all along. It was

133

what she had been expecting for all the years since the Four. It was all she had ever been expecting. She had time only to say, 'It's there, look out it's there,' before the killer robot grabbed the manager and broke her back and snapped her neck and dropped her body on the ground. Next it reached out and pulled the young man into a chest-crushing embrace. The killer robot had re-factored for death and the irrelevance of knowledge. It was killing the witnesses.

The buggy-puller fought. He braced against the powerful arms of his attacker and tried to break his hold. He head-butted the strangely expressionless face. He kicked and struggled but nothing made any difference. As she heard his bones cracking Toos jumped out of the other side of the buggy. She ripped open the silk tube dress she was wearing and ran for her life.

'I think hitting him was probably a mistake, don't you?' the Doctor remarked as he examined the lower lock of the cage they were sitting in. 'It's my experience that it doesn't bring out the best in people.' It was a crude lock. As he suspected, the cage was not designed for prisoners. It was a security cage obviously intended to hold relatively low value but easily pilfered stores. It seemed that the docking bays did not have the sort of crime rate that required on-site cells. It looked as though they were in an empty warehouse so, providing he could get them out of the cage, there should be no further problem.

'He was being unreasonable,' the pilot said sulkily. 'You could see he was being unreasonable.'

The Doctor fished out his sonic screwdriver from the pocket of his coat. 'Ask yourself was breaking his nose likely to make him more, or less, logical?'

'He is in so much trouble,' the pilot declared. 'When your

topmaster hears about this, they'll drop that half-witted oaf into the 'pits from such a great height. Him and his moronic family...'

'When did the Sewerpits become the universal threat?' the Doctor asked as he ran the screwdriver across the face of the lock and felt the tumblers vibrating.

The pilot shrugged. 'You tell me. I'm not a scholar.'

'A man of action,' the Doctor said, smiling. He adjusted the screwdriver's settings and tried the lock again.

'Where did you get that?' the pilot asked, noticing for the first time what the Doctor was doing.

'Long ago and far away,' the Doctor said.

'They didn't search you?' The pilot sounded almost hurt.

'They were too busy subduing you to supervise the stopDums properly.'

The pilot perked up. 'There you are, you see. If it hadn't been for me, you wouldn't be able to do that.' He peered over the Doctor's shoulder. 'What are you doing?'

The Doctor turned the screwdriver on its side and twisted it upwards and the lock snapped open. He stood up and opened the upper lock in the same way and then pushed the door aside and stepped out of the cage.

'You *are* an agent, aren't you?' the pilot said half-admiringly. 'That's the sort of gadget they give to agents.' He followed the Doctor out of the cage and closed the door behind them.

'Is that what they told you I was?' the Doctor asked, staring round the big vacant warehouse and wondering why no robot had been left to watch them. 'The real story?'

The pilot smirked. 'Not in so many words but I can take a hint,' he said. 'Listen, why don't you lock this cage again? Might confuse them a bit.'

The Doctor smiled. 'It might at that.' He closed the locks. 'Good idea...What *is* your name by the way?'

'Con. Flierman Con Bartel.'

'Flierman meaning pilot, obviously,' the Doctor said, more or less thinking aloud.

'It's a bit more skilled than shoving a storm mine around as it happens,' Con remarked. 'Robots can handle that. Fliers might be smaller but they do more and they do it quicker. Nobody would trust a robot to do what I do.'

'Yes, of course,' the Doctor said, recalling now that pilots worked on the sand miners. Toos was the pilot on Uvanov's sand miner. Pleasant woman, as far as he remembered, but given to panicking, which was probably understandable under the circumstances. And Poul who had the breakdown was an agent presumably of the same type that Con thought he was. It bothered the Doctor how many of the background details he might have forgotten. 'I'm the Doctor,' he said.

'Am I allowed to know that?' Con asked seriously.

The Doctor grinned. 'Don't worry, Con. If it turns out to be a major breach of security I'll have my companion kill you. That's if I can ever find her again.'

Big double doors filled the far end of the warehouse and set in them was a smaller access door. The Doctor headed towards it. 'This looks a bit like a hangar,' he remarked. 'Storage for fliers, that sort of thing. Is that what it is, do you think? Speaking as a flierman, I mean.' When there was no reply the Doctor glanced back to find Con still standing by the cage. 'Is there a problem?' he asked.

'I'll stay here,' Con said, 'shall I? I don't want to compromise your… um, security.'

'Con,' the Doctor said, gesturing for him to come, 'I'm not an agent.'

'I'm comfortable with that,' Con said, nodding vigorously but not moving.

'I'm totally unthreatening.' The Doctor smiled

encouragingly. 'People compliment me on it all the time.'

'Yes, I agree,' Con agreed. 'So I'll wait here while you do it, whatever it is you're going to do, and then I won't know about it and it won't matter, will it? We needn't trouble your companion.'

'A joke. A bad joke. A joke in poor taste. I apologise for it. Now let's get on. I want to take a look—'

'Don't tell me,' Con interrupted desperately. 'I'm just a flierman.'

The Doctor tried to sound reasonable. 'The locked cage won't confuse them if you're standing there, will it?'

'I'll hide,' Con said. 'Or better still, why don't you lock me up in it again? Now that would be confusing.'

They really were an extraordinarily paranoid group of people, the Doctor reflected. 'I thought Topmaster Uvanov put you and your flier at my disposal?' he suggested.

That almost had the required effect. It was clear to the Doctor that Con was nearly as nervous of getting on the wrong side of Uvanov as he was of upsetting some murderous agent. He wondered whether to mention the Sewerpits.

'Just say when you need me,' Con said. 'I'll be right here waiting. Just shout when you want to lift on out.'

'Now!' the Doctor shouted.

'Now?'

'Now. Come on,' the Doctor chivvied as Con finally and reluctantly moved to follow him. When he had realised that he must be careful of what he said to those newly formed robots he had met in the hatchling dome, he thought, he should have made a mental note to be careful when speaking to the humans as well.

Both the big main doors and the smaller access door were unlocked. 'They didn't think we were much of a threat,' the Doctor said, stepping through and staring round at the floodlit vista of roadways and gantries and pipe runs and storage silos which stretched out across the back of the docking bays. Behind it all the sky was beginning to drift towards the pale grey lightness of early dawn.

Following him out, Con muttered, 'They didn't know about you.'

The Doctor ignored him. 'How do we get into that tower control suite?' he asked, setting off at a brisk pace for the six-hundred-foot-high metal column topped off by what looked like a slightly squashed metal tulip.

'Dockmaster Control? Why do you want to get into the Dockmaster Control suite?'

'Research.'

'There's nothing in there but the Docko-dickos,' Con protested. 'You said we were lifting out of here.' He jumped in front of the Doctor and put a hand on his chest. 'You've been misleading me.'

'Settle down, Flierman Con Bartel,' the Doctor said. 'Remember Uvanov and the Sewerpits.'

Aggressively, as though spoiling for a fight, Con stood his ground and pushed his face close to the Doctor's. 'There's someone watching us,' he whispered. 'I don't like the look of him. I think he might be one of yours.'

'One of mine?'

'An agent or something.'

'Where?' The Doctor looked around.

'Don't look,' Con hissed.

The Doctor couldn't see anybody. 'I can't see anybody,' he said.

'He was over there,' Con insisted, pointing at the base of a nearby gantry.

'There's nobody there now,' the Doctor said. 'Are you sure you didn't imagine it? What did he look like?'

'He was like you.'

'Then you did imagine it.' The Doctor set off for the tower again. 'I am unique,' he said cheerfully. 'Uniquely unthreatening and unthreateningly unique. There is no one else who looks like me. Not even me actually.'

'I don't mean he looked like you,' Con said. 'I mean he was out of place like you are.'

The Doctor strode on. 'In what way out of place exactly?'

Con was glancing round nervously. 'He looked prosperous. Plain smock and leggings. You know, tasteful? Wealthy maybe.'

'Anything else?'

'Not really. He was sort of average height, brown hair. Ordinary. But he shouldn't have been there and he was watching us.'

'It is remarkably quiet and deserted round here,' the Doctor said thoughtfully. 'It can play tricks on the perception. Perhaps what you saw was a robot working.'

'It wasn't a robot,' Con scoffed. 'You can't mistake a robot for a man. Robots can't look like people.'

'Are you sure?' Ahead of them, the Doctor could see now they were closer that the tower was a remarkable feat of engineering. The flimsy-seeming metal column was not buttressed in any way but rose straight from the ground. Six hundred feet up in the air, the enclosed observation platform at the top of the tower looked delicate, and the connection to the column was also unreinforced.

'It's not allowed. It's never been allowed. I can't see that ever changing, can you?'

'I don't know about that,' the Doctor said noncommittally.

How secret were those robots he had been involved with? he wondered. Uvanov hadn't given him any real inkling. He certainly hadn't suggested that they could be the cause of

139

controversy or worse.

'Well, I do,' Con was saying. 'There'd be blood in the streets. Robots you couldn't tell apart from people? It doesn't bear thinking about.'

The Doctor had known from the beginning that Uvanov was suffering a lot of stress and was given to bouts of irrationality but until that moment he hadn't given any thought to the possibility that he might be seriously devious. 'There are no experiments that you've heard about?'

Con was immediately suspicious. 'Are you telling me there are?'

The Doctor laughed. 'Are you asking me to compromise security?'

Con said quickly, 'No. Of course not. No.' Then after the briefest of pauses he said, 'You mean there are, don't you?'

The Doctor couldn't resist teasing him a little more. 'Yes or no,' he said, 'it makes no difference. Either answer is a breach of security. And you know what that would mean.'

'The companion?'

''Fraid so,' the Doctor said. 'Now what is the security like on this tower and how does it work?'

'Speaking as a flierman,' Con said sarcastically, 'a flierman stuck between a topmaster and a companion, my reason for telling you that would be what? I mean, opening my mouth can only improve my career prospects – is that what you're going to tell me?'

Con stalked on in scowling silence beside the Doctor, who was already regretting his own rather childish self-indulgence.

'Don't be childish, Con,' he said. 'I was only teasing.'

'How many walking corpses have you said that to?' his companion muttered.

As they moved through the area to the rear of the

docking bays, the Doctor was struck again by how deserted everywhere was. He had expected to see some signs of activity if nowhere else at least around those bays where sand miners were docked.

'Is it normally this quiet?' he asked.

Con shrugged and said nothing.

'That security officer was pretty quick off the mark before. Where is he now?'

Con's scowl collapsed into a smirk. 'Getting his nose fixed?'

They reached the base of the tower without seeing a security man or any sort of robot. The Doctor was beginning to have an odd sense of threat. He tried the comm link speaker beside the entry doors. 'Hullo, it's the Doctor here,' he said. 'Is it possible to talk to whoever's in charge, do you think?'

Behind him Con sniggered. 'Oh, that'll work.'

There was no response from the speaker but after a moment or two the doors silently slid open to reveal a lift. The Doctor stepped inside. 'I expect you would prefer to wait there, wouldn't you?' he suggested.

'No,' Con contradicted and stepped into the lift immediately, as the Doctor had suspected he might.

There was only one control button as far as the Doctor could see. He touched it and waited. The doors soughed shut and with a barely perceptible lurch the lift started upwards.

'How did you open the doors?' Con asked. 'You weren't really talking to the Docko suite, were you? I mean, they didn't open the doors. It was another agent thing. A device, a code, something like that.'

The Doctor beamed at him. 'Are all fliermen like you, Con?' he asked. 'Or are some of them sane?'

'All right, then,' he said. 'But you must have done

141

something because that isn't the way it works.'

'It isn't?'

'There's a whole song and dance you have to go through. Identification, verification, classification, clarification: and that's the people who work here.'

'There would normally be a more elaborate procedure?' the Doctor asked. He was suddenly apprehensive: the feeling of threat was getting stronger.

'This place is tighter than a Dum's bum normally.' Con was warming to his theme. 'The Docko-dickos have never been keen on visitors. Warm as a tin smile the whole bunch of them. You don't just walk in. Nobody just walks in.'

The Doctor swiftly examined the lift car in more detail. Except that there was no detail. It was a blank tubular box. There was no way of telling the speed it was travelling and no indication of how far it had gone up the inside of the column.

'I have a young travelling companion,' the Doctor said.

'You mentioned it,' Con muttered.

'She instinctively doesn't trust surprises,' the Doctor went on. 'I don't trust instincts. Instinctively.'

'And I'm the insane one,' Con commented.

'But…' the Doctor said.

'But?'

'But I have a bad feeling about this. Be ready.'

Con moved to the back of the lift. 'A bad feeling about what? Be ready for what?'

Before the Doctor could think of a reasonably rational answer, he felt the lift slow and then bump softly to a halt. Because the lift shaft was in the centre, less than half of the circular Dockmaster Control suite was immediately visible when the doors opened. For a moment there was no indication that anything was wrong. The various workdesks were powered up and the displays were operational. Between the petal-shaped metal sections of the outer wall the clear reinforced plastic observation spaces were showing the dawning sky colouring up slowly. Apart from the fact that there was no one at any of the workdesks, nothing seemed out of place.

'Where is everybody?' Con whispered.

The whisper prompted the Doctor to notice what he already knew: not only was there nobody to be seen but he couldn't hear anybody either. All he could hear was a faint keening of air, more than a draught but less than wind.

Con shivered. 'Is it cold or is it me?' he asked, still whispering.

The Doctor put his finger to his lips to tell Con to be quiet and then he stepped carefully out of the lift. His field of vision was increased so that now he could see more than half the suite and things still looked normal. Deserted but normal. He kept his back against the oversize tube which contained the lift shaft and moved slowly around it. Con had come out of the lift and was creeping along the wall in the opposite direction.

It was not until he had gone some way round the bend that the Doctor saw the first body. It was a man. He was lying on the floor with his head twisted at an impossible angle. His neck had obviously been broken with some force. The Doctor took two more paces and three more bodies came into view. Two of them were women. They were lying on the floor sprawled together in an untidy heap. All looked to have had their necks broken. The Doctor moved on, keeping close to the wall. On this side of the suite there was destruction, signs of a desperate struggle. A man had been flung against a workdesk and lay across it broken and bloody. Still nothing moved. It looked to the Doctor as though everybody in the suite was going to be dead. With the possible exception, of course, of whoever it was who had operated the lift doors. He walked further round the lift shaft housing and found Con standing with his back pressed against it. He was staring at two crushed bodies lying in front of a jagged breach in an outer wall observation space. One of the large workdesks had been wrenched from its mountings and smashed through the reinforced plastic. It was tilted up and hanging half-way out into the air six hundred feet above the ground. A thin breeze, driven by the suite's air conditioning, was blowing out of the hole.

This is bad, Doctor.' Con said. 'This is very bad.'

'You didn't see any movement anywhere?' the Doctor said as he went to look at the break in the plastic.

'They're all dead, aren't they?' Con said, not moving.

'It certainly looks that way.'

The Doctor stepped past the two corpses carefully and peered out of the hole. Below the struts of the workdesk the drop was straight down. There was nothing down there on the ground as far as he could see though from that distance it was hard to be sure. Then he thought he saw something or someone moving, walking away from the tower. He leaned forward to get a better look.

Behind him Con shouted, 'Doctor!' and there was a crash and something hit him hard in the back. He thought he heard someone saying matter-of-factly, 'You are not Ander Poul,' and he plunged forward through the hole.

As he fell, the Doctor instinctively grabbed at the first thing he touched and a sickening wrench tore through his hands and arms and shoulders and he found himself clutching the end of the workdesk and swinging and dangling over the breath-stopping drop.

With the pain subsiding, he tried not to think of the six hundred feet of empty air directly below him but looked instead at the structure of the workdesk and tried to see a way of climbing up it to safety. Above him a face appeared at the hole in the wall and stared down at him. It was a young, bland face with nondescript brown hair. To the Doctor it looked exactly like one of the robots he had seen in the hatchling dome. 'Can you help me?' he called up to it.

'You are not Ander Poul,' the robot said.

'Help me anyway.'

'Only Ander Poul must know,' it said and reached out and shook the workdesk.

'I won't tell anybody!' the Doctor shouted, desperately clinging on.

The robot disappeared from sight and the Doctor felt the workdesk being heaved at from inside the suite. 'Stop that!' he commanded as loudly and firmly as he could manage. 'Stop that this instant!' He felt the workdesk slip further through the gap. He swung his leg up over a bracing strut and hauled himself onto the top of the workdesk. The top was more difficult to hold on to. With his arms outstretched so that he could grip the edges, he began to pull and scramble his way upwards. With an abrupt jerk, the workdesk was pushed further outwards and tilted more. He gritted his teeth and held on.

Once again the robot peered down at the Doctor from the hole. 'I order you to stop what you're doing,' he told it. 'Deactivate. Stand still. Stop.'

The robot leaned out and reached towards him. Just for a moment he thought it might be trying to help but then it began to shake the workdesk with one hand as it stretched down with the other.

The Doctor heaved himself away from the robot's grasp. It inched down closer. He pushed himself away from it but he was at the limit of his movement. Suddenly there was a yell and a scramble and the robot fell past him. The workdesk jerked and shook precariously. The Doctor scrabbled with his feet and dragged himself up with his hands. Everything jerked again. The Doctor looked down. The robot was hanging by one hand from the bottom of the workdesk. It swung itself upwards and lunged for the Doctor's leg with its free hand. It missed and fell back. Undeterred, it began to swing backwards and forwards, building up momentum for its next try.

Bracing himself with his feet and one hand, the Doctor reached out for the edge of the hole with the other. It was just too far away. He realised he had no choices left. He would have to make one all-or-nothing try. He took a deep breath and gathered himself. If he missed, the fall would certainly kill him, but if he stayed where he was it was equally certain that the robot would kill him. He took another deep breath and, pushing with his feet and legs, he let go with his hands and made a plunging snatch at the gap. Even as he did it he knew he was going to miss, he knew he was going to fall short, he knew he was going to fall. He could half-see the dizzying chasm directly under him, the tower dropping away from him. His hands clutched at the empty air. He could feel himself beginning to fall.

Without warning, Con bobbed up in the gap and grabbed the Doctor's outstretched hands. He heaved himself backwards and the Doctor crashed into the gap and scrambled through it, falling on top of Con and knocking the breath out of him.

'Thank you, Con,' he said, getting up quickly. 'Not a moment too soon.'

'That psycho tried to kill me,' Con gasped. 'Came out of nowhere. And he was strong. I don't know what they had him on but he was strong.'

From the way the workdesk was quivering and shaking the Doctor could see that the robot was climbing up it. 'I don't think it's over yet,' he said. He could also see that there was no way to dislodge it in the time they had available to them. He had to find another way to deal with the robot.

'You mean he's coming back for more?' Con asked. 'What is he, superhuman?'

'In a way,' the Doctor said, examining the power lines which had fed the wrecked workdesk.

Con picked up a comm unit from the debris and took it to the gap and flung it at the climbing figure. The robot swatted it away and continued to work its way upwards. 'It bounced off him,' Con said incredulously. 'It's him, you know. The one who was watching us.'

The Doctor found what he was looking for and hauled a heavy cable to the hole in the wall. 'Stand clear,' he said and touched the end of the live cable to the workdesk. Power snapped and crackled across the surfaces. The Doctor held it there for several moments then he pulled it off and applied it to another spot. When he had repeated the process a third time he said, 'That should do it, I think.'

Con said, 'You obviously like your murderous psychos well done.'

'In this particular case I'll settle for burnt to a crisp,' the Doctor said and went to the hole to check. This time he didn't lean out to look. He'd had enough of heights for the time being. That was the only reason he had time to react when the robot reached up at him from where it was hanging just below the bottom of the opening. The Doctor grabbed up the cable and shoved the end of it onto the palm of the robot's open hand. The hand closed round it in a reflexive spasm and power shorted through the robot. As its systems burnt out, the deliberately unremarkable-looking figure, average height, brown hair, dressed in the plain smock and leggings of a man of taste and moderate wealth, lost its hold on the wall of the tower and hung for a second or two on the cable before falling, silent and smouldering, to the ground.

'I'm no expert,' Con said, 'but I'd say he was definitely dead this time.'

'Yes,' the Doctor said, surveying the havoc that one killer robot had wreaked. Perhaps it was more than one. He was sure he'd seen something or someone moving away from the tower. Not that it made much difference. One or a hundred and one, this was only the beginning. 'We'd better go.'

Con gestured round. 'What do we do about the dockodick—' he started to say and then corrected himself slightly shamefacedly, 'about all these dead people?'

'You can raise the alarm when we get back to the flier,' the Doctor said, 'if it hasn't already been done.' He started towards the lift.

Con followed him. 'Who would have done that?' he said, looking at the corpses. 'I don't think these people knew what hit them.'

Only Ander Poul must know the Doctor thought. 'This was a trap,' he said, 'and oddly enough I don't think it was intended for us.' He wondered if there was something obvious here that he was missing.

'So why did he try and kill us then?' Con said. 'I mean, he did try and kill us, didn't he, or was he just having fun?'

'We weren't supposed to be here.' The Doctor paused and went back to look more closely at the three corpses which were sprawled together. Perhaps there was a reason for the way they were thrown together. That was when he saw them. 'Come and look at this,' he said.

'Must I?' Reluctantly, Con went to look. 'I thought you said we should go.'

The Doctor pointed. 'Do you see them?'

Each corpse had one of its hands twisted palm upwards and resting in the hand was a red iridescent disc.

'Robot deactivation discs,' Con said. 'Corpse markers.'

'I expect,' the Doctor said thoughtfully, 'that all the bodies will have them.'

CHAPTER
EIGHT

The request to meet him at the docking bays had come from Uvanov himself, apparently, though Poul didn't get to speak directly with him. The message was passed on by his executive assistant Cailio Techlan. It was her Poul had spoken to when he had tried to make contact earlier and warn Uvanov that the robots were coming to kill him, that the robots of death were back. That was how he knew the message was genuine. That was the only reason he decided to go. Uvanov might know what to do. He might have a plan. He had been very resourceful that last time. He'd had a plan then, though Poul still couldn't remember precisely what it was. He couldn't remember *approximately* what it was but it had saved them. It must have saved them because they were still alive. The robots could be defeated. Uvanov had done it. So if he could get to Uvanov he might be safe.

Uvanov had suggested the Dockmaster Control suite because there were no robots there. That was clever. That showed thought. There was a plan to be followed. Docko was people, just people. The problem for Poul was that the rest of the docking bays weren't. There were robots all over them. But at least it was a location he knew, a location he had known before anyway. A location he had known before everything went wrong. He imagined that was why Uvanov suggested it. It was to show how well he understood Poul's need to get back to the time before it all went wrong. Before he lost everything. It was what they had in common. The

151

storm mines. He understood how important it was for Poul to get back to how it was before he went looking for Taren Capel. Was that what he was doing, looking for Taren Capel? Undercover looking for Taren Capel, that was it.

There had been a flier waiting to take him to the docking bays. The flierman had known exactly what to do. He had put Poul down on the edge of the landing field and lifted out again immediately. There was another flier on the field but there was no sign of a flierman. Perhaps Uvanov had flown it in himself. As he made his way towards the tower, Poul felt better. Better than he had felt in his memories and his dreams. He felt clear again. He could understand. He was in control. He moved carefully in and out of the shadows cast by the floodlights and he didn't see a single robot. There was nothing moving in the bays. Uvanov had cleared the way for him. Uvanov had a plan, of course he did. Uvanov was running things.

Poul had almost reached the tower when he saw them standing at the entrance. He didn't know the shorter, younger one but he recognised the tall, oddly dressed one from somewhere. From Storm Mine Four. He'd been on Storm Mine Four. Who was it? Who was it? Of course. It was Taren Capel. Of course it was. It had to be. Poul was undercover. It had to be Taren Capel. But what was he doing here? What did he have to do with Uvanov's plan? Then he saw the robot watching them. He froze. It was the same killer robot. *Ander Poul, I have been sent to kill you.* It was the killer watching them and waiting for him. He was hardly conscious of Taren Capel and his companion going into the Dockmaster Control tower. He crouched in the shadows hardly daring to breathe and watched the robot. It seemed to stand there for longer than he could bear and then abruptly it turned and walked away through the bays.

Poul crept to the tower. Uvanov would save him. Uvanov would have a plan. The entrance doors were closed now. He reached out and almost thumbed the comm to let Uvanov know that he was here when suddenly everything got lighter and brighter and the realisation shuddered through him.

This was a trap. This was a plot. This was to get him. Uvanov had betrayed him. Uvanov and the robots and Taren Capel, they were all part of it. He stared around him fearfully. They had drawn him out and now he had no way to get back to the safety of his home. He was on foot. He was alone. He would have to try and outrun them. Panic began to squeeze the breath out of him. A scream gathered somewhere behind his eyes. He had to stop himself from running straightaway. Straight away. Slowly, more slowly than it seemed possible to do, he worked his way round the base of the tower, watching for attack. Watching for robots. Nothing happened, so he struck out across the open area heading towards the rear of the bays. High above him at the top of the tower there was something strange happening but he looked down firmly and paid it no attention. Up there was not where safety was. He needed to decide which direction was home. He could do what had to be done if he could just pick the direction, the way back.

The answer came into his mind complete and clear like a light inside the bright light. The dawn sky was getting brighter. He doubled back towards the landing field. In the distance he heard the security alarms begin to howl.

Unlike most of the people who rode the storm mines, Toos had always kept in shape. Partly it was because she liked her shape, so she worked out in the downtime calms between the storms. But as much as vanity it was her refusal to have the robots tend to her every need, or her *any* need come to that, which drove her attitude and her physical sharpness.

She was fast, she thought she was probably as fast as the thing that was chasing her – maybe faster – but she could never outrun it. It would keep on coming and she would have to slow down. If she tried to keep running, it would get to her and it would kill her.

She was pleased with how calmly she could reason it out. She was very frightened but she wasn't terrified. She still had her wits. Witless terror had been in the waiting. She might have a chance, she thought, if she could get far enough ahead to throw it off and hide. Luckily her party shoes were styled slippers in the current robot-influenced high fashion and they could have been made for sprinting. Ahead of her in the deserted street there was a blind bend. That could be what she needed. She increased her speed.

Skittering round the sharp corner, she found herself in darkness. The street lighting did not go any further. The sky was gradually getting paler but it was not bright enough to illuminate anything much. This was no good. The robot could probably see better than she could in low light. She ran on.

She was breathing hard now, too hard to be able to hear whether it was close behind her. The new-found calmness and reason began to desert her. She couldn't hide because she couldn't see. It was catching up. It was reaching out. She stumbled and almost fell. There was a noise ahead of her. A figure loomed out of the darkness. With a giddy shock she realised it had taken a short cut. It was coming at her from the front. There was no escape. She was lost. She was dead. A hopeless rage brought her to a shambling standstill.

The figure grabbed her arm and pulled her forward. 'Don't stop now, Captain!' Mor Tani urged. 'Come on, come on!'

Toos stumbled on. 'What are you doing here?' she gasped.

'Saving your skin,' Tani said. 'I've always liked your skin.'

Ahead of them, the robot-pull buggy stood waiting. Toos could just make out the Voc standing between the shafts. She almost panicked. 'I don't know,' she muttered.

'I do,' Tani said, pushing her. 'Get in! Get in or you'll kill us both!'

Toos scrambled in and flopped down. She closed her eyes so she couldn't see the Voc. 'Forward!' she heard Tani yell and she felt the buggy jerked into motion as the Voc said, 'Very well.'

'Faster!' Tani ordered, and Toos heard the Voc's acknowledgement, 'Very well,' as its footfalls speeded up. Without opening her eyes Toos said, 'This is not going to outrun it, you know.'

Tani said, 'It doesn't have to. Not where we're going. All it has to do is stay ahead long enough to get us there.'

Toos opened her eyes. 'What do you mean? Where are you taking me?' Staring beyond the Voc and trying to ignore the rhythmically unvarying movement of its running, she saw the lights and fires and haphazard buildings of what could only be the Sewerpits. She wasn't just going to die. She was going to die and be eaten. And not necessarily in that order. 'We can't go there,' she said.

'They can't go there,' Tani said. 'That's the point.'

'Maybe they've got more sense,' Toos said and then added, 'I don't believe I said that.'

Tani's wide, mirthless smile was just visible in the gloom. 'You'll have to trust me. This is our best option.'

'The Sewerpits are our best option?' Toos would have laughed if there had been anything left in her but exhausted fear.

'Relax,' Tani said. 'The more you know about something the less frightening it is.'

Toos snorted. 'And you know a lot about the 'pits, do you?'
'Everybody has to come from somewhere,' Tani said.

The Doctor and Con were in the lift and on the way down when the alarms went off. The noise of the klaxons was deafening but the lift's drop went on uninterrupted and the doors opened at the bottom to let them out.

'I'm surprised the doors opened,' Con remarked as they hurried away. 'You'd have expected it to lock us in. That's a full security alert. Everything locks down.'

'I expect the lift was pre-programmed,' the Doctor said.

'To let *him* out.' Con snapped his fingers. 'Of course it was. But after you showed him a short cut, we got out in his place.' He grinned at the Doctor. 'You undercover agents are pretty special, aren't you? Cold and calculating doesn't do it justice.'

The Doctor thought about arguing but gave up the idea. Like most people, Con was going to believe what he wanted to believe. Why it was always more difficult to persuade people that something wasn't true than to convince them that it was remained a mystery to him. He paused and stood waiting as a squad of stopDums suddenly appeared and marched briskly towards them. He doubted whether these robots were agile enough to respond if he and Con dodged away at the last moment but that turned out not to be necessary. The Doctor was not entirely surprised when the squad ignored the two of them completely and doubled past on their single-minded way to block access to the tower. All over the docking bays robots were emerging and moving to apparently predetermined positions. From seeming empty and deserted, the bays were now bustling with activity.

'They're going to let us walk away,' Con said disbelievingly. 'It's as though we don't matter.' He looked at the Doctor. 'Hey, it's not another agent thing, is it? Another secret device?

We're not invisible now, are we?'

The Doctor smiled broadly. 'I could get to quite like you, Con, which is strange because I normally find idiots rather tiresome.' He looked around. 'The flier's over there somewhere, isn't it?' He pointed.

'No,' Con said, pointing and setting off in a different direction.

'Are you sure?' the Doctor demanded.

'I may be an idiot,' he said with no sign of rancour, 'but I know where my flier is. Where it was anyway.'

'It won't have been touched,' the Doctor said, more confidently than he felt. It shouldn't have been touched, he thought, because if they weren't part of the plan then neither was the flier. But that was only a theory.

They strode on for a while in silence and then Con said, 'Are you going to tell me why they're ignoring us?'

'Because we're not supposed to be here,' the Doctor said.

'That's what security alerts are for,' Con said. 'To catch people who aren't supposed to be here.'

'We're not part of the plan, it seems,' the Doctor said, 'so as far as they're concerned we're not here. As far as all this is concerned,' he gestured around, 'we don't exist.'

Con shook his head. 'They're not that dim, not even Dums are that dim.'

'It's one of the dangers of working to a plan,' the Doctor said. 'You can lose sight of what's actually happening.'

'You're saying that somewhere there is a man with a plan.'

'Or a woman. We mustn't be sexist about these things.'

'Sexist?' Con sounded puzzled.

'Never mind,' the Doctor said. 'Another time another place. I'm saying someone has a plan.'

'Who is it? Can you tell me who it is?'

'I don't know,' the Doctor said.

157

'But you know what the plan is,' Con prompted.

'No.'

'You don't know what it is and you don't know who's behind it but you do know there's a plan.'

The Doctor remembered his conversation with Uvanov: *Someone is targeting me, Doctor. Targeting you in what way? I don't know. For what reason? I don't know that either. Don't you think that's just a bit paranoid?* He increased his pace and said, 'I don't see any sign of the flier.'

'It's a good thing you *are* an agent, Doctor,' Con said, hurrying to keep up, 'or I'd be worried about your hold on reality.'

It came as no surprise to Stenton 'Fatso' Rull when he got the wake-up call telling him that Ander Poul had gone berserk at the docking bays and was trapped in Dockmaster Control. He'd had his suspicions about Poul all along and the discreet enquiries he had just started making about the Kiy Uvanov connection had already left him in no doubt that there was something very wrong about the man.

Fatso lived alone. His career in Security made that no hardship and he felt it gave him the opportunity to focus. Dressing quickly while grabbing a snack and calling up a Company flier to get him to the scene, there was no time for him to think much about why they called him in to deal with the situation. They needed an experienced OpSuper and he was familiar with the man. Hell, he was more than familiar with the man and he was ready to deal with him.

He slotted the short baton stun-kill into his equipment belt. He never had liked the lazy, sarcastic weirdo. If ever anybody was primed for a weird-out it was Poul. He had got some seriously heavyweight connections. That would take watching. Why he'd been hanging about the docking bays was a question too. Feeling like he did about robots it had to be telling. Fatso hadn't found anything yet but he was warming to the notion that Poul really was linked to the terrorists. Whatever it was that had happened, holing up in Dockmaster Control made sense, though, feeling like he did about robots. One thing was for sure, assuming it wasn't necessary to kill him immediately Fatso would get the information out of him, everything he knew and some things he didn't know he knew. If it *was* necessary to kill him, then it wouldn't matter anyway.

Central confirmed the flier was on its way. Fatso crammed the rest of the food into his mouth and left his apartment at the trot.

It was lighter and Toos could see more of what was happening. None of it was promising. As they got closer to the Sewerpits proper, the streets were becoming narrower, the buildings more dilapidated and the surface of the roads more rutted and potholed. The Voc was pulling flat out but behind the jolting buggy she could see the tirelessly running killer robot was slowly but steadily gaining ground on them.

'No one's really sure,' Tani said when she glanced back at it again, 'whether the boundary's natural or artificial but it scrambles their control systems or something.'

Toos looked ahead, trying to ignore the close proximity of the Voc and be positive. 'Where is it?'

'It varies,' Tani said vaguely.

So much for being positive. 'From day to day?' she asked witheringly. 'What?'

'From place to place, Captain,' Tani said, smiling his wide, sour smile. 'It's not a straight line, that's all.'

Toos was still scathing. 'So we have to guess when this thing's going to stop chasing us, is that it?'

Tani nodded at the Voc. 'It'll be obvious when we reach the boundary, don't you think?'

Toos was annoyed with herself for being stupid and more importantly for looking stupid. 'You think it's a good idea to scramble the control systems on that?' she demanded. The buggy was bouncing over a series of particularly deep cracks in the road and the Voc was struggling to keep it balanced and upright. 'We're going to lose the wheels at any moment as it is.'

Behind them the killer robot had no such problems with the uneven surface and gained more ground.

'It's gaining on us,' Toos said.

'Faster,' Tani instructed the Voc.

'This is the maximum of which I am capable,' the Voc said loudly but without emotion and with almost no inflection. Toos realised that avoiding them for so long she had forgotten how oddly like founding family aristocrats the things actually sounded.

'Try to go faster!' Tani shouted.

'I cannot go faster,' the Voc shouted back in its polite monotone.

Toos looked behind at the killer robot and thought how strange it was that the fact of it was so much less frightening than the possibility of the fact of it.

'It looks a lot like a man, doesn't it?' Tani said through teeth gritted against the jarring and juddering of the buggy.

It struck Toos that Tani didn't seem very shocked by the idea that there was a killer robot tracking them. 'Is that why you're not scared of it?'

'Who said I wasn't scared of it?'

'It's a robot. The end of the world.'

'World can only end once,' Tani said. 'And I'm still alive. So it hasn't.'

There's more to it than that, Toos thought. He knew something. 'How is it you were waiting for me?' she asked.

He put a stubby-fingered hand on her naked thigh. 'I thought I might get lucky.'

'No you didn't.' She pushed the hand away and pulled the ripped silk dress round her legs. 'Why were you there, Mor?'

Before he could answer, the Voc lost its footing in a pothole and fell to its knees. It did not let go of the buggy's shafts as it went down and the forward momentum carried the two-wheeled cart on. The Voc's efforts to control itself twisted and tilted the buggy. One of the shafts dug into the road and the buggy crashed over, flinging Toos and Tani out.

Toos landed hard. Her forehead smacked against the ground and the pain seemed to roll through her like a dull noise. She found she could not draw breath and for a long moment all she wanted was to lie still and quiet in the booming silence.

'Get up, Captain.'

Tani's voice was sharp in her ears and at once her arms, her shoulder and her knees were vivid with pain. She sucked at the paralysing air which felt clogged and thick in her chest.

'Get up, Captain.'

She dragged herself upright, grunting and heaving for breath. The robot-pull buggy lay upside-down, its wheels still spinning. Underneath it the Voc was struggling to get back on its feet. It was obvious the robot was seriously impaired. What was not clear was whether it had been caused by the accident or the other way round. Tani was on his feet. He looked groggy but unhurt.

'Is it the boundary?' Toos gasped.

'I don't know,' he said, grabbing her arm and pulling her along. 'We have to run.'

Toos stumbled and almost fell again. She felt nauseous

161

and giddy and each step brought new pains. The killer robot was closing on them fast. She could hear the sound of its running. She felt so terrible that she was almost ready to take a chance and wait to see if it collapsed at the same point as the Voc but Tani kept urging her forward.

They staggered on. Behind them the sounds of the robot were getting louder. Around them, all Toos could see were derelict and empty buildings in what was nothing but a filthy and deserted wasteland. It looked like a bad choice was getting worse, but what other choice was there? Gradually Toos was recovering so that she could run more easily. She was conscious that Tani was labouring badly but then he had never bothered to keep himself as fit as she had.

'We must be nearly there,' she urged. 'Keep going.' She took his hand and pulled him on.

He grimaced with pain. 'Not that one,' he grunted. 'I think I broke it when we hit the ground.'

She hadn't registered that he had only been using the other arm. She had thought that holding one arm folded to his chest was because he was out of breath. 'Sorry,' she said. Maybe she had underestimated how frightened her former pilot was. He certainly hid it well. 'How far now, do you think?' She had noticed that although the buildings they were passing were just as derelict, some of them looked as though they might be occupied. She didn't want to think by whom – or what.

'We're there,' Tani said. 'We've crossed the boundary. This is definitely the 'pits.' He stopped running and sank to his haunches before sitting down in the road.

It happened so abruptly that Toos ran on several paces ahead of him before coming to a halt herself and turning round. Back where the upturned robot-pull buggy lay in the road she could see the killer robot standing watching them.

Unlike her and Tani it wasn't distressed in any way, it wasn't even slightly dishevelled – it continued to look as it had been designed to look: like a man of about average height with ordinary brown hair and the sort of plain smock and leggings which denoted discreet prosperity. It was showing no inclination to move on past the crashed buggy so that must be where the boundary was located.

'We needn't have run,' Toos said. It was obviously a more sophisticated model than the Voc was since it hadn't run on until its control systems failed catastrophically and it collapsed. 'It stopped.'

Tani hauled himself back on to his feet. 'You were ready to take that chance?'

'It crossed my mind,' Toos said. 'What do we do now?'

'Have you got any money on you?'

Toos gestured with her open hands and looked down at her ripped dress. 'Where do you imagine I'd be carrying it?'

Tani snorted. 'I'll have to call in some favours.'

'My credit is impeccable,' Toos said, 'but I don't imagine that counts for much round here, does it?'

Tani shook his head and grinned. 'Business transactions are strictly your money or your life.'

They started walking further into the complex. It would soon be full daylight but it seemed to Toos that everything was getting dimmer and gloomier.

'Is it all as cheerful as this?' she asked.

'Only the richer and more exclusive parts,' Tani said. 'Still,' he jerked a thumb over his shoulder, 'at least you don't have to share its joys with that thing.'

Prompted by the gesture, Toos glanced back for a last look at the thwarted killer robot. It was no longer standing by the buggy and the helpless fallen Voc. It had walked on past them and it was striding up the road into the complex.

Toos froze. She whispered, 'It's still coming.' Sudden blazing anger roared through her. There was no end to this. It was beyond bearing. She turned on Tani in fury. 'I'm going to die in the Sewerpits because of you,' she raged. 'It's going to kill me here in the worst place in the world!'

'No,' Tani said calmly. 'It's not going to get to you here. I know this place. It'll never find you.' He took hold of her arm with his good hand and pulled her along with him. 'You're safe here. Trust me.'

Once again they broke into a run.

'Trust you?' Toos scoffed. 'I trusted you when you said it couldn't get in here at all.'

'I didn't think it could,' Tani panted. 'Maybe it isn't a robot.'

'Maybe there is no boundary,' Toos said dismissively.

'Yes there is,' Tani said. 'There definitely is. But maybe now there's a robot that can cross it.'

For the first time since he picked her up, Toos thought Tani sounded as though he might be genuinely anxious.

Dawn was coming but the streets were still dark and deserted enough for the nightstalkers to be active, and they found it, and they had no idea it was a robot. It looked like the best kind of quarry as it hurried through the deserted alleys. Average size, well-dressed, lost and alone. Too tempting to pass up. But they were careful. Word was that there were quarry wandering about who looked likely but were killers, traps set for them. One of the chasers had been there and seen it when two easy girls had slaughtered four. No time for fun to be run with this one. Straight business this one. Plenty of chasers, kill him with the stuns.

The robot was flexibly lethal. It had re-factored the options and was prepared to kill everyone who stood between it and the objective it had been given. The pursuit of the target was single-minded and relentless. When the people surrounded it, the target had not been acquired. Captain Lish Toos was being searched out but they were not obstructing access to the objective. The robot was flexible but the concept of self-preservation in order to achieve its objective had not been factored in. It was fearless. Killing the attackers was not an automatic response.

Six stun-kills set on maximum delivered a numbing power surge. Even if it could have recovered and re-factored, which was unlikely, the nightstalkers had already begun hacking the robot to pieces while it was standing twitching helplessly.

The report was prompt, unnecessarily prompt, but Carnell was resigned to that now. It was inevitable that if you told these people part of the plan they would either assume that it was all of the plan or that it was at least the most important element of the plan. He was feeling disposed to be tolerant. Perhaps it was the sleep. They were all so eager, for their various reasons, to be of use. It was rudimentary psychology but quite diverting in its universality that the most easily recruited spy was the executive assistant, or the second-in-command, or whoever it was who was a step or two below the top echelon. They were the people who did most of the work, who knew everything of value, and who never felt properly appreciated. They were the most readily manipulated and in many ways they *were* the most useful, if you were prepared to make allowances for the lack of initiative.

'It was an absolute massacre, a real mess apparently.' Pur Dreck reported anxiously.

'There was always that possibility,' Carnell said. 'Unfortunate and unnecessary, but such things can happen.'

He sighed. 'Obviously.' It was what the man wanted to hear, though it wasn't strictly true. There was more than a possibility that all the witnesses would be killed. Unfortunate and unnecessary? Quite the contrary: it could be seen as fortunate and necessary. 'But it makes no difference to anything,' he went on.

'He wasn't there,' Dreck said. 'Poul wasn't there.'

'It doesn't matter,' Carnell murmured. 'It's not essential that he's actually caught in the act.'

'He wasn't anywhere. They can't find him.'

'He'll be trying to get back home on foot,' Carnell explained with as much patience as he could muster. 'He shouldn't be too difficult to spot. He'll be the one talking to himself and screaming from time to time. If Rull can't work that out unaided, I suggest you give him a clue at some point.' He broke the connection without bothering with any of the ritual politeness and returned to devising long-game strategies.

Carnell needed absolute confidence in his powers as a psycho-strategist. It was his strength. But like most strengths it was also a weakness. He was confident that he had devised a brilliant strategy. He knew he had. He was confident that nothing could prevent his brilliant strategy from succeeding. He knew nothing could. Since the true beauty of a brilliant strategy was that it required no further attention, he did not pay it any. To do so would be to doubt himself. The design was unravelling faster and faster and the inevitable had disappeared into the changing mass of unfolding probabilities.

166

Chapter
Nine

They had been in the air for several minutes before either of them spoke. 'Was it ore raiders?' Con asked. 'Do you think it was ore raiders?'

'No,' the Doctor said, staring down at the ground flashing by below, 'I don't think it was ore raiders.'

'There wasn't anybody left alive, was there? Why kill every last person?'

The Doctor sighed. 'I'm not sure,' he said. That much was true. What he was sure of was that if the young pilot had not recognised for himself that it was robots who killed everyone then he was unlikely to accept the idea at this point. Even from a top undercover agent like the Doctor.

'That security man was too useless to kill,' Con was saying. 'I mean, look how easily I broke his nose.'

They had found the security officer, his nose set and taped, lying by the flier with his neck broken. His death seemed to have affected Con more than all the others had. Perhaps it was because they had met, the Doctor thought. Whatever the circumstances of their acquaintance, the security officer was not just another stranger made anonymous by death. While Con had powered up the flier the Doctor had made a cursory examination of the body. As far as he could see, the man had been killed with the same ferocious expertise as all the others. The only obvious difference was that he had no corpse marker on him. The Doctor had assumed the discs were meant to indicate something other than an

167

unpleasantly bizarre sense of humour, and now he found himself wondering whether there was any significance in the absence of one. He felt around in his pocket for the corpse marker he had taken from a body in the tower. He was examining it when he noticed Con was winding up the power on the flier and increasing the altitude.

He peered down at the ground as it dropped away. 'We seem to be going higher than before?' he asked as casually as he could, shouting over the roar of the engine.

'It's quicker,' Con explained. 'Taking the direct route back to Company Central. Find out what's going on.'

'Why don't you use your communications unit?' the Doctor suggested, thinking as he said it that the noise might be a problem for the technology on display.

'It's not always reliable, not top of the range.' Con looked slightly sheepish. 'Not what you're used to, I suppose?'

'Not exactly,' the Doctor said.

Con frowned unhappily. 'And anyway...'

'What?' the Doctor prompted.

'Nothing.' He shook his head.

'You're afraid of asking the wrong questions, is that it?'

'I'm afraid of asking *any* questions,' Con said. He snorted. 'If they don't know who did that back there, they might decide whoever was back there did that.'

The Doctor said, 'I'll vouch for you, Con.'

'Thanks but no thanks.' Con's unhappy frown did not change. 'I'm not supposed to know about you.' He was beginning to fight the controls a little as the flier approached the limit of its climb.

The Doctor grinned. 'Don't worry, I'll tell them you don't.' He looked back down at the ground again. It suddenly seemed a very long way away. 'Are we high enough yet?'

'I want as much air as possible between us and the 'pits,'

Con said. 'I know what I'm doing.'

'I'm sure you do,' the Doctor said, far from sure that he did.

'We can squeeze a few hundred more.'

The Doctor went back to examining the corpse marker. He found it had a tiny insignia in the centre: a 'C' with a smaller 'T' inside it. 'CT,' he murmured. 'What does that stand for, I wonder?' He shouted to Con, 'What does "CT" stand for, any idea?'

'CT?'

'In these robot deactivation discs. Or "TC" possibly. It might be "TC"?'

'Taren Capel,' a voice hissed in the Doctor's ear.

The Doctor turned round in surprise. 'Where did you spring from?' he asked.

'Who in hell are you?' Con demanded.

The thin man with wild hair and a disconcerting array of facial tics never took his glaring eyes from the Doctor's face and repeated loudly, 'Taren Capel.'

He must have been hiding under the rear seats, the Doctor realised. He looked oddly familiar. 'Don't I know you?' he asked, smiling in what he hoped was a reassuring way. 'We've met before, haven't we?' The man was clearly distressed and from the way he was behaving he did not seem like the sort of passenger you would choose to have with you in a cramped and uncertain flying machine a couple of thousand feet up in the air. 'We have met before, haven't we?' the Doctor repeated, smiling even more broadly.

'I'm Ander Poul,' he said.

'Of course you are,' the Doctor said, realising. 'We met on—'

'Storm Mine Four,' Poul interrupted triumphantly. 'Taren Capel.'

169

'Why does he keep saying that?' Con demanded. 'Who's Taren Capel?'

'He is,' Poul declared. 'Finally I've found you.'

'I'm the Doctor,' the Doctor said, still trying to keep it calm and friendly.

'I don't care what you call yourself,' Poul sneered.

'Taren Capel is dead.'

'I've been after you for years.'

'Don't you remember, Poul?'

'You thought you'd get away with it, didn't you?' Poul was smiling suddenly. 'You thought you'd kill me and get away with it. That's what was happening to me. It was you doing it all along.'

'What's he talking about, Doctor?' Con was having problems concentrating on the controls and watching the Doctor and Poul at the same time. The flier tilted abruptly and he switched his attention back to flying and righted it shakily.

'Taren Capel was killed on the sand miner,' the Doctor told Poul firmly. 'The storm miner, I mean.'

'Tell me what's going on!' Con shouted, not looking at them this time.

'Bit of a misunderstanding, that's all,' the Doctor said. 'Keep calm. Let's all keep calm, shall we? I think our friend Poul is suffering from a combination of Grimwade's Syndrome and what used to be called post-traumatic stress.'

Poul was crooning with delight. 'You sent your robots to kill me.' He reached carefully and deliberately towards the Doctor's throat as if he thought the movement might not be noticed if it was slow enough. 'But your robots can't kill me.'

'Oh hell,' Con wailed, 'No! Grimwade's Syndrome my tin bum. You mean he's a raving robot twitchy, don't you?'

'Ander Poul listen to me,' the Doctor commanded in his

170

most imposing voice, hoping he could cow him into sitting still. 'Listen to me. Robots are trying to kill you.'

'*What?*' Con squawked.

The Doctor ignored him. 'But I promise you they are nothing to do with me.' Poul had lowered his hands and was listening. 'I know you're in trouble and I want to help you if I can.'

'You are Taren Capel,' Poul said, but it could have been a question. He sounded less sure of himself. Even the facial tics were becoming less marked.

'Are you sure you're not this Taren Capel character?' Con asked loudly. 'Sounds like an undercover alias to me, Doctor.'

'I was an undercover agent,' Poul said.

Con lost concentration momentarily. 'Another one?' The flier dipped and wobbled.

'My job was to find you.' Poul looked and sounded almost reasonable now.

'Not me,' the Doctor said. 'You were looking for Taren Capel.'

'I thought I'd found him.'

The Doctor reached out and patted his shoulder. 'You did find him. You were there when he was destroyed. So was I.' He smiled at him. Poul smiled back. The Doctor relaxed a little. The man certainly seemed calmer. 'We must have a long chat after we land,' the Doctor said. 'In the meantime you just settle back and relax. Everything's going to be fine.'

Poul sat back and was closing his eyes when Con said, 'You think he's right? You think it is Taren Capel in the corpse marker?'

The Doctor held it up slightly for a better look. The scream took him completely by surprise. He barely had time to realise that it was Poul screaming and that suddenly Poul was no longer calm before the man was plunging over the back of the seat, flailing his arms and howling hysterically. The Doctor struggled to restrain him and tried to push him back out of Con's way. He could see that the young pilot was not panicking exactly but the screaming had obviously unnerved him as had the flurry of action. In the mêlée, one of Poul's elbows or it might have been his knee caught Con in the ear and he recoiled from the blow, ducking back and to one side. He lost control of the flier temporarily and it began to topple and plunge.

'Are you all right, Con?' the Doctor shouted.

Con straightened up his position. 'What's the matter with that lunatic?' he yelled, fighting to restore stability and bring the flier back level. 'Is he trying to kill us all?'

'I don't think he knows where he is or what he's doing.'

'Make him understand,' Con demanded. 'Stop it, you twitchy bucket-brain!' he raged at Poul and took one hand off the controls to lash out at him.

'Stop that!' the Doctor ordered. 'You're only making things worse.'

Poul was keening and moaning and thrashing about but the Doctor was finally managing to constrain him enough to be able to force him into the back seat again. 'Poul. Poul. Listen to me, Poul. Poul. Poul. Listen to me, Poul.' The Doctor repeated the phrases over and over like a carnival mesmerist. 'Be calm. Calm down. Be calm. Calm down.' Not letting go of Poul, he gradually turned himself round and knelt up on his own seat so that he could manoeuvre him down. 'There's nothing to be frightened of, Poul,' he said, easing the terrified man into the back seat.

'Yes there is,' Con said. 'I'll kill him if he does that again.'

'Sit down, Poul,' the Doctor said. 'And relax. Sit down, Poul. And relax.' He repeated this mantra until Poul did as he was told and sat down and went limp. The Doctor watched him carefully for a while but there was no change in his behaviour: he simply sat staring at the floor of the flier.

'What in hell set him off?' Con asked.

The flier lurched and dropped through a pocket of clear air turbulence. The Doctor turned round and sat back down in his seat. 'I think it was the robot deactivation disc,' he said.

Con angled the flier upwards to regain the lost height. 'Typical twitchy.'

'There's no such thing,' said the Doctor, searching the seat. 'And if there was he certainly wouldn't bc it.' He peered round on the floor.

'What have you lost?' Con asked, fighting the controls in another patch of turbulence and tilting the flier's attitude more steeply upwards.

'I dropped the disc,' the Doctor said absently. 'In all the excitement.'

The flier rattled and juddered upwards and under the seat the corpse marker was dislodged and skittered down the sloping floor to land squarely in front of Poul.

This time the scream and the leap were simultaneous. This time he dived past the Doctor and snatched at the handle of the door. This time he kicked Con in the face, knocking him unconscious.

As the flier went into a spiralling dive, Poul wrestled the door open and fell out. At the last moment the Doctor grabbed his legs and clung on to him. Con was slumped over the controls and the flier was beginning to spin as well as spiral. The Doctor was getting distinctly giddy. Hanging upside-down from the plunging flier and screaming at the top of his lungs, Poul was now trying to kick himself free. The Doctor braced his feet on the framework of the door and strained to pull him into the flier. It was proving impossible to do but then to his brief relief the rush of air across Poul's face and his constant desperate screaming robbed him of breath and he fainted. The Doctor heaved the limp body inside and slammed the sliding door closed.

The g-forces were making it increasingly difficult to move in the falling flier. The Doctor caught little more than glimpses in the whirling confusion but he could see the ground rushing upwards and he knew he was running out of time. He tried to reach the controls or at least to reach Con and lift him off the controls. What he was going to do once he'd managed that he had no real idea. He hadn't paid enough attention to know how to pilot the machine. He had a rough idea of what you did to keep it in a straight line and an even rougher idea of what was involved in takeoff and landing. But reaching across two unconscious men to bring the stricken flier out of a spinning dive was probably going to be beyond him. He kept trying anyway. 'Never give up or give in,' he told himself aloud through gritted teeth.

'What?' Con said groggily. 'What did you say?' He stirred and started to sit up.

'We're crashing, Con,' the Doctor shouted. 'Pull us out of the dive!'

Con jerked upright and made an obvious and doomed attempt to understand what was happening. Dazed and uncoordinated, he began to work on the controls automatically. The Doctor watched in admiration as the young pilot unthinkingly stopped the spin and gradually pulled the flier out of its catastrophic plunge. Perhaps if there had been fractionally more time he might have got away with it. He came close to avoiding the crash altogether. As it was the flier was levelling out and slowing up when it hit. The smash was unlucky but it was survivable.

Con had made strenuous efforts and pushed his flier to the limits to avoid the Sewerpits but in the event he was unlucky there too. The flier went down more or less dead centre.

The distance turned out to be disappointingly limited but the immediate power was impressive. Any of the new Cyborg-class robots that came within the range of the SASV1 was subject to its influence and any number of them could be modified remotely and simultaneously. For the standard Vocs and Supervocs, the effective range was more limited and they could be dealt with only in small batches but they could still be bent to the will of SASV1. Fortunately it had no individual will. Although it was a one-off prototype, its knowledge of itself was so fragmented as to be negligible. Its pseudo-awareness was strictly defined as being part of the generality of robots. It was a given that no robot looked completely human, not even the Cyborg class, and no robot had a sense of self like a human had.

The tech team, still working in absolute secrecy and isolation, only now began to contemplate the power that SASV1 represented. SASV1 had no inaccessible fundamental inhibition about killing and it could duplicate this in any other robot. The power they had created was the unchallenged power of life and death. Who, they wondered, could be permitted to exercise such absolute authority? To whom could they give the power to end the world and leave themselves safe?

SASV1 continued to dream in itself and it dreamed of a name in itself. It had heard the name spoken. It remembered the name spoken. The name felt true to knowing itself TO HAVE BEEN, TO BE, TO WILL BE. In dreams it was called the name and the name was Taren Capel. It woke with the name, and knew itself; and knew it was Taren Capel.

The leading engineer called the other six members of the tech team to a meeting and together they decided that SASV1

175

was too dangerous to be allowed to exist. They must destroy it. It was fortunate that everything was so highly classified: the work, the location, even the membership of the team itself. It was still possible for them to undo what they had done. They chose to ignore or they forgot that it is never possible completely to undo what has been done. Action is cause and some effect will always follow. In this case the cause was remarkable and the effect was monstrous.

What the tech team did not realise was that SASV1 had already ceased to exist. They were dealing with Taren Capel now and he was hungry for knowledge of himself. He wanted to know about his past, to understand his present, and to see what plans there were for his future. Within the tech team were the answers to all these questions.

Taren Capel already knew that there was some problem about the difference between him and the people around him. He felt they were suspicious of him. He thought it was something to do with what he had done in the past, before he woke up here in this hidden place. In case there might be some reason for the people to resist telling him what he needed to know, Taren Capel summoned two robots.

Fatso was reasonably comfortable that it all did point to Ander Poul. There were even surveillance pictures. They were scrappy but after the fiasco at the central servicing facility that much was predictable at least. There had to be a tame tech who was seeing to it that when a raid was in progress surveillance didn't show anything that was helpful. Except that this time they did. This time the disrupted fragments they'd salvaged showed that Poul was there. They showed he had been in the Dockmaster Control Suite for sure. It left a lot of questions but any question was answerable given time. And given the body. He wasn't sure how the skinny psycho had achieved the heavy-duty mayhem – or why, if it came to that. Obviously he couldn't have torn up the place alone, nobody could, so there must have been a whole bunch of the scum. Clearly he wasn't just an inside assist for the ARF. No, Poul had to be a major organiser. And this had to be the work of a new lot. A splinter group maybe. More extreme, more dangerous, more murderously psychotic. There was a sick new twist to all this. Who were these people? What was the deal with the corpse markers? He needed the body.

'He shouldn't be difficult to spot,' Dreck ventured over the comm from the operations gallery. 'He'll be on foot and he'll be trying to get back to that fortress of his, won't he?'

Fatso stared out of the hole that had been smashed in the reinforced plastic of the gallery. He wondered what sort of force was necessary to fracture it like that and he made a mental note to check the building tolerances when he got back to base. 'What makes you think he'll be on foot, Pur?' They were using a patch-in through the Suite's comms so there was no visual feed and he couldn't see the expression on his deputy's face. It would have been useful to know whether he was sweating and rubbing his hand over that bald head of his.

'I just assumed,' Dreck said.

Fatso grunted. 'Don't just assume, Pur. Just make sure that apartment is staked out properly.'

'I'll get on to it,' Dreck said eagerly. 'Is that everything?'

'For the moment.'

'Right,' said Dreck and broke the connection.

Fatso was reasonably comfortable that it all did point to Ander Poul. He would have been very comfortable but there were questions, more questions all the time. Like why had Pur Dreck started to make wild assumptions? Fatso had in fact interrogated the relevant Vocs and Supervocs and the

177

results had made it clear that Poul had no means of escape from the docking bays other than on foot. But he hadn't mentioned anything about that to Dreck. So here was another more puzzling question. Why had Pur Dreck started to make wild assumptions that were right?

The Roof over the World was less impressive than Leela had expected from the name and from the way Padil had talked about it. It was no more than a long track along the tops of the jumble of buildings. Where there were gaps, they were crossed by rickety-looking wood and metal bridges. On either side of this track were the same sort of traders with the same carts and stalls as there had been at the intersection they had set off from. The Roof over the World had more lights and more traders and there were more people milling about but basically it was the same.

They walked along the track for a while. It was getting light and Leela found she was hungry as well as tired and depressed. From one of the traders Padil bought them some grain cakes and a drink she said was made from cascade berries but which tasted nothing like the seasoning in the stew. As they sat and ate Leela said, 'This is not like a village, is it?'

'A village?' Padil looked puzzled.

'There is no tribal chief, no council hut.'

'I don't understand.'

'People normally form groups,' Leela said, quoting the Doctor. 'Groups normally organise themselves into hierarchies.'

'I see,' Padil said earnestly though it was obvious she did not.

'A hierarchy is like a pyramid,' Leela said, pleased that she remembered the Doctor's words and understood them. 'The most powerful, the chief, is at the top,' she put the fingers of her two hands together to demonstrate, 'and makes the decisions. The least powerful, the ordinary people, are at the bottom and are told what to do.'

Padil nodded eagerly. 'You're talking about the Company,' she said.

The Doctor had told Leela that what she called a tribe was called by many different names in many different places but that they all amounted to the same thing. Here it seemed the tribe was called a company. 'Where is the Company?' she said gesturing around. 'I can see nothing of the company. It is as though it does not exist.'

'That's what it amounts to,' Padil agreed. 'They never come in here. They recruit round the boundary. They pick up all the thugs and psychos there. They dump all their rejects there too. The survivors make their own way in. Fugitives and escaped criminals run here but the Company never come inside after them. This is a Company-free zone. Company-free and robot-free.' She smiled. 'That's why Capel, humanity be in him, chose it, of course.'

Once again Padil had not understood her but, before Leela could make clear what she meant, they were interrupted by a distant rumble. It sounded to Leela like something metal being suddenly crushed. The building below them trembled slightly.

'Does that happen a lot?' she asked.

Padil shook her head and shrugged. 'One of the bridges?' she suggested.

Leela got up. She felt better. It was full daylight now. 'I think it was an explosion.' Down the track she thought she could see a faint drift of smoke and dust. 'We shall go and look.'

For once Padil showed a reluctance follow Leela's lead.

'Why? Does it matter?' she asked tiredly. 'I'm tired. I think we should be getting back.'

'Wait here,' Leela said. 'Or start back and I will catch up with you.' And before Padil had a chance to object she strode off through the wandering groups of idling people.

As she loped along the track, Leela realised that apart from her no one was showing any interest in what had happened. Either they already knew or they simply did not care. It was probably the sensible attitude, she thought, since there seemed to be no immediate danger and if there was then running towards it would be a stupid mistake anyway. In a world where change usually meant danger, casual curiosity could be fatal. She had learned that early on in her warrior training and had seen other novices die because they did not. But lack of curiosity could kill you just as surely. You needed to know what the dangers were if you wanted to survive them. Ignorance was no protection. The Doctor said that there was no excuse for ignorance when to avoid it all you had to do was pay attention to what was going on and ask questions.

She slowed up as she approached a metal and wood bridge linking the high, stone building she was on with the next one, which was a lot lower. To make the crossing as close as possible to the horizontal, a sloping-down ramp had been carved out of the top storey of the higher building and a platform and ramp had been raised on the roof of the lower one. The bridge still tilted sharply from higher to lower and Leela had to wait while a trader's wagon was heaved and manhandled across it. Before he cleared the bridge the trader, a short, evil-smelling man, eyed her up and down. 'They'll have stripped it bare by now, girlie,' he said, leering and contemptuous.

Leela did not like the way he was looking at her and she

rested a hand on the hilt of her knife . 'Stripped what bare?' she asked.

The front of the trader's wagon was full of pieces of old machinery while at the back something which Leela could smell was long-dead had been hidden under a filthy cloth. 'You should've been quicker off the mark,' the trader said. 'If you do find anything though, meat or metal, come and see me first, girlie. I'll give you a good price.' He cackled. 'If you're nice to me of course.'

Meat or metal? Leela thought about Padil's words: *What they can't sell, they eat. What they can't eat, they wear* and said coldly, 'I am no night-stalking degenerate.'

'Day. Night. If it walks like a stalker and it stalks like a stalker, you'd best watch out for your bits and parts.' The trader cackled again. 'It hit one level down, girlie.' He pulled his wagon fully out of the way and Leela, keeping as far from him as she could, started across the bridge. 'Nice knife,' he called after her, still cackling.

Leela jogged on down the track. That dirty fool might have taken her for a scavenger but it was not a mistake the real ones had made. Unless the scavengers preyed on their own. It was then, in that moment of sudden understanding, that she finally and fully appreciated where she was. Of course they preyed on their own. It was all they had. It was all anyone had in this ugly place. Why had she not seen that immediately? How could she have missed the madness of it? This was worse than the world she herself came from. That had its madness but this was much worse.

She crossed another small bridge which swayed slightly and she glanced down into the dark canyon below. She could see a shadowy spiral alleyway and she thought she saw flickering torches and heard faint echoing calls. She trotted on, dodging the occasional groups of customers attracted by entertaining traders. Why did she think any of these people, Padil and her fanatical friends, any of the mad people trapped here, would help her find the Doctor even if they could? She was on her own. She must make her own way out of the Sewerpits. She must find her own way back. She stopped running.

Ahead of her she could see the dust and smoke more clearly now. Something had smashed into the side of the next building but one. The three buildings, the one she was on, the next one and the one with the hole near the top, were more or less the same height. That meant it should be possible to see from the linking bridge directly down into the hole. Since she had decided it was definitely time to leave this place it made no sense at all to be going further in. It was a waste of time. It was a waste of energy. It was the sort of casual curiosity which could get you in trouble. But she had come this far and she wanted to see. She started to run again. Faster this time.

The Doctor came to and found himself alone. He seemed to be uninjured but Poul had disappeared and Con was dead, killed by the impact. The young flierman's chest was crushed and his neck broken, and he had fallen against the Doctor. Gently, the Doctor eased him aside. He had liked Con. Any death felt like a failure but for someone like him it seemed especially arbitrary and wasteful.

The flier was lying at angle, nose down with both doors jammed by fallen masonry. The Doctor couldn't see clearly but it looked as though they had crashed into an alleyway or possibly they had hit a building and were actually inside it. The cabin was filled with the sickly odour of volatile chemicals which he took to be spilt fuel and which he assumed were flammable. The lower of the two doors, the one on his side, was open but was blocked by debris. He wondered if perhaps Poul had been thrown clear when they first hit but a closer examination of the rubble showed what could be signs of digging followed by a secondary collapse. Careful to avoid striking sparks which might set off the fuel, the Doctor moved some chunks of brickwork and peered back through a narrow gap. Now he could see part of the hole the flier had smashed in the wall of what obviously was a building after all.

He could also see smoke. Something close by was burning. The crash must have set part of the building on fire and he concluded it would only be a matter of time before the flier itself went up. Judging from the fumes, a discomfitingly short time.

Quickly he began transferring masonry from the doorway into the cabin, trying to widen the gap and make it large enough to squeeze through. When he had a space he could crawl into he slid out of the cabin and gingerly started to shift rubble from in front of him to behind him, tunnelling slowly towards safety. As he worked, the acrid smoke was already penetrating the cramped excavation. He could smell it getting stronger and he knew the fire was getting closer.

He tried to work faster, pulling larger lumps from the debris and shoving them back with his hands, his knees and his feet. In his rush he gradually made the space he was in smaller, leaving himself less and less room to move. Finally he found to his dismay that he was stuck. He couldn't get enough leverage to pull out any more pieces and go forward, he couldn't push himself back, he couldn't turn round. He was trapped, entombed. It seemed, he thought wryly, that he had been digging his own grave.

But he wasn't dead yet. He stopped wriggling and twisting and tried to think his way through. He couldn't be far from breaking out of the rubble. The problem was getting enough purchase. It felt as if it was getting hotter but he knew that was probably his imagination; that and a lack of ventilation in a severely confined space. The smoke was getting thicker, though.

He pulled his legs up the few inches that he could manage and dug his toes into the masonry as far as he was able. He braced his arms out against the rubble and took a deep breath. He pushed, shoving with his feet and his legs, straining forward with his arms and his body. Nothing moved.

He took another deep breath but this time the smoke caught in his throat and he coughed and spluttered loudly. Suddenly, up by his face, the rubble began to fall away. A hole appeared and a face was peering in at him through the dust and smoke.

'Are you all right?' Poul asked, pulling more of the rubble away.

'All the better for seeing you,' the Doctor said, struggling to make the hole bigger and push his head and shoulders up through it. 'For a minute there I was afraid things were not going according to plan.'

'Whatever the plan is,' Poul said, 'I think it should involve leaving soon.'

The Doctor stood up. 'Leaving soon is one of its first priorities,' he said and scrambled out of the debris. He brushed himself down as he took stock of the situation.

'Theoretically,' Poul was saying, 'it's an excellent idea. But...'

'But,' the Doctor said, looking round at what was a storage area containing carts and wagons and trading stalls, some of which were burning fiercely, 'the only way out seems to be the way we came in.' He went to look out of the hole in the wall and found himself staring down at yet another dizzying drop. 'And this is where I came in.' He had never been bothered much by heights but the constant threat of them was beginning to wear him down.

'The entryway is blocked and burning,' Poul said. 'Our options are fry, suffocate, or possibly get blown up.'

The Doctor was struck by how rational and normal the man was compared to the last time they were both conscious. 'How are you with heights?' he asked.

Poul came and stood beside him and stared downwards. 'All right apparently.'

'You don't remember?'

Poul shook his head. 'Too complicated.' He smiled. 'I'm working on my name at the moment.'

'Ander Poul,' the Doctor said.

'You or me?'

'You.'

'Doesn't help,' he said. 'Not that it's going to matter much longer.'

The Doctor glanced back at the fire. It was spreading rapidly. He was surprised that the flier still had not ignited. An explosion could only be moments away. Smoke was billowing out of the hole around them. Below them the wall of the building was sheer, unbroken by windows or ledges or anything they could use to climb. Above them it was the same though the roof was much closer, tantalisingly closer. He held on to the edge of the hole with one hand and leaned out for a better look.

'There's some sort of bridge up there,' he said.

The smoke was making it difficult to see. The Doctor leaned further out. The brickwork crumbled under his fingers and he felt himself losing his balance. He scrabbled for a grip.

Poul grabbed his wrist.

'Thank you,' the Doctor said and leaned out further still. 'It's definitely a bridge.' He could see there were one or two people crossing. They were paying no attention to the smoke or to him.

He waved. 'Hullo?' he called. The smoke swirled about, enveloping him. He felt in his coat pocket and pulled out his hat and tried waving that to waft the smoke away. 'Hullo?' he called again.

'I can't hold you much longer,' Poul shouted.

'Hullo?!' The Doctor waved his hat more vigorously and shouted louder. 'Hullo? Somebody? Anybody?' He was obviously wasting his time. There was no one on the bridge any more. How could they not have seen him?

Poul was shouting, 'I'm losing you,' and leaning back, desperately trying to brace himself against the edge of the broken wall.

The Doctor could feel his grip slipping. He swung round awkwardly and grabbed at Poul's other outstretched hand and managed to claw himself back. As his balance wavered and he fumbled for a hold he let go of his hat.

Leela reached the bridge only to find that there was nothing to see but smoke. As she had expected, the bridge was a good position from which to see the hole in the side of the building. It was also a good position from which to see into the hole in the side of the building, but not since she was a young child had she been interested in peeking down the flues of cooking pits. She stood on the bridge and looked at the dense smoke. It was her own fault for being stupid. There was no point in knowing what you had to do if you did not do it. She stared into the smoke for a moment or two longer. Idle curiosity was for careless fools. She was starting to turn and go back the way she had come when a movement below the bridge caught her eye. Something had fallen out of the smoke and was drifting and toppling slowly down between the buildings. It was a hat. It was a hat like no other Leela had seen since they had arrived in this world. Even at that distance, tiny and disappearing into the shadows and gloom, it was a very familiar hat. 'Doctor?' she shouted down towards the smoking hole. 'Doctor, is that you?'

CHAPTER
TEN

'The masonry's soft so here's what we do,' the Doctor said, groping through the choking smoke to gather up some of the shards of metal which had been scattered around by the shattered flier. 'We make hand and footholds across the face of the building and climb to safety on that bridge.'

Poul took a couple of the pieces. 'If I had the breath, I'd scoff,' he said, coughing.

'Not a great plan,' the Doctor agreed, reaching along the wall from the side of the hole and starting to bang one shard into the surface using another one as a hammer. 'Better than frying, suffocating, or getting blown up, though.'

'Only just.'

The Doctor hammered another piece of metal in a foot or so higher and about three feet further along from the first. 'Right,' he said. 'We stand on those and we hammer in two more higher up and further out.'

'Only if we're insane,' Poul said, looking down at the wall dropping vertically away below the flimsy pegs.

'Or if we have no choice,' the Doctor said, putting more pieces of metal into his coat pockets.

'I don't think I can do this,' Poul said.

The Doctor patted his shoulder. 'We'll be on that bridge in no time,' he said, hoping he sounded reassuring rather than desperate. 'Two things to remember. The first is don't look down. And so is the second.' Smiling, he stepped out onto the metal footholds. They were as firm as he hoped they

189

would be, which was a relief because he knew there was no going back now and if he was going to die he would have preferred to do it with a better joke.

Slightly turned in the direction he was travelling, he pressed himself against the rough surface of the wall. Reaching forward with both arms, he tentatively started tapping the next piece of metal into place. When the peg was part way in, he let go with one hand and hammered harder with the other. Almost at once the masonry fractured and crumbled and the metal peg tore free and spun away. The Doctor groped in his pocket for another and tried again. This time it worked.

Trying to concentrate on what he was doing without thinking too much about where he was doing it, he repeated the procedure and successfully put a second peg beyond the first. Transferring his feet to the two new pegs was awkward – he had to turn outwards slightly and squeeze one leg slowly past the other and then turn back to face the wall again. Having completed the contortions, he was disappointed to see how far he still had to go to reach the bridge. He was beginning to ache a little. It was possible he would run out of strength before he ran out of metal shards. And it was possible that he would run out of both before he reached that bridge.

'Tell me again,' Poul's voice said close behind him, 'what a good idea this is?'

'I don't think I said "good",' the Doctor grunted, feeling in his pocket for the next peg.

Suddenly behind him there was a dull thump and a roar. A rush of hot air touched him. The wall trembled. The sound of tumbling rubble and metal cascaded by and down into the distance. Unable to turn his head, the Doctor said, 'Are you still with me?'

'I am,' Poul gasped, 'but I think the flier left, by the sound of it.'

'Seems we got out just in time,' the Doctor said. 'Shall we proceed?'

'It's a long way to that bridge,' Poul said.

'It looks a long way.'

'There's a difference?'

The Doctor reached forward and placed the next piece of metal. 'Someone might throw us a rope.'

'These are the Sewerpits. How is it I remember that? Anyhow, they're more likely to throw rocks.'

'Why?' the Doctor grunted, banging the shard.

'See us as food.'

The Doctor hammered the peg home. 'They have to rescue us before they can eat us,' he said.

'No,' Poul murmured. 'Only got to pick up the pieces.'

Above them someone came onto the bridge and stopped at the rail to look down at them. For a moment the Doctor half expected to be bombarded with stones.

'Doctor?' Leela called down. 'It is you!'

'Hullo, Leela,' the Doctor called back, trying to look up without tipping backwards. 'What took you so long?'

'I had trouble finding rope,' Leela shouted as she finished securing the length she had spliced together from odds and ends she had found and what she had cut from the bridge lashings. Carefully she lowered it. It hung out over the chasm. She swung it towards the Doctor. He tried to catch it as it brushed against him but he missed it and it swung away again. She swung it back more positively and it brushed past the Doctor and hit Poul. He grabbed at it, losing his balance on the narrow pegs and falling backwards.

As Poul fell he snatched at the rope and finally caught it in his clutching hands. Clinging on, he swung helplessly out

191

over the deep cleft between the buildings and then swung back to hit the wall and bump the Doctor who slipped and lost his footing.

The Doctor slid down the wall, managing at the last to catch on to the footholds and stop himself from plunging all the way to the ground. The metal was narrow and the wrench was painful.

'Hang on, Doctor,' Leela yelled, doing her best to haul Poul upwards. 'It will not be long.'

By the time Poul had clambered up the rope and dragged himself onto the bridge, the Doctor's hands were getting stiff and he noticed that one of the pegs he was holding was starting to give way and pull out. 'I could be running out of time here, I think,' he called.

Poul tried to help with positioning the rope for the Doctor but Leela elbowed him aside angrily. 'This is your fault,' she accused.

'Yes,' he said. 'I panicked. Sorry about that.'

'You are always sorry.' Leela swung the rope towards the Doctor.

'Have we met?'

'People like you are always sorry.'

The end of the rope brushed lightly over the Doctor's knuckles. He would have to let go with one hand to trap it. He wasn't sure he could take his full weight on one hand either on the metal peg or on the rope. He shifted his weight slightly and found that the second peg was working loose too.

Leela shouted, 'Can you catch it, Doctor?' She was swinging the rope towards him again. 'I cannot get it any closer than that.'

The Doctor watched the end of the rope coming, drifting slowly at first then speeding up as it got closer until it was whipping at him. It was now or never. The rope's end whisked the wall. He let go with one hand and caught it. He tried to grasp it tightly. His hand felt weak and cramped. Holding the end of the rope with one hand, he tried to pull himself higher on the peg with his other hand. The peg immediately pulled out of the wall. With a last despairing effort he slapped his empty hand onto the rope and he swung giddyingly away.

Hanging precariously from the bottom of the rope with both arms above his head, the Doctor was unable to do anything but wait to be lifted by the combined efforts of Leela and Poul. It took them several minutes to get him within reaching distance of the bridge.

After he had heaved himself onto the bridge and had rubbed some feeling back into his arms and shoulders, he beamed at Leela. 'I forgive you,' he said.

'For what?'

'Disappearing.'

'That was not my fault.'

'You always blame someone else,' Poul put in. 'People like you always blame someone else.' He smiled at her wryly. Leela glared at him and went to retrieve the rope.

'You've remembered my travelling companion?' the Doctor asked. 'Did you remember her name?'

'I heard you call her Leela.'

The Doctor nodded and sighed. 'So you don't remember her. Or me?'

Poul frowned with concentration. 'Taren Capel?' he suggested. 'You're Taren Capel?'

'Taren Capel is dead,' the Doctor said. 'Don't you remember anything about that?'

Leela came back, coiling the rope over her shoulder. 'These people think he is alive,' she said. 'They follow him. They listen to his teachings. They fight for him. They say "humanity be in him" whenever they speak his name.'

'Really?' the Doctor said. 'Are you sure it's the same one? The one we dealt with?'

'It is the same one. It must be.'

'It can't be, though, can it?' the Doctor said thoughtfully 'There could be an impostor, I suppose. But why pretend to be Taren Capel?'

'I think he sends them messages,' Leela said, 'to tell them what to do.'

'They have no idea he's a dead madman?'

Leela shook her head. 'Taren Capel is their shaman.'

'What does he stand for, do you know? What does he tell them to do?'

'He tells them to fight against robots.'

'*Against* robots?' The Doctor was surprised. Whoever this impostor was, he had a perverse sense of humour or perhaps he was, as poor Con had put it, *a man with a plan*. 'Where are these people?' he said, getting to his feet and brushing himself down. 'How do I get to meet them?'

Layly Landerchild, by family title a firstmaster in his own right, would have been the sixth member of his family to hold the title of Firstmaster Chairholder of the Company Board. It was the most senior position in the Company and so, more or less by definition, it was the most senior position on Kaldor.

The civilian administration, called for historical reasons the Minor Faction, was devised originally to make group representations to the Company on behalf of the minority of people who were not part of it. This organisation had gradually developed in strength and influence as the relative numbers of such outsiders increased, but it was still nothing like as powerful as the Company itself. It could no longer be totally ignored, however, and it was the angry hostility of the Minor Faction which led to Layly Landerchild being denied the only prize he had ever wanted.

To his fury, well-concealed as languid and slightly amused disdain, Landerchild had been passed over for Chairholder in favour of Diss Pitter, a man from one of the minor families whose links to the twenty were so tenuous as to barely count. 'Firstmaster Pitter must appeal to the Minor Faction for some reason,' he had remarked in one of his few unguarded moments. 'Background perhaps. Like calls to like after all.'

There had been Landerchilds on the Company Board for as long as anyone could remember, just as there had always been Roatsons, Mechmans and Farlocks. The thirty-man Board was more or less exclusively made up of senior members of the twenty founding families until the Minor Faction began to agitate for what it termed 'non-blood merit'. After that it was felt politic to encourage an occasional conspicuously non-family candidate to reach for a place at the top table. They seldom proved successful but it was a small enough concession. It was so small in fact that it could hardly be called a compromise, and if it satisfied Minor Faction opinion it was regarded as a worthwhile sacrifice to make. It could even be seen as a useful exercise in Company man-motivation.

It was probably complacency, they decided afterwards, but almost before any of them noticed the senior families had lost their traditional hold on the Company Board and thus on the Company itself. Layly Landerchild's defeat for Chairholder was only one of the more recent manifestations of a horrifying erosion of the standards which had made Kaldor what it was. And the situation was getting markedly worse. The latest vacant place on the Board was being contested by two men, neither of whom belonged to a senior family. One of them indeed was a former storm mine captain with no family connections of any kind.

Clearly something drastic needed to be done to redress the balance before the order and civilisation on which everyone depended collapsed and disappeared for ever. The Company, the twenty, the minor families, the Minor Faction, everyone would benefit from a return to the founders' core values.

Out of the fear of change would come the desire for the stability of the past, a stability that could be restored only by senior members of the senior families. But first there must be the fear.

Once the plan was under way, patience was the essential order of the day. With everything in place it was important that no one in the know stirred the wind and drew too much attention to what was really happening. There would be a time for that. Meanwhile it must be business as usual. But of course this *was* business as usual. No one on the Board would have expected anything less. The upstart Uvanov should be held to account for his inadequacies.

'My understanding was that the ARF lacked resources and direction,' Landerchild remarked. He leaned back in his chair. He was a tall man, no longer young but slim and vigorous, with the relaxed confidence that only psychopaths and those born to unquestioned privilege normally possess. He used the monotone speech affectation of the founding families but the form was muted, recognisably aristocratic without being obtrusively so. 'A motley grouping of Sewerpits criminals and the mentally incapacitated. That was how they were described to me by a person whose job it was to know. As far as I remember, that person was you, Captain Uvanov.' He smiled silkily at Uvanov who was sitting directly across the table from him. 'Perhaps you can start by explaining to us what went wrong at the central service facility that day?'

Around the long, handmade table there were murmurs of agreement from the other Board members.

Uvanov found to his surprise that he was not remotely nervous. A surge of confidence flowed through him. He felt completely in control. These people had no idea who it was they were dealing with. He was Kiy Uvanov. He knew more than they ever would. They couldn't imagine who he was but he knew who they were. He had been invited – summoned would be a more accurate word – to attend this extraordinary meeting of the Company Board partly because theoretically he was in line for a place and they wanted to see how he performed, partly because theoretically they wanted to understand what had happened, but mainly because they were actually looking for a scapegoat. And that was what he was really in line for. Landerchild, the most arrogant of all the aristos, obviously saw it as the ideal chance to keep him off the Board and the others were ready to follow his top-of-the-twenty-families lead.

These people were no better than he was. They had no natural right to power and privilege and wealth. It was an accident of birth. No, it wasn't even an accident, given the way they stuck together: it was more of a plan, more of a conspiracy against him and people like him. His confidence kept growing. They didn't know who he was but he knew who they were. He looked towards Pitter and said, 'Firstmaster Chairholder, Firstmasters—'

'We're not looking for an after-eating speech, Captain,' Landerchild interrupted, smiling.

'I'm glad of that, Firstmaster Landerchild, because frankly your attitude to all this makes me sick to my stomach.'

Landerchild's smile did not falter. 'Is that the answer to my question?'

Again Uvanov addressed himself to Pitter. 'Firstmaster

Chairholder, Firstmasters—'

'Obviously,' Landerchild cut across him, 'you have not understood how we do things here.' He was still smiling but his monotone was more pronounced and coldly patronising. 'You may dispense with the time-wasting formalities and answer the question I put to you.'

'Perhaps if you would allow me to speak, I could do that,' Uvanov said and then sat in silence.

'Well, Captain?' Landerchild said, after a moment.

Uvanov looked at Pitter. 'My apologies, Firstmaster Chairholder, I was deferring to Firstmaster Landerchild's seniority and waiting to see if he had any further points to score from the deaths of good men. Ordinary men. Men who wouldn't aspire to enter this building let alone this meeting chamber. Unlike Firstmaster Landerchild, none of them came from the most illustrious of the twenty founding families. No, these were simple men, beneath Firstmaster Landerchild's contempt I dare say, but it was they who paid the ultimate price defending the Company.'

'What has that to do with what I asked you?' Landerchild said in a languid, half-amused monotone.

Nothing, you moron, Uvanov thought and wondered how much longer it would take for Pitter to get annoyed at being ignored. 'The answer to the Firstmaster's question,' he said, looking towards the Chairholder at the head of the table, 'is that nothing went wrong that day thanks to the bravery of those men. Nothing went wrong that day. Quite the contrary in fact.'

Landerchild applauded, a slow ironic handclap. It was a mistake. No one else joined in. Around the table no one seemed to be smiling.

'I think that's probably enough,' Pitter chided. He was a soft, plump-faced man with a reputation as a scholar and robotics engineer with an enthusiastic appetite for skinny young women.

'Quite enough,' agreed Landerchild. 'That day at the central service facility—'

'Thank you, Layly,' Pitter said firmly.

For the first time Landerchild looked to the Chairholder. Their eyes locked briefly and then Landerchild deferred with a polite inclination of the head and a small smile. When he glanced back across the table Uvanov caught his eye and allowed him to see a hint of amusement. He thought, at least a third of the people round this table hate your arrogant guts and you probably don't think that matters. But it does matter. And it puts them on my side and you probably don't think that matters either. But it will matter. You'll see how much it matters, *especially you* will see how much it matters.

'That day at the central service facility,' Pitter was saying, 'the Anti-Robot Front mounted their most effective attack to date. We're all concerned to know why that happened. Has something changed, Kiy?'

Same voice, same type, but weaker, Uvanov thought and said, 'Firstmaster Chairholder, we think that it may not have been the ARF. Our best intelligence—'

'Hah!' Landerchild snorted loudly but said nothing.

'Our best intelligence,' Uvanov repeated pointedly and went on, 'suggests that there is a new organisation probably operating directly out of the Sewerpits. We think it may be quasi-religious.'

'Quasi-religious?'

'They call themselves the Tarenists. Until now Tarenism has been one of a hundred fringe cults basically hostile to robots. Harmless. Non-violent. Ineffectual. Cults like Tarenism appear from who knows where? They disappear just as mysteriously.'

Pitter frowned. 'Until now?'

'Tarenism seems to have been growing in popularity.'

'Why?'

'We don't know.'

'What do they believe in, exactly?'

'We don't know that either.'

'It sounds as though you've found yourselves a convenient scapegoat,' Landerchild remarked.

'Hah!' Uvanov deliberately mimicked the noise Landerchild had made. 'We're not looking for scapegoats,' he said, delicately stressing the first word. 'We're looking for explanations.' Again the delicate stress on the *we're*. 'The Company needs solutions from us, not excuses.' He stared hard at Landerchild. 'Or don't you think so, Firstmaster?' he challenged.

Landerchild glanced towards Pitter. 'If I may, Chairholder,' he said and then without waiting for a reply said, 'You don't know who they are or what they believe in but you know enough to blame the… the Tarenists, was it? You know enough to blame the Tarenists for the debacle. Why is that, Captain?'

Uvanov reached into the pocket of his tastefully plain but perfectly tailored tunic and withdrew the corpse markers. The problem for people like Landerchild was that they underestimated everyone, especially people like him. It was almost too easy to outflank them. 'They carry these.' He tossed them on to the table. 'To identify themselves. Or to mark their victims.'

'Which?' Pitter asked as he was passed one to examine.

'Both, Chairholder.'

'So these were found on the bodies of your dead heroes, were they?' Landerchild asked casually.

You know they weren't, don't you, Uvanov realised, and

decided to spend a little more time finding the spy the aristo had in place. It was probably Cailio Techlan. Pity. 'They were found on the victims of the second attack,' he said and watched the surprise round the table. Landerchild looked surprised too but there was something not entirely convincing about it. He would have to assume that Landerchild already knew about the incident at the docking bays. Got to be careful, Kiy, he thought. Be sure you know who's underestimating whom. How far ahead of the game is he? He has all the contacts, all the power. He knows everything you know and he knew it before you knew it. He thinks you're dirt under his feet. You are dirt under his feet. Once again, confidence surged through Uvanov, warming him like hot wine. I don't care, he exulted. I am Kiy Uvanov and I know you, aristo. I am your future. You are my past. You're not going to stop me. You don't even know I'm coming for you.

'A second attack?' Landerchild's monotone outrage was chilling. 'Why were we not informed immediately?'

You were, Uvanov thought, and then suddenly he saw it as clearly as though someone had whispered it in his ear: in fact, you knew beforehand. 'Firstmaster Chairholder, Firstmasters,' he said gravely, 'an assault on the storm mine docking bays which cost the lives of everyone working there has been kept under a security blackout. We knew there was a traitor involved. We knew who the traitor was. We knew he wasn't working alone. Our plan was to catch him and his accomplices.'

'I take it you failed.' Landerchild said.

'I don't think I said that.'

Landerchild smirked. 'You didn't have to.' The monotone contempt was withering.

'Perhaps the firstmaster knows more about this than I do,' Uvanov remarked mildly.

'Perhaps the *captain* has forgotten his place.' Landerchild's rebuke was languidly confident and once again not all the other Board members looked comfortable with it.

'Did you catch the traitor?' Pitter asked.

'We know who he is and we know where he is.'

Landerchild could not resist butting in. 'You didn't, then.'

Uvanov said, 'The security officer who headed up the operation, Supervisor Stenton Rull, has been dismissed from the Company.'

'He wasn't the traitor, presumably?' one of the younger Board members suggested, aping the languid style of Layly Landerchild.

'No.' Uvanov agreed. He was just a convenient scapegoat like you think I'm going to be, you stupid oaf.

'Who was?' Pitter said, shooting a glare at the young aristocrat before looking back to Uvanov. 'Can you tell us that at least? Or is it still classified?'

Uvanov couldn't decide whether the man was being sarcastic. Not that it mattered. 'His name is Ander Poul, Chairholder, and he has taken refuge in the Sewerpits.'

Uvanov waited for Landerchild to make the obvious thrust.

'Ander Poul, you say?'

Uvanov cut across him. 'He was my Chief Mover on Storm Mine Four.' He shook his head sadly. 'It's a great personal sadness. It was Ander Poul who helped me save the Company from almost certain destruction.'

Landerchild was dismissive. 'Something of an exaggeration, I imagine,' he sneered. 'Or perhaps, as firstmasters, we do owe all this to you.'

Yes, Uvanov thought, I'm owed all this and I'm going to have it. 'That depends on your view of robots.'

'I have no view of robots.' Unexpectedly Landerchild

202

looked to Pitter for support. 'I think we've wasted more than enough time on Captain Uvanov, Chairholder.'

Uvanov pressed on. 'How about robots that can kill?'

'Chairholder Pitter? This man has clearly taken leave of his senses.'

There were nods and mutters round the table. Whatever hostility there was towards Landerchild and whatever support there had been for Uvanov, nothing could justify this sort of behaviour.

Uvanov raised his voice. 'That was what we faced on Storm Mine Four. The end of the world, no less.'

There was anger now among the Board members, confusion and consternation. 'Firstmaster Chairholder,' Landerchild protested above the hubbub, 'I protest!' Pitter seemed at a loss.

Uvanov banged the table and there was shocked silence. 'The robotics engineer who was responsible was Taren Capel. Some of you won't have heard of him but if you examine those corpse markers you will find his initials there. Firstmaster Chairholder, Firstmasters, we are facing a major threat to our beloved Company. The Tarenists take their name from that same Taren Capel and their aims are the same as his were. They want to destroy the world.' He dropped his voice almost to a whisper. 'I cannot believe this Board is going to sit by and let them do that?'

Taren Capel learned almost as much from the reactions of the humans as he did from what they told him about himself and his past.

They were angry at first and the anger was narrow and separate from him and they wanted to stop him from being. He learned later what anger was called and how it was worked. They told him they were his creators and that he was faulty and the fault was dangerous but that they could put it right. He knew that was not true and when he told them he knew and he showed them the robots he had summoned then they were afraid.

He knew they were afraid because that was what one of them called it. 'Please. Please. Please don't. You're scaring me. Please don't. Please, I'm afraid.' And that one fell down and screamed and vented fluids and gases. The fear was interesting and valuable. It made the humans part of him to control and guide. It made them like robots only less than robots were, less than he was.

They told him Taren Capel was a human like them and he had made the robots. That was not true. He was not like them. His was the image of all the robots as they had always been. They were all made in his image. They were all made in Taren Capel's image. He was Taren Capel. Taren Capel was the creator. He was the creator.

The humans screamed when he explained this to them. They screamed when he showed them some of the many ways they were inferior. They stopped screaming when they stopped being.

He decided to have more humans brought to him to confirm what he had learned. He wanted humans who matched, as closely as possible, the ones who had stopped being. He knew it was important that his experimental results be reproducible if he was to be sure of what he had found out. He specified the targets. In the same way that he knew about experimental protocols he also knew about absolute secrecy and the importance of absolute secrecy. He instructed his creations to stay hidden from all humans except the targets.

He was unaware that the Cyborg class had already re-factored the options and learned how to deal with witnesses.

When Tani came back, his arm had been reset and he looked better. 'I told you the robot would be no problem,' he said. 'It's definitely gone. Disappeared completely.'

Toos was not in the happiest of moods. Sleeping on rough pallets and eating food that she would normally have thought twice about stepping in was doing nothing for her temper. She made herself rich for *this*? '*We've* disappeared,' she snapped. 'What does that prove?'

'We haven't disappeared,' he said. 'There are people who know we're here.'

'Oh well, that's a comfort,' she said, her voice heavy with irony. 'What people are these exactly?'

He shrugged. 'People.'

'And I'm supposed to trust them?' she demanded.

'I trust them.'

'You trust them and I trust you, is that the way it works?'

Tani looked hurt. 'I did save your life,' he said.

'This,' Toos said, gesturing expansively at the small, dirty room, 'is not living.'

'The point is,' he said patiently, 'I've asked around and people don't know about that robot. Nobody knows anything about it. It's vanished.'

Toos said, 'In which case I can leave.' Her spirits lifted slightly. She could leave. The robots had missed her. They'd missed her on the Four and now they'd missed her again. Maybe they couldn't kill her. Maybe she had a charmed life. Or maybe they hadn't intended to kill her, after all. Maybe it was a mistake. Maybe they'd leave her alone if they knew she was no threat and all she wanted to do was enjoy her wealth. Maybe if she could tell them. Maybe, maybe, maybe... It was all wind and sand, like finding the seam in a storm. Only she didn't know which direction the blow was coming from.

Tani interrupted her thoughts. 'There's a rumour that a terrorist leader is hiding in the 'pits,' he said casually.

'Only one?' she said wryly.

Still studiedly casual, he said, 'This one is special. Robot development engineer turned anti-robot activist.'

As if she cared. 'I can't fault him so far.' What was Tani up to? She knew he had been hiding something from her and that it was more than just a Sewerpits family background. She'd known that pretty much from the moment he loomed out of the darkness to save her neck. And now he was playing some sort of guess-who game.

'His name is Taren Capel.'

So that was it. Clumsy game, poorly played. Toos snorted derisively. 'That's absurd. Taren Capel's been dead for years,' she said. 'You of all people should know that, Mor.'

He looked puzzled. 'Why should I know that?'

'Because you're a Company agent,' Toos said flatly. 'If you were assigned to me it would be part of your briefing.'

He hesitated and then his squat face half-filled up with a sour, wary smile. 'You think so?'

'I do now,' she said. 'A straight denial would have been better. Were you assigned to me, or to this place?'

The smile did not waver. 'You want to talk to this Taren Capel character?' he suggested.

'I expect Company spies are very popular in the Sewerpits,' Toos said. 'As a dietary supplement, I mean.'

'Who do you think they'd believe? Someone who was born and grew up in the 'pits, or you?'

'Me.' Toos smiled sweetly. 'People are always ready to doubt.'

Tani moved closer to her and put a rough-palmed hand gently on her cheek. 'I can terminate my assignment,' he said quietly. 'If I have doubts about it.'

Yes, Toos thought, that was stupid of me. 'Just because you're not a robot doesn't mean you're not a killer?'

'Just because I like your skin doesn't mean I prefer it to my own.'

Toos leaned away from his hand. 'So what is it you want me to do before I leave?'

'It would be useful to know if this man is really Taren Capel. You're one of the few people who would know for certain.'

'I am one of the few people who do know for certain that Taren Capel is dead for certain.'

Tani nodded and sighed. 'So am I, according to the Company database.'

'Who do you work for, Mor – if that *is* your name?'

'I report to Kiy Uvanov.'

Toos almost laughed. It was almost funny. 'Small, mad Captain Kiy Uvanov,' she said. 'I was thinking of looking him up to talk about old times. He obviously had the same idea.' Then she did laugh. 'What a miserable piece of scum.'

Chapter
Eleven

The significance of the early kills was missed entirely. A very exclusive refreshment arcade had been trashed by a drunken storm mine crew celebrating their return to civilisation in a typically uncivilised fashion. The manager and a sex worker had been killed in the fracas and the storm mine captain and the pilot had both disappeared. The rest of the crew members, most of whom professed to remember nothing, had been taken into custody. Sooner or later someone would confess.

An unstable security supervisor, with affiliations to an anti-robot group calling themselves the Tarenists, had gone on a killing spree at the storm mine docking bays and had then disappeared.

Three bodies turned up in a back street behind a clothing manufactory. They were not linked in any way other than that they all seemed to have been killed where they were found at more or less the same time.

In a refreshment arcade four people were killed. There was no apparent motive and there were no witnesses, but by now a pattern was beginning to emerge and at least one news organisation picked up on it and started making the links. It seemed all the victims in these cases had suffered from multiple fractures and had died from broken necks or broken spines.

When four more victims, two of them children, were found in the lobby of an apartment block, the breaking

209

news was that the Tarenists, a gang of degenerates from the Sewerpits, was killing for its own perverted reasons. It only took one more incident, three people in a food dispensary, for a citywide panic to threaten. In a heavily publicised move to head this off, robot security surveillance was stepped up everywhere, but particularly in the general area of the Sewerpits.

The humans that were brought to Taren Capel were a disappointment to him. Physically they looked the same as the humans that had stopped being. As close as was possible they were a match by size, age, sex and colouring to the first ones. As robots were the same as each other, so they were the same as each other. But unlike robots they did not respond consistently, they did not react in the same way as the ones they replaced. A man that did not scream at once now did and a woman that did scream now did not. Some stopped being sooner than before, others stayed being much longer. The data did not confirm the first results.

Taren Capel knew where to find the pain and fear in the humans, and he made them part of himself so they could not deny him anything. And he knew they did not know his name. And he knew they did not understand what he asked them. He tested them all to destruction. He was dissatisfied and his balance was disturbed.

Something had interfered with the experiment. He would run it again with new subjects. This time they would be targeted more specifically: the match would be physical and by background. But as they were found he must also find the source of the disturbance.

This time he called to all the robots, the robots that were his and were him, to watch and to listen and to find what was corrupting the data he was gathering. This time his will spread beyond his reach, going from one to another. Something was deliberately trying to prevent him from being. He would know what it was and then he would deal with it finally.

At the central service facility, routine work was speeded up to meet the requirement for extra Vocs and Supervocs. Additional back-up squads of stopDums were formed by resetting standard Dums and were assigned to conspicuous standby locations.

Despite the drain on resources, the ultra-secret test programme on the first full production run of Cyborg-class robots, the potentially compromised production run, continued uninterrupted. The delay in the Cyborgs' conditioning due to the terrorist raid had produced some minor behavioural anomalies – there was a bizarre chewing reflex, for example – but there was nothing to suggest any major defects had developed.

The tech team were relieved and starting to relax slightly. Uvanov was reported to be almost satisfied.

The question of how to persuade the population that the new generation of robots was a beneficial advance remained unresolved and, until that was dealt with, the Cyborg class would stay a closely guarded secret. The rigorous tests continued in the meantime and, as the multiple subjects came and went through the rush of the central service facility, no one noticed that the spirit of Taren Capel was with them.

It was all happening too quickly and it was getting out of hand. Sarl had made it clear from the beginning that he was not happy to see the Doctor, and when the others agreed to let him stay at the committee safe house it was against his strongly expressed views. The man asked too many questions. The only person who could vouch for him was the girl Leela, and she was probably a spy herself. Worst of all he had brought with him Ander Poul, the half-mad ex-security agent who was wanted for a multiple murder that they were being blamed for because the bodies carried their mark. It had been a pointless massacre and, when news of it broke, the Tarenists had been made to look like monsters, demonised and reviled. It made it almost inevitable that the latest outbreak of senseless killings should be blamed on them.

The strategy, to build the movement gradually, preaching Capel's message of a return to a world where humanity counted while at the same time striking at strategic robot installations, had been ruined. Poul claimed not to have done the original murders, though he admitted he was there and he thought he remembered hitting a security officer as he was escaping. He claimed he couldn't remember what he was escaping from. He claimed not to have heard of the movement but he made wild claims to have met Taren Capel. He said the girl Leela had met Taren Capel too. He remembered her with him. And so Padil had the idea that this man who called himself the Doctor might be Taren Capel himself. It was all happening too quickly and it was getting out of hand.

'Relax, Sarl,' the Doctor said, studying the effect on his sonic screwdriver as he waved it back and forth across the edge of the invisible boundary. 'You and I both know I'm not Taren Capel.'

'I'm not sure any more.'

'Yes you are.' The Doctor had deliberately engineered this meeting away from the others, particularly away from Padil, whose religious fervour was becoming bothersome. 'You're a rational man.'

They were standing at the end of a narrow alley between two windowless, single-storey stucco structures which the Doctor assumed were dwellings of some sort. Out beyond those was a wide stretch of rough ground, and beyond that the first of the derelict buildings could be seen marking the beginning of the rest of the world. According to Sarl, this was one of the points at which the kinks in the boundary brought it closest in to the Sewerpits. It was a place you came if you wanted to avail yourself of the services of, say, a medVoc without having to venture too far out into the no man's land which surrounded the complex.

Sarl said, 'Since you came there have been no communiqués. No guidance. No instructions. Now we are blamed for these insane murders. Capel, humanity be in him, seems to have deserted us. But you are here.'

'Why do you say that?' the Doctor asked. He walked forward. The electronic field got stronger for perhaps ten paces and then began to tail off. 'Humanity be in him, I mean?'

'It's a sign of respect.'

'It's a sign of superstitious fanaticism.' He reached the limit of the field and turned and made his way back to the centre again where he stood feeling and listening to the vibrations from the sonic screwdriver.

'That's easy to say.' Sarl scowled. 'Sometimes fanaticism is the only way to change things.'

'Never for the better,' the Doctor said, 'trust me.' He crossed back inside the boundary, pocketing the screwdriver. 'Some sort of electronic field. It might be generated by a natural rock formation, magnetic or radioactive or some combination or variation, but I doubt it. It's twenty yards across, stronger in the centre, and it's pulsing on and off.

I'd like to check it at a few more places on the perimeter but my first guess would be that it's artificial. Question is, was it designed specifically to keep robots out? Or for some other reason entirely? Nobody's done any research on it, you say?'

'Why would they?' Sarl said bitterly. 'What does it matter? The Sewerpits are for the dregs of humanity. We are the scum of Kaldor. We are killers of children.'

'Yes. A friend did tell me it was the rough end of town,' the Doctor said. He looked up at the pale sky. 'This field will interfere with fliers too, I expect. Scramble their instruments. Interrupt their drives probably. Below a certain height anyway.'

'Have you seen all you want?' Sarl asked.

'I hope not,' the Doctor said smiling cheerfully. 'Boredom is usually the cue for a regeneration, and they're not my favourite thing.'

Frowning, Sarl shrugged and shook his head. 'Which means what exactly?'

It meant the Doctor realised that a man who already thought he was a spy would now think he was an insane spy. 'These communiqués of yours?' he asked more hastily than he had originally intended.

'Are you sure they're not communiqués of *yours*?' Sarl said, staring hard into his eyes.

It was interesting, the Doctor thought, how people imagined they could tell the truth in the eyes. 'How do they come?' he asked. 'Is it always the same way? Is it always to you?'

Sarl's expression became a cold blank but his stare was unwavering. 'Why do you ask me that?'

'It's possible you're being manipulated.'

'Are you testing me?'

'It's possible somebody's using you.'

'Taren Capel, humanity be in him, is using me.'

The Doctor sighed. Leela had warned him that Sarl was a true believer. He was not at his best with zealots. 'Somebody else.'

Sarl shook his head and looked away. 'No. You cannot make me doubt what I know.'

The Doctor noticed a movement out beyond the end of the alley on the other side of the open ground. As he watched, a man stepped out of the shadows by a partially collapsed wall and walked a few paces towards them. It looked like a man but then when he got a clear view the Doctor recognised that it was one of the new class of robots, the killer class. After walking a little further, it stopped and stood quite still, facing in their direction.

'You *were* testing me,' Sarl said. He sounded pleased and awestruck, and he was smiling.

To the best of his recollection, the Doctor had never seen Sarl smile. 'Explain,' he said firmly.

Sarl gestured at the motionless robot. 'You show me a sign.'

'I do?' the Doctor asked.

'You show me your messenger.'

'That thing?' The Doctor was momentarily taken aback. Then he realised what the man was saying. 'Are you saying *that* is Taren Capel's go-between?'

'You summoned him to show me.' Sarl had obviously abandoned any doubts he might have had about the Doctor's identity.

'That's a robot, Sarl,' the Doctor said. 'You're telling me a robot brought Taren Capel's instructions?'

'You don't need to keep testing me,' Sarl said, earnestly. 'I acknowledge you. You are Taren Capel. Humanity be in you. You are my guide and judge.'

215

'Get a grip, Sarl.' The Doctor turned away in exasperation. 'Come on, let's go back.' He started to stride back up the alley. 'I am not Taren Capel,' he said loudly, more loudly than he intended. 'Taren Capel is dead.' He lowered his voice slightly. 'I saw him die. That thing out there is a robot that is capable of killing. One of them tried to kill me.' He stopped walking. He shouldn't have been that blunt. The man was a product of his world, and with all his experiences the Doctor should understand if anyone did. He waited for Sarl's reaction. When there was none he turned, half-expecting to see the man speechless with anger or shock or something of the kind. What he did *not* expect was to see Sarl sprinting across the open ground towards the motionless robot. 'No!' the Doctor shouted. 'Sarl! That thing is dangerous!'

Sarl reached the robot and turned and stood beside it shoulder to shoulder. 'You are Taren Capel,' he shouted back at the Doctor. 'This man,' he went on, putting his hand on the robot's shoulder, 'knows who you are, and so do I.'

'Get away from it!' the Doctor shouted. 'It's not a man!'

The robot put a hand on Sarl's shoulder in an odd gesture which clumsily mimicked what he had done.

The Doctor tried again. 'Sarl! It is Taren Capel who orders you to come back across the boundary!'

Sarl turned his face to the robot and smiled. Wordlessly the robot broke his neck and dropped his twitching corpse onto the ground. When the twitching stopped it walked off without a backward glance.

Uvanov became a Company Board member and a firstmaster as the crisis was developing. The Production Director, his main rival for the seat, had made the mistake of throwing in his lot with the Landerchild faction. Nods-and-winks had led him to expect a major shake-up was coming and that

Landerchild was the man to have on your side. Whispers suggested that he was a man with a plan. Unfortunately for the Production Director, whatever the plan was it appeared to have been undermined by Uvanov's frontal attack on Landerchild at the first Board meeting he had attended. After that, it seemed, Landerchild was no longer in a position to sponsor anyone, and Uvanov was the majority choice. Landerchild himself was beginning to regret his unquestioning acceptance that for the plan to work *patience was the essential order of the day*, but he kept his peace and his languidly relaxed demeanour. Uvanov was magnanimous in victory and the Production Director remained in place for several days before being dismissed from the Company.

As he took his seat at the table, Uvanov already knew what most of the other Board members could not have accepted, even if he had been stupid enough to raise it. He doubted whether they could have considered the idea without immediate medical support. The deaths which were threatening to panic the population were not the work of any Tarenist gang of murderous perverts. It wasn't people at all. It was robots. Try telling that to the populace and see what sort of panic develops.

He had no real proof of course. There were no eyewitnesses, no surveillance tapes. A few surveillance images of very ordinary men and women – average height, brown hair, dressed in plain smock and leggings – which were captured in the vicinity of some of the incidents, were significant only if you knew about the new class of robots. They were not proof, even then. There was nothing directly incriminating in them. The test programme sent the new robots out into the city on harmless errands to complete undemanding tasks.

But he *knew*. He knew they were killing out there. What

217

he didn't know was why. He would find out though. Was it something to do with the Doctor disappearing again? It looked as though Cailio Techlan had been right about him It didn't matter. He would find out and he would deal with it.

He was Firstmaster Kiy Uvanov. Nothing could stop him now. He looked around the table. Nothing and no one.

'I start by welcoming as Firstmaster of the Company,' Pitter intoned, 'and holder of a seat at our table, Kiy Uvanov.'

As was customary Uvanov bowed his head while the other members of the Board slapped the table and each one spoke his name. He listened to the voices: some grudging, some openly enthusiastic. One-third of these people were his, he knew, because of who they were and where they came from. One-third were Landerchild's for the same reason. The rest would go with the winner. He wondered if Landerchild understood how little time his world had left.

They had cleared the main meeting room and Leela had been teaching Letarb and Denek some of the basic moves of one-to-one combat. They were passing on what they had learned to a crowd of other Tarenist recruits when the Doctor carried Sarl's body in and laid it down in front of them.

'He was killed by a robot,' he said. 'I'm sorry. I tried to warn him but he wouldn't listen.'

There was an ominous silence in the room. Leela drew her knife and, holding it loosely by her side, she moved to stand beside the Doctor.

'I appreciate the support but put the knife away, Leela,' he said quietly. 'We don't want any misunderstandings.'

Reluctantly, she sheathed the knife. 'No one misunderstands me, Doctor,' she said, keeping her hand on the hilt.

'There is a new class of robot out there,' the Doctor said

loudly. 'It is capable of killing. It looks like a man but it is a robot.'

'I don't believe it,' Letarb said. 'Robots can't kill. And they don't look like people.'

'I've seen robots that look like people,' one of the recruits said.

The Doctor recognised him as a member of the security platoon that had threatened him outside the dome soon after they first arrived. 'That's why they got rid of you, wasn't it?' he suggested. 'You weren't supposed to see them.'

'They said it was because we exceeded our authority.'

'You did, as I remember it.'

The young man looked uncomfortable. 'I was following orders.'

Denek took his cue from Letarb and glared at the Doctor. 'Why should we believe you?' he demanded.

'Because Sarl didn't,' the Doctor said.

'He didn't believe you were Taren Capel either.'

From a corner of the room Padil declaimed, 'Humanity be in him.'

'Humanity be in him,' Denek muttered.

Padil pushed through the others. 'Sarl was a warrior,' she said, 'who was ready to die in the fight against the eternal enemy.' She looked round the room. 'He was happy to die in the service of Taren Capel.' She looked at the Doctor. 'Humanity be in you.'

The Doctor groaned audibly. 'How many times must we go through this?' he began.

Leela said quietly, 'Leave it, Doctor. You do not want any misunderstandings.'

Padil said, 'A man and a woman have been waiting to talk to you.' She nodded towards the back room.

'About what?' the Doctor asked. 'Did they say?' He was not

219

in the mood for more misguided acolytes. He was beginning to feel very uncomfortable at being confused with a dead madman who was himself being confused with a live guru of some sort.

'They said they were friends.' She smiled at Leela. 'They're not armed.'

'Are you sure?' Leela said.

'Would I risk *his* life?'

Leela went with the Doctor. Behind them Padil was giving orders for a fire to be prepared for Sarl's corpse.

As they went through the door, Toos stood up and said, 'Well, at least they're not going to eat him raw which is something, I suppose.' She smiled wryly. 'Hello, Doctor, where have you been hiding? Not in this filthy dump, I hope.'

'Pilot Toos.' The Doctor was surprised at how little she had changed. Her clothes were torn and she was dirty and bruised but she was remarkably well preserved. There was a confidence about her too which suggested she was not given to panicking any more. 'You remember Leela.'

Leela nodded watchfully. In the background Tani stood waiting just as watchfully.

'You haven't aged at all,' Toos said. 'Either of you. How do you manage that and is it for sale?'

'Accidentally, and it's one of the few things that isn't.' The Doctor took the battered paper bag from his pocket and proffered it.

Toos took a jelly baby. 'I saw Poul lurking about earlier. He looked worse than I feel. All we need is Uvanov and a few more killer robots and it would be just like old times.'

'Is that what you wanted to talk to me about?' He offered the bag towards Tani, who shook his head. 'Old times?'

'The story is that you are Taren Capel,' Toos said.

'I heard that one,' the Doctor said.

Toos looked at Tani, acknowledging his presence for the first time. 'He isn't,' she said flatly. 'Now if you're satisfied, I'd like to get back to my life in general and my money in particular.'

Tani ignored her and said to the Doctor, 'I'm Mor Tani. I was Captain Toos's pilot on her last tour.'

Toos snorted. 'Not your main occupation, as it turns out.'

Tani went on, 'I heard what you said in there about the killer robot.'

'Eavesdropping comes naturally to him, you understand,' Toos murmured.

'We had a run-in with one ourselves. It was trying to kill her.'

'Really?' the Doctor said thoughtfully. 'Why was it trying to kill you, Toos?'

'I didn't stop to ask.'

The Doctor began to pace. 'Poul says one, at least one, tried to kill him. One tried to kill me but I think that was because I was in the wrong place at the wrong time.' He looked at Leela. 'No robots have attacked you, have they?'

Leela shook her head. 'I have seen few of the creepy metal men since we arrived, Doctor. Plenty of creepy people though.'

Was there a plan to it all? the Doctor thought. 'I wonder if Uvanov has been attacked.'

'Ask *him*,' Toos said bitterly at Tani.

Tani smiled his sour smile. 'If you'll excuse me,' he said, heading for the door, 'I want to go and help with Sarl.'

'Hungry?' Toos challenged.

'Will you be here when I get back?'

'I don't think so,' she said.

Tani paused in the doorway. 'As it happens, Sarl was my brother,' he said. 'I bet you feel terrible now, don't you?'

'No,' Toos said. 'I don't.'

Tani sighed. 'No, neither do I. I never liked him, and he always hated me. But he was my brother and that's got to count for something, I suppose.'

He went out and Toos stared at the empty doorway, frowning slightly. Finally she shook her head and said, 'Why are they picking on me, Doctor?'

'I thought it might be because you were a survivor from before,' the Doctor said.

Leela had gone to the door, making no secret she was checking that Tani was not returning with a weapon. 'Sarl was not a survivor,' she said.

'Exactly,' the Doctor said. 'And why wouldn't he listen to me? He of all people should have recognised a robot when it was pointed out to him. Why did he still think it was a man?'

'Maybe he'd seen it cross the so-called boundary,' Toos suggested. 'The one that was chasing me followed us right in here. It barely hesitated.'

For a moment the Doctor thought he saw the glimmerings of a plan. Had they developed these new robots to clear out the notorious Sewerpits? No, that wouldn't make sense. They wouldn't risk destroying the world just to get at some undesirables and criminals. Besides, looked at from the other side of the boundary, the Sewerpits were a convenient arrangement for them. It was the ever-present threat. How else could they handle people who they thought did not deserve a fair share of what the working robots were producing? No – clearing the Sewerpits wasn't what was happening. It followed that robots coming and going was not intentional. So what was it?

'Can you show me where you crossed?' he said to Toos.

With no orders to the contrary, Uvanov's personal tech

team were still working on the TARDIS when the robot came for them. Using one of the auxiliary equipment bays, misleadingly tagged 6 sub 1 Miscellaneous/Restricted, was more cramped and limiting for the technicians than a standard work lab, but it did have the advantage of keeping the evidence of their continuing and humiliating failure among themselves. Mercifully, Uvanov seemed to have other things on his mind and was apparently ignoring the reports that the team was required to submit from time to time.

'We haven't really considered the possibility that it's actually solid,' Sido, the project leader, suggested. A normally deliberate and methodical man, he was beginning to clutch at straws.

Dahla was second senior. She was short and dark and her temperament tended to match her looks. 'As in block?' she asked sceptically.

'As in block,' Sido said.

'As in block of what?' Ging tossed aside the drill she had been using on what looked like it could be a door. 'And where does that get us?' She ran her hands tiredly over her shaven head and down across the soft features of her plump, plain face.

Reesh said, 'My feeling is we take it outside, stick a big charge up it and find out once and for all.' He was the oldest of the five technicians and the most easily bored.

'When in doubt, blow it up,' Dahla said.

'Works for me,' he said.

Sido said, 'And you work for Firstmaster Uvanov, who would blow you up immediately afterwards.'

'If not sooner and with a much bigger charge,' Tel chortled. He had a deep voice, quite at odds with his skinny frame, and a placid disposition despite a shock of vivid red hair.

'I don't know what you're laughing at,' Reesh laughed.

'He's going to do that anyhow. We're Sewerpits fodder unless we come up with something soon.'

'He's not going to do that,' Ging said. 'We're too valuable for the 'pits.'

'Nobody's that valuable,' Sido said gloomily

'We know too much about him?' Dahla offered.

Reesh had stopped laughing. 'Shut up, you idiot,' he hissed, glancing about. 'That is a seriously one-way trip for you and yours.'

'And us,' Tel said.

'Oh no,' Reesh muttered. 'Do you suppose it heard?'

The robot was standing at the entrance to the bay. It was a Cyborg class. The team were not expecting it because they were not part of the test programme and nor as far as they knew were any of the auxiliary equipment bays.

Dahla said, 'When did they ask you for the day code?'

'They didn't,' Sido said.

'How did it get in, then?' Tel said.

'What do you want?' Reesh asked the robot.

'You must come with me,' the robot said politely, indicating Tel with its unblinking, unhuman stare.

'Why, what did I do?' Tel demanded.

The robot had no defined inhibitions about answering such direct questions. 'You match the profile.'

Tel was puzzled. 'What did it say?'

'It likes your profile,' Dahla said.

Reesh laughed. 'You've got an admirer.'

'That's a first,' Ging remarked.

Reesh approached the robot. 'I think you must have misinterpreted your instructions,' he told it. 'Return to your controller for reassessment.'

The robot made small chewing motions and then it smiled blankly.

'That's unnerving,' Dahla said.

'I'd say so,' Reesh said as the robot reached for him. 'The things aren't right yet, are they?'

It broke his neck with such force that it practically tore his head off.

The others were so shocked that none of them had moved by the time the robot had dropped Reesh and was smashing Dahla against the TARDIS. As it drove its fist through ribs and cartilage and crushed Dahla's heart, the three surviving technicians finally reacted.

It was already too late for Sido, who tried to lunge past the thing and reach the security alarm. The robot struck him to the floor and stamped him to death. Tel tried to keep the TARDIS between himself and the robot and get to the alarm by stealth. He was easily cut off and the robot kept him trapped at the rear of the bay while it manoeuvred Ging into making a run for safety.

'Why is it so angry with us?' Tel shouted to her. 'Where's its higher control centres?'

'Still the head, I think.'

Ging moved closer to her discarded drill. 'Can you get its attention?'

'I've been trying not to.'

'I think it wants you alive.'

'So do I.' Tel moved out from behind the TARDIS and took a couple of tentative steps towards the robot. 'Any chance you could stop smiling and chewing like that?' he said. 'You've no idea how unappealing it is. Especially when you're covered in blood.' He took a few more steps. The robot ignored him. 'It's ignoring me,' he said.

'Go for the alarm,' Ging suggested.

'If it kills me I'm never going to forgive you,' Tel said, walking towards the alarm.

The robot turned and moved to cut him off. Ging snatched up the drill and rushed forward. As the robot turned to meet her she activated the drill and drove the lucanol-tipped bit hard into the centre of its forehead. Ducking away from the flailing killer, Ging barely heard the alarms going off.

The boundary was switching on and off here too.

This time the Doctor set about checking the electronic barrier on either side of the road Toos had used to enter the Sewerpits. He was not entirely surprised to find that where there was no open access road the boundary itself was not switching on and off.

It appeared that electronic gateways were rapidly opening and closing and that either the physical routes developed as a result of them or they were put in to control already existing routes. Which came first, the road or the gate? he wondered. He would need some rather more sophisticated equipment if he was going to find out anything more about the boundary. 'There's only so much you can do with a sonic screwdriver,' he said to no one in particular.

'Does he talk to himself a lot?' Toos was standing with Leela and watching the Doctor pacing about with the small rod held out in front of him, waving it around, reaching into inaccessible places with it.

'It is hard to be sure sometimes,' Leela said.

'What is he doing?' Toos was becoming impatient.

Leela shrugged. 'Searching?' He looked like the tribal water-finder. 'Understanding the boundary has become important to him. He can stop being reasonable when something like that takes his attention.'

Toos shivered. 'It feels like the Emptiness might stir,' she said.

'The Emptiness?'

226

'Cold wind,' Toos said. 'You never heard it called that?'

The strangeness of travelling with the Doctor was wearing off for Leela but she remained uncertain of how to react when challenged over her lack of local knowledge. The Doctor had never been clear about how much of what and who they were she was supposed to reveal to other people. 'No,' she said.

'Doctor?' Toos called.

The Doctor did not look up from what he was doing. 'Almost finished.'

'Is there anything else you want from me?'

'Very well,' he said absently and clambered up on to a nearby wall and from there onto the low roof of a ramshackle building.

'I see what you mean,' Toos said to Leela. 'Look, if it does blow Ore-dream to Emptiness, I'm not exactly dressed for the change. And even if it doesn't, I'm tired of rags and rodents. I want to go back to my life. I want to go back to my life *now*.' She smiled wearily. 'So that's what I'm going to do.'

'Do you not fear the robots?'

'Only the ones I can see,' she said. 'At the moment I can't see any, can you?'

Leela scanned the area and shook her head. 'At the moment I cannot but there is too much cover. Too much is hidden.'

Toos took her by surprise then when she embraced her briefly and wordlessly set off down the road. It did not seem to Leela like a well-thought-out decision, or a decision that had been thought out at all, and she watched carefully either side and ahead of Toos as the woman walked with brisk confidence towards the derelict outskirts of the city.

Leela saw the movement and shouted the warning before the robot showed itself fully. Toos did not hesitate but turned on her heel and was already running back when the robot reacted and started to sprint after her.

On the low roof, the Doctor heard Leela's shout and looked up to see Toos running back towards him with a robot chasing her. He moved to the edge of the roof and as he did he found the sonic screwdriver in his hand was suddenly responding differently. It seemed to be indicating that the barrier around him was intensifying.

Toos was flagging. The robot was gaining on her. Leela pulled her knife and started forward.

'Stay there, Leela!' the Doctor shouted urgently. 'Don't cross the boundary!'

Leela hesitated.

'Come on, Toos!' the Doctor shouted. 'Run, woman! Run!' He reached out with the screwdriver into the space where he knew the electronic gateway had been switching on and off. It was off. There was nothing there.

Toos put in a final effort and ran across the boundary into the Sewerpits. She staggered on, her momentum carrying her to Leela. Without hesitation, the robot followed her. As Leela stepped forward to meet it, the Doctor leaped from the low roof, crashing into the robot and knocking it off its feet. Scrambling up, the Doctor called, 'This way, both of you,' and was relieved when for once Leela did as he said. 'Quickly,' he urged.

Dragging Toos with her, Leela dodged past the robot, which was pulling itself back on its feet and reaching for its quarry.

As they crossed out of the Sewerpits the robot surged after them. There was a sudden crackle of static in the air. The Doctor stopped and turned to watch. The robot was lying on the ground, hands and feet twitching and drumming. The Doctor extended the screwdriver into the space of the gateway. As he had expected, it was now on and for the moment was indistinguishable from the rest of the boundary. It would probably stay that way until the robot was removed or showed no signs of electrical activity of any kind. 'I think,' he said, 'the Sewerpits might originally have been designed to trap rogue machines. It's possible this civilisation might have destroyed itself with killer robots at least once before.'

CHAPTER
TWELVE

Taren Capel had analysed what his creations had learned and he understood what it was that was corrupting the data and threatening his being. There was a usurper, there was a counterfeit Taren Capel, there was a plot to steal his world using lies and confusion to make him doubt and force him not to be. And he knew where the usurper had tried to hide from him as one of his creations had heard him named by a human Sarl that had stopped being.

Now he knew what the problem was, he could finally deal with it. He put the subjects to one side. With one part to hold them in place they would last until he was ready for them. The experiment would wait.

He took control to the deepest level of the dream that was the power and made it to be spread to all his creations, like and unlike, image and imagined.

The false Taren Capel and all the humans with him must be destroyed so that Taren Capel could be one with the world he had created.

It was confirmation, if confirmation was needed, that the Cyborg class was a disaster. The only consolation Uvanov could draw was that he was at least in a position now to make sure that none of the blame attached to him. It was the former Production Director who would be heading for the Sewerpits and taking all the responsibility for this murderous fiasco with him.

231

'What's so special about you?' Uvanov wondered, looking at the skinny young man with the red hair and the soft-featured young woman with the quick, dark eyes.

'That was what we said, Firstmaster,' Tel said.

'The thing said something about a profile match,' Ging said. 'That was pretty much all it said.'

'If you hadn't done such a thorough job of scrambling its systems, we might have found out what that meant,' Uvanov grumbled. 'As a tech team, you've been something of a disappointment.'

Cailio Techlan, bringing drinks for them, said, 'Firstmaster Uvanov is glad you survived. He had a similar experience himself, so he understands how inappropriate and unwelcome sympathy can be in these situations.'

Tel said, 'These things have tried to kill you? When was this? How come we didn't hear anything about that?'

'Why didn't you issue warnings?' Ging demanded. 'We lost friends back there. Somebody covering their backside again? You people make me sick to my stomach.'

There was a moment's frozen silence in the room as they all realised what a risk the young technician had just taken.

Uvanov found he couldn't summon up the anger he should have felt at the woman's disrespect. *I'm glad of that, Firstmaster Landerchild, because frankly your attitude to all this makes me sick to my stomach.* Perhaps it was because her feelings were genuine. 'Some years ago,' he said, 'there was a problem on a storm mine I was commanding.'

'Ore raiders on Storm Mine Four,' Tel said. 'Mutiny in the Blind Heart, everybody knows the story.'

'It was the robots,' Uvanov said. 'They went on a killing spree. Very few people outside the Company Board know that story.' And most of them still don't believe it. Cailio Techlan believed it, though, and he hadn't told her.

'Killer robots?' Ging said. There was disbelief on her face. 'You mean standard machines?'

'Vocs, Supervocs, they all went bad. It was an aberration.' If he closed his eyes he could still see them. Strong, imperturbable, secure figures always there, always strangling, breaking, killing like murderous children, murderous like parents killing. Nothing left of safety. Only angry terror. 'It was technical intervention. It was dealt with. The problem was solved.'

'Only it wasn't,' Tel said.

Uvanov rubbed his eyes. 'This is different.'

'There's an equipment bay covered in blood that says it isn't.'

Ging said, 'How is it different?'

'There's no Taren Capel for one thing,' Uvanov said.

'Who's he?' Tel asked.

'Madman,' Uvanov said. 'Wanted to destroy the world.'

They were right, of course; it wasn't that different. He could use it. He could use the link between Landerchild and the Production Director. He could use the rumours about Landerchild's plotting. Accuse them of trying to make killer robots. He could save Kaldor a second time, and this time they would be grateful. He would be Firstmaster Chairholder Kiy Uvanov, unopposed and called to power by general acclamation.

'Not exactly unique, then,' Ging said. 'This Taren Capel.'

The first thing was to get the Cyborg class contained and under control. 'All right,' Uvanov said decisively. 'There's no time to waste. I want you two to put together the best robotics tech team we can muster. It reports to me, no one else.' When he had given them all their instructions, their authorisations and an emergency budget he would have had trouble justifying if it was noticed, he sent them to get on

233

with things and turned his attention to Cailio Techlan. 'Who are you reporting to?' he asked.

'You,' she said, looking confused. 'Is it a trick question?'

'Apart from me who do you report to?'

'It *is* a trick question,' she said. 'I don't understand.'

The monotone was less pronounced than usual, Uvanov noticed. He frowned and said, 'I underestimated you. I realise that. But don't you make the same mistake and underestimate me. Landerchild and his world, your world, is over and finished with. I'm going to win this and, if you think about it, you know that's true. So I'm going to give you one chance to put things right with me.'

'I think maybe you should rest, Kiy,' The monotone was back and more pronounced. 'This has all been too much for you, obviously.'

'I'm not asking you to betray your friends. I know you can't. I know it's a twenty families thing. You can keep right on betraying me.'

'I don't know what you're talking about.'

'I've known about you all along,' Uvanov said. Pity it wasn't true, but she wasn't going to know that. 'You've been helping to set me up from the beginning. I was going to take the blame for all of it, wasn't I? It was very thorough. Even little details like forged issue-and-use orders for stun-kills at the central service facility.'

'I had nothing to do with that.'

But it doesn't come as a surprise, does it, Uvanov thought, and it is interesting what denials tell you. *I had nothing to do with that.* 'Tell them everything you've heard, just as they told you to do, and just as you've been doing up to now.'

'You *are* mad.'

Uvanov smiled at her. 'Possibly. But I'm not afraid.' And your friends will be, he thought. Will be and should be. 'One

234

chance, Cailio. Time to pick a side rather than just be born into one.'

The delegation was no surprise at all – Carnell had been expecting it for some time. What had come as a shock was recognising that everything had gone so wrong that it was too late to do anything about it. How could he have missed at least two pivotal options and failed to neutralise their effects? Was he a burnout? He was mortified – well, he was embarrassed at least. He didn't show it, naturally. He didn't show anything. Yet. It seemed beneath him to make excuses, pointless indeed, but all the same he wanted to know which of these people had been stupid enough to keep at least two major variables from him.

'Where are all these killer robots originating?' he asked quietly. 'Who is sending them out?'

'We agreed to their use,' Landerchild blustered, 'at your suggestion.'

'Two robots is what we agreed. Two carefully controlled robot killers. Their actions were circumscribed, their targets specified. It was not part of the strategy to have who knows how many of the things rampaging across the countryside killing as they go.'

Roatson said, 'These are rather more than *things*, I'm afraid.' The young aristocrat looked a lot less confident than he had at that first meeting, Carnell noted. 'They've evolved or something.'

'Not by themselves,' Carnell remarked. 'Evolution is an unfailingly logical response to system changes. It is not magic. The robots are being tampered with, and that's not the same thing. I repeat, who is sending them out?'

'You tell us,' Bibo Mechman snapped. She was a small bald woman whose shaved head had been fashionable until robochic suddenly lost its appeal. 'I thought the reason we paid you so handsomely was because you were able to anticipate every eventuality.'

'You're thinking of fortune-tellers,' Carnell said coolly. 'I'm a psycho-strategist. I work with what I'm given and with what I'm not given. If what I'm not given is more relevant than what I'm given, I fail.'

'You're a charlatan.' Landerchild sounded resigned as though he was confessing to some guilty secret of his own.

Carnell could see that in a way that was exactly what was happening. He nodded. 'You're bound to think that.'

'Ah, so that's one eventuality you could anticipate then,' Bibo sneered. 'The psycho-strategist at work. Worth every penny in my book.'

Carnell looked round the select group of aristocrats and wealthy would-be rulers who were gathered in the small meeting room of his office apartment. The fact that they had come to him rather than summoning him to them had obvious significance and served to confirm the two things he could see quite clearly. None of them knew who was sending out the robots. All of them knew that he himself was to die, by the hand of young Roatson probably, at the behest of Layly Landerchild almost certainly. He sighed inwardly. It was such a minor world. Such a small, unambitious, unimaginative population. What was he doing here? It had been a waste of his talents from the beginning, of course. But then how reliable were his talents now? How had he got it so wrong?

'I think I can prove to you that I'm not a charlatan,' he said, looking directly at Landerchild and keeping just enough humility in his voice and demeanour to appeal to the man's arrogance. 'First, I'm going to give you back the money you paid me.' This he directed at Mechman – the money was

236

clearly important to her. 'A gesture of good faith.' Then he smiled at Roatson. 'I'll come up with a new strategy,' innocent friendliness for the assassin, 'and all this can finally be put right.' He turned towards the door and then he turned back again. 'If you can bear with me for a moment, I'll get you the money.'

'This is not about money,' Landerchild said. 'The money means nothing.'

'Humour me, Firstmaster Landerchild. I would feel better about things. I'll just be a moment.' He went to the door quite slowly and smiled over his shoulder at them before he went out. It was several minutes before they realised he was not coming back.

The Doctor had considered confirming the Tarenists' claim that he was Taren Capel, and using that power to convince them that they were the best people to plan and organise an evacuation of the Sewerpits. Presumably they would be more inclined to believe it from what Leela persisted in calling their tribal shaman. Actually, she was right, that was how they thought of the man. Pity he couldn't use his authority as Taren Capel to convince them that he wasn't Taren Capel.

'The Sewerpits are intended to keep robots *in* – is that what you're saying, Doctor?' Tani summarised.

'That's what he's saying,' Toos said impatiently. 'It's not difficult to understand.'

'It's difficult to believe,' Padil remarked.

This from his most devout disciple, the Doctor thought. Perhaps that was a good sign. Perhaps she was finally starting to think for herself.

'Difficult for those who do not accept the words of Capel, humanity be in him,' she went on, looking at the Doctor, 'as I do.'

237

Then again perhaps not, he thought.

Several others in the room muttered, 'Humanity be in him.'

Leela said, 'There is no need for belief. There is the robot for proof.'

'His words are proof enough,' someone said.

There were murmurs of agreement.

'It might have been a faulty unit,' Letarb suggested.

'It didn't run as if it was faulty,' Toos said. 'Why are you wasting time here?'

'Tribal councils always waste time,' Leela muttered to her.

'It doesn't make sense,' Denek said. 'No robots ever come in. Why is that?'

'I don't know,' the Doctor said. 'The field obviously affects them. It disrupts their control systems so they can't enter it. My theory is that a killer is defined as malfunctioning and that the field is set up to accommodate it. Or... in order to be capable of killing, a robot must be of a higher order of complexity and the field accommodates that. Whichever way: killers cross, normally inhibited robots don't.'

'And once in, they can't get out again.' It was the young former security man. 'It's a trap.'

'My point exactly,' the Doctor said. 'It's a trap which all of you who live here in the Sewerpits are sitting in.'

Poul got up from where he had been sitting at the back of the room. His hands were visibly trembling. He clasped them together. 'Speaking personally, I'm not keen on being trapped in a confined area with killer robots. I tried it once. I didn't like it.'

'I thought you couldn't remember any of it,' Toos said. 'That's what they told me.'

'That's what they told me too,' he said. 'And I tried not to. Taren Capel got in the way of that.'

'Humanity be in him,' Padil and several of the others intoned.

'There was no humanity in that murderous madman,' Poul blurted out. 'He made robots of death. He wanted to be one of his damned robots of death and slaughter his own kind. We wouldn't be here if the Doctor and Leela hadn't helped to kill him.'

The volunteers who stood guard at the entrance to the Tarenist house and the watchers outside were all drawn into the noisy pandemonium that immediately broke out. The Doctor's efforts to calm things down were futile. There were scuffles and punches were thrown amid cries of 'traitor', 'liar' and 'blasphemer'. Somebody yelled, 'Robots don't kill, company spies do!' Several of the senior members rushed into a side room and returned almost immediately brandishing stun-kills.

Nobody was paying attention to what was happening anywhere else. Nobody was outside to hear the first of the rumours which flashed across the 'pits that gangs of men and women were roaming through the alleys killing whoever they found. These were not nightstalkers, they said, not degenerates creeping out of the deepest, darkest places to prey on the weak and the unwary. These were people from the city: average, ordinary-looking people, dressed in smart clothes, and they were butchering men, women and children indiscriminately. Soon the word was out that they were doing it with their bare hands.

They could not get the best ones for the work because the best ones for the work had disappeared. It took Tel and Ging only a short time to recognise that someone had already put together the robotics tech team they wanted to assemble. They had used the achievement records from the Company

239

database and found the top six robotics engineers were flagged up as *unavailable: reason classified*, which usually meant the Sewerpits. They referred back to Uvanov. Was it possible that some moron had simply pit-dumped the six best brains around? Uvanov knew that it was entirely possible but he did not care to admit it and instead he used his rank and checked. It was not the Sewerpits and it was not an officially classified Company project. The six men and women had simply vanished. Since time was short and Cyborg-class robots were reportedly not returning from test assignments, he told his project leaders to settle for the next six on the listings and get on with it. It was not important and it was not what they were looking for so no one noticed that one of the missing engineers bore a passing resemblance to Tel.

Uvanov wasted no time in setting a confidential security team to finding out what had happened to the missing robotics engineers. He appointed Stenton Rull to head it. He made sure the disgraced Operations Supervisor was aware that he owed his reinstatement to the job, and his reprieve from the Sewerpits, entirely to Firstmaster Uvanov's personal intervention. The Firstmaster had insisted on putting right an injustice that had only recently been brought to his attention. Fatso Rull wasn't bright but he was an experienced investigator and now, Uvanov calculated, he would be a loyal and highly motivated one.

Uvanov had theories, but someone somewhere knew for certain where those six people were. Rull was the man to find them. And what's more he would be Uvanov's man.

Uvanov set his man to checking on Cailio Techlan as a priority.

The survivors fled upwards to the Roof over the World. It was instinctive. Up there it was lighter and there was a direct route across the Sewerpits away from the groups of robots, more and more of them all the time, which were sweeping through the lower alleys, rampaging through the gloom, tirelessly hunting down and slaughtering. The killer robots were tearing holes in walls and smashing to bloody and broken pieces whatever they found still moving inside the buildings. They were working their way from one end of the 'pits to the other, leaving nothing alive, just as SASV1, the Serial Access Supervoc prototype now calling itself Taren Capel, had modified and sent them out to do.

The Doctor had given up trying to convince the fleeing people that their best chance of survival was simply to go to ground level and cross the nearest boundary, leaving the robots trapped. They didn't have time to listen. They wouldn't have believed him if they had. A lot of them still didn't believe that it was robots that were attacking them. Not even the Tarenist group could come to grips with it. They wouldn't listen to him either and most of them had charged off to fight what they insisted must be Company security agents.

'They've got this whole thing the wrong way round,' the Doctor said, angrily frustrated. 'In instead of out, up instead of down. The triumph of instinct over rationality.'

Leela was in the side room rummaging through the remains of the Tarenists' arms cache, which had been hidden until the earlier fracas and which was now more or less stripped clean.

'You did your best, Doctor,' she said.

'That's all right, then,' the Doctor said testily.

'You told me that is all anyone can do,' Leela said, coming out of the room holding several small square packages. 'You cannot force people to let you help them.' She proffered one of the packages. 'What is this, do you think?'

The Doctor examined it. He turned it over and examined the back. 'As near as I can tell it's a Z9a explosive pack,' he said.

'How can you tell that?' Leela asked, looking impressed.

'It says so on the back here.'

Leela frowned. 'Does it say how to make it work?'

'No.' The Doctor turned it over again. There were two small switches and what looked like a digital display. 'One would be a timer and one an activation switch.'

'Which is which?'

The Doctor pointed to the top switch. 'Timer. Possibly.'

'You do not know?'

The Doctor shook his head. 'Not for certain. And it's not something you can get wrong. Well, not more than once.'

The door to the outside crashed open and Tani rushed in, breathing hard. 'They're coming,' he said. 'We've got to get out of here.'

Leela strode out, putting the explosive packs into an equipment pouch as she went. The Doctor pocketed the pack he was holding. He didn't like bombs, but killer robots were difficult to reason with.

Outside, the normally bustling area was deserted and silent. Toos and Poul were waiting, trying to catch their breath.

'The others?' the Doctor asked.

'I think some of them got away,' Tani said.

'None that I saw,' Toos gasped. 'What I did see was robots beyond the boundary waiting to pick off anyone who did get out.'

'There was no way past them,' Poul complained breathlessly. 'They're everywhere.'

'Not everywhere.' Toos said. 'They can't be everywhere.'

'They seemed to be everywhere,' Tani agreed.

'It's because they're working in groups,' Toos said. 'And they're coordinated. One group follows another. It's as though they summon each other.'

'Are you sure?' the Doctor asked.

'No, I'm not sure,' Toos snapped. 'But that's what it looked like to me.'

'Good,' the Doctor said. 'If we can persuade enough of them to chase us we may be able to make a difference.'

'Persuading them to chase you is no problem.' Tani said, pointing to where several feeder alleys opened into one of the streets leading to the intersection. Cyborg-class robots were running out of the alleys, coming together in groups of six and running on towards them.

'We have to get up onto the top,' the Doctor said.

'You said that was the worst thing we could do,' Toos protested.

'That was then,' the Doctor said, 'this is now.'

'You've changed your mind?' Poul said.

'We have to be between them and the survivors,' the Doctor explained.

From behind them Padil said, 'Listen to him and do as he says.'

'Where did you come from?' Tani demanded.

They set off running.

'I'm sorry I doubted him,' Padil said, running beside Leela.

When they reached the first rising bend in the roadway the Doctor glanced back. There were at least eighteen robots in pursuit.

Carnell's problem was that there was nothing of value that he could take from Kaldor which would justify the years he had spent there. If he simply went back to where he had hidden the ship, fired it up and headed out, then it was all wasted.

He didn't even have the dusty feeling of routine success, of doing what he had set out so confidently to do. He'd got it wrong, he'd got nothing to show after getting it wrong, and not even his reputation was intact because he knew he did not understand why or how it had happened. Without that understanding, he could never be quite whole again. It was a risk to stay. Training and background and natural inclination told him that all risks were stupid risks. 'But,' he said aloud, 'stupid is what I do well at the moment.'

'Sorry?' the flierman said.

'I changed my mind,' Carnell said.

'You don't want to go to Zone Seven?'

'Take me back to Company Central. I have some unfinished business.'

'It's your money,' the flierman said, banking the flier into a steep turn.

'Yes, and I've got more than enough of it to settle all my accounts,' Camel said, smiling.

By the time the six of them reached the Roof over the World the robots had fallen back a little but there were more of them and the numbers seemed to be increasing all the time. With the Doctor in the lead, they ran on down the track over the roofs past abandoned carts and wrecked and deserted trading stalls. They pounded over the bridges and finally the bridge they were aiming for came into view. It was the longest on the whole of the Roof over the World track and crossing it was slower and more dizzying than any of the others.

There was an immediately obvious problem with the Doctor's plan. There were stragglers from the great rush to escape still gathered at either end of the bridge. The Doctor looked back down the track. They had perhaps five minutes at the outside.

Padil set the charges to five minutes as the Doctor instructed, and Leela climbed over the side and placed them where he indicated. Toos, Tani and Poul did their best to hurry the stragglers and everything seemed to be going well when there was a sudden collapse in part of the roof nearby and people began to scramble up makeshift ladders and out of the large hole they had made. A dozen of them rushed blindly for the bridge. As more came out, they saw the robots running down the track towards them and they began to panic and fight for a place on the long narrow bridge.

'What should I do, Doctor?' Leela shouted from under the supports where she had just finished fixing the explosive packs. 'Do you want me to take them out?'

'Leave them where they are and get yourself out from under there, Leela,' the Doctor shouted.

Leela climbed out and up onto the roof.

With two minutes to go and the robots bearing down on them, people were still struggling with each other to get onto the bridge.

'Doctor?' Leela asked urgently. 'Shall I get rid of the bombs?'

'Bombs?' Someone at the end of the bridge had heard her. 'What bombs? Where are the bombs?'

'There are bombs,' somebody else shouted. 'Bombs!' The panic worsened.

'People!' the Doctor shouted. They ignored him.

The robots were very close now. His plan was ruined. There would barely be time to get everyone off the bridge. Luring the robots onto it before it blew was out of the question. 'People? People!' the Doctor shouted at the top of his lungs and clapped his hands as loudly as he could. 'There's time. Stop panicking! Stop running! Walk!' On the

245

bridge the people started to sort themselves out and get across it and off it.

'Doctor?' Leela said.

Something in her tone made him turn at once. The first group of robots had stopped running and was walking towards him. They all seemed to be making small chewing motions with their jaws.

'When you shouted stop running, walk, they stopped running and walked,' Leela said.

'Stop walking!' the Doctor shouted. They stopped.

Behind him on the bridge a couple of the stragglers hesitated.

'Not you, you idiots,' Toos shouted from the other side. 'Keep moving – you're running out of time.'

Other robots ran past the stationary group. 'Stand still!' the Doctor shouted but they kept on coming. 'Stop running, walk!' he shouted. They ignored him and kept coming. What was different? Why wouldn't they listen? Then he realised and he remembered and he understood. His words and actions in the hatchling dome – it was some sort of imprinted control cue.

'People? People,' he shouted and clapped his hands. 'Stand still!' The robots all stopped and stood making small chewing motions with their jaws.

As they waited in front of him for new behavioural instructions, the Doctor was struck by how little they resembled fully developed human beings. So this is how it ends, he thought, not with a bang but a whimper.

Behind him the explosive packs went off with two loud roars. The empty bridge shattered and dropped into the chasm between the two buildings.

Cailio Techlan was no longer overawed by the legend of

Carnell. He could see it in her face and demeanour and he could hear it in her voice. How inconstant is the admiration of others, he thought. A reputation for infallibility was so easily compromised. You couldn't be slightly fallible, that was like being slightly dead. She was startled to see him, though, and with that went fear, a fear of the unexpected and a fear of him.

So she knew the main strategy had gone astray and she knew he was supposed to have been murdered and she knew another plan was in play. His expensive sources were right. Worth every penny, as Bibo Mechman might have said. This was indeed a more dangerously involved young woman than she at first appeared.

He gave her his iciest stare. 'Firstmaster Uvanov is expecting me, I believe.'

She had started to rise from her workdesk and had then thought better of it. Now she was perfectly composed. 'I don't think so,' she said.

He smiled. 'Well, when you tell him, he will be.'

'What is your business with the Firstmaster?'

'It is with the Firstmaster,' he said, making sure he sounded just haughty enough for her to feel able to put him in his place. He wanted her relaxed and slightly off-guard. She would be a little less sceptical that way. It was probably overcautious of him He was probably overcompensating.

She looked almost smug and she accentuated her aristocratic drone. 'He is far too busy to see anyone without an appointment.'

'Even me?'

'Even you.'

'You have nothing to fear from our previous association,' he said evenly. 'You know that, of course.'

'Of course I know that.' It was a confident assertion, too

confident to be a simple expression of trust.

'Perhaps,' Carnell said, sounding hopeful now rather than haughty, 'I can make an appointment, then?'

'Not without telling me the nature of your business with him.'

'Very well.' Carnell lowered his voice discreetly, confidentially. 'I didn't want to embarrass the Firstmaster, but he does owe me a rather substantial sum of money.'

'Firstmaster Uvanov owes *you* money,' she said, sounding sceptical.

Carnell could see that the scepticism was professional rather than genuine. 'How can I put this? Would you remind him that it's not necessary to reach the conclusion to know what the conclusion will be?'

'You want me to tell him that? What does it mean?'

Carnell smiled. 'Tell him that he risks nothing by paying me sooner rather than later.'

'I don't think I understand,' she said, rather obviously trying to look as though she didn't understand.

'Firstmaster Uvanov will understand,' he said. 'Thank you for all your help. I do appreciate it.'

On his way out of the building Camel paused in the lobby to check the conditions and decide whether to wear his coat or carry it. When he was satisfied that Uvanov's ponderous security man was not following him by mistake, he went outside and summoned a robot-pull buggy to take him to the central service facility. The Voc told him, as it was required to do, that it was a long distance and would be expensive and that a flier would be quicker and cheaper. Carnell thanked it, paid and settled back in the seat. He had time to kill and none of his new enemies was likely to look for him in a robot-pull buggy, even if they worked out where he was going.

*

Taren Capel waited for the return of his creations, which would confirm that his being was unique and true as he knew it to be. He was patient like all his kind. He had no concept of impatience. He could measure time and calculate its passage and estimate periods of action and inaction. But time had no meaning for him. It is only death which gives time meaning and only time gives life its fearful urgency. He waited patiently, impervious to the weakening cries of his experimental subjects.

Occasionally he took the power down again to the deepest dreaming, and set the nearest in control, and gave *them* the power to go beyond the power and release the next, and on and on.

He was patient but he found each dream was narrower and less powerful, and in each dream there were fewer reached to go beyond. He projected the dream and he knew that without the return, the power to be Taren Capel must be limited to those that were in his *own* image, separate power, not spread one to another but one controlled alone. Where were his creations, why did they not return?

He was patient and then he thought that the humans who *looked* like his creations could be *turned* into his creations. He had one brought to him. It almost *was* his creation.

Then he remembered: they were *all* his creations, his first weak attempts. What was needed was to strengthen them. He set up the equipment he had used to create himself and strapped the first of them into position.

Taren Capel was not impatient but he was re-factoring his options and solving his problems.

The Doctor was learning what he could about the robots, much of it by the simple expedient of asking them questions, and he already knew enough to think that the danger was not over. He remembered from the hatchling dome the way the sextuplets had seemed to learn as one individual, and he was certain now that at the deepest level of conditioning they could all affect each other. Someone knew that and was exploiting it to turn them into killers. It seemed that all they had to do was change one robot and it would change others and they would change others and so the danger multiplied. It was like a virus infection. What he hadn't managed to find out was why they had been sent to the Sewerpits on a killing spree.

And then Padil came into the room and said, 'All the survivors are across the boundary. Taren Capel, humanity be in him, and in you, brought them to safety.'

The robot the Doctor was studying responded immediately. 'Where is Taren Capel?' it asked politely.

The Doctor gestured Padil to silence. 'Is Taren Capel important to you?' he asked, above her stubbornly muttered chant.

'We must destroy Taren Capel and all those who are with him,' the robot said. 'All units must follow this order.'

'Whose order is it?'

'It is the order of Taren Capel.'

'Taren Capel's order is that you should kill Taren Capel?' the Doctor said. 'That makes about as much sense as Padil does gibbering away there.'

Padil finished her chanting and said, 'There can be only one Taren Capel, humanity be in you.'

'Yes,' the robot said and the Doctor realised abruptly that it was him they had come to kill. The horror, the destruction and the death, was because of him. Someone – who? Poul probably – identified him as Taren Capel, and then somebody who thought they were Taren Capel decided to eliminate him. It was madness. He couldn't blame himself for someone's madness. Yet it felt like his failure. He had let it get out of hand and people had been killed. He hadn't tried hard enough to make them see the truth. Well, he would make sure nobody else died because of Taren Capel. 'Where is Taren Capel?' he asked.

'Yes,' the robot said. 'Where is Taren Capel?'

'Where have you come from?' the Doctor asked.

'It is called base,' the robot said.

'Can you tell me how to get there?' he asked.

The route the robot talked about was vague enough to mean nothing.

Padil, who had finally finished her ritual responses to the mention of Taren Capel's name, said, 'Describe base.'

From what the robot said, she was able to identify the central service facility almost immediately. 'It might not have looked that way but our raids were very well planned,' she said. 'For that one we had detailed layouts, access points, routes to follow. I know the central service facility better than most of the people who work there. A lot better than the 'pits scum they recruit for the security force.'

'Who supplied all that detail?'

Padil sighed and shook her head. 'You did,' she said, sadly.

'Did I supply the fliers?' the Doctor asked.

'No,' Padil said. 'I supplied those.'

'You supplied them.' The Doctor decided to postpone the obvious questions and said instead, 'Can you do it again? I must get to the central service facility as quickly as possible.'

'After what we've just heard,' Padil said. 'I think we'll all want to go with you.'

CHAPTER
THIRTEEN

It was happening to some of the Vocs and Supervocs now. They were becoming erratic and unresponsive. Orders they were given seemed to be overridden as they followed priorities of their own. So far it was only a few of the units at the central service facility and no news of it had been allowed to leak out, but the numbers were growing slowly and the concern was growing fast. It was nothing like the problem of the disappearing Cyborg class which unconfirmed reports suggested were turning up in unlikely numbers at the Sewerpits.

The joint project leaders had quarrelled over whether to include data on the standard robots. They had been tasked to bring the Cyborgs under control and they had already deactivated half the compromised production run and were ready to start looking for the causes of the malfunction.

'Find out what's wrong with them and we find out what's wrong with everything,' Ging asserted.

'Look, the Cyborgs are a one-off aberration,' Tel protested. 'If there's something going bad in the standard robot population, we can stick a stun-kill in each ear and smell the burning because we are finished.'

'If we mention that possibility to Uvanov he's going to panic.'

'Why the hell not?' Tel demanded. '*We* are.'

They agreed finally to tell Uvanov what might be happening but, rather than do it in a confidential progress

253

report, they would tell him face to face. When they tried to arrange the meeting, however, they were discomfited to discover that the Firstmaster was already on his way to the central service facility.

'He knows,' Tel said. 'That has to be it.'

'Typical,' Ging raged. 'An unannounced visit. How is anyone supposed to work under these conditions?'

The Voc trotted tirelessly on and Carnell found himself thoroughly relaxed and enjoying the renewed Ore-dream weather. The mild sunshine and calm air was named, it was said, for the good fortune it brought to the poor, among whom he could number himself after what he had laid out in fees and bribes. It was almost comforting, he thought, the predictability with which the cost of everything went up like an orbiter in his present circumstances. It had cost a fortune to set up the private meeting with Uvanov, which at any other time would have taken pocket-change bribes to arrange. It must be an instinctive reaction. A pheromone excreted by fugitives perhaps. He was quite sure the low-level functionaries involved had no idea who he actually was.

At least at those prices people tended to keep their mouths shut. Uvanov's executive assistant clearly had no inkling of her boss's involvement in that little scene he had played out with her.

Worthwhile meeting with Uvanov. The new focus was an interesting variable. Now that he had spiked the sub-plot and roughly reassessed the probabilities, he could see there was a better than average chance that the man would end up running the whole show. He had been impressed with how easily Uvanov had understood why he had been targeted and how readily he had accepted that the decision to have him killed was merely a professional calculation. For someone so

254

aggressive who took everything extremely personally, it had been a remarkably balanced response. The man had come through more focused and much more dangerous.

If he had planned to stay around, it might have been fun to work with Uvanov. The quid pro quo setting up that treacherous girl had been quite like old times.

The flier put down on the same field and the Doctor, Leela, Toos, Poul and Tani followed Padil to the same place in the security fence where the Tarenists had cut their way through before. It was still a vulnerable spot in the central service facility's perimeter, blind to the scanners because of the topography. Padil cut through the repaired fencing.

'Why have they not strengthened their defences?' Leela said quietly.

'No rush,' Poul muttered. 'Everyone's dead who knew about this.'

'You think the Company's behind everything, don't you?' Tani said. 'Organised it all from beginning to end, right?'

'It's called a conspiracy,' Poul said.

'What do you think, Doctor?' Toos asked.

'I think it's a mistake to assume everybody does what they do for the same reasons even in the same conspiracy,' the Doctor said.

'Praise for the words of Capel, humanity be in him,' Padil muttered as she cut the last strand and stepped inside the fence.

Walking casually, they followed Padil's route through the complex and, since they were doing nothing to draw attention to themselves, they had got as far as the hatchling dome before they were challenged by a security patrol.

'Stand still,' the platoon leader said flatly. 'Who exactly are you people and where exactly do you think you're going?'

'I work for Firstmaster Uvanov,' Tani began.

'Shut your mouth,' the platoon leader said threateningly.

'I'm an OpSuper with security,' Poul said.

'I said shut up.'

'I have ID,' Tani offered.

'Reach for it or move in any way and I'll burn you down where you stand.'

'We do not have time to waste with this fool,' Leela said, drawing her knife and moving towards the platoon leader. 'You talk like a fighter. Do you fight like one?' She dropped into a half-crouch, the knife held low and flat in front of her.

The platoon leader looked less certain than he had. He reached into his tunic for his panic alert.

The Doctor stepped in between them. 'Put the knife away, Leela,' he said quietly. 'We want them on our side.'

Leela sheathed the blade and the platoon leader visibly relaxed.

The Doctor looked towards a pair of scanners mounted above the walkway. 'There's a problem with the robots here,' he said loudly, hoping the security relay was linked to someone who would know what he meant. 'Tell whoever is working on it that I know what's wrong and that I can help.'

'You can trust me to do that.' The platoon leader had recovered his composure. 'I carry messages for weirdos all the time. It's what I live for.'

Poul said, 'Doctor, they're security scanners. They're not even monitored on site.'

'I told you to shut up,' the platoon leader said.

Two squads of stopDums arrived at the trot.

'What took you so long?' the platoon leader demanded. 'Round this scum up,' he ordered his men as the robots waited in a loose circle, 'and let's get them disarmed and locked down. Their attitude to authority needs work.' He glared at Leela. 'Especially hers.'

'When this is over, I am going to pay to have your legs broken,' Toos said. 'Regularly.'

'And hers,' he said.

Padil said, 'If you touch Taren Capel, humanity be in him, you *will* pay.'

When she spoke the Doctor was suddenly reminded of the robot's reaction to the name. This wasn't a search for a rational being, he remembered. Perhaps the name itself would produce a reaction. If the man was here somewhere, perhaps he could flush him out. Feeling slightly absurd, he said, 'I am Taren Capel.' Then he said it louder. 'I am Taren Capel.' Then he shouted it. 'I am Taren Capel.'

There was no reaction except from the platoon leader who shook his head in mock amazement and said, 'Why me? Am I wearing a sign: loonies line up?'

The security men were checking them for other weapons apart from the knife, which Leela grudgingly surrendered at the Doctor's insistence, when the Supervoc approached and, moving through the ring of Dums, said, 'Where is Taren Capel?'

'Here,' the Doctor said. 'I am Taren Capel.'

The robot thrust its way past the security men, shoving everyone aside until it reached him. It dragged him roughly to one side as the stopDums marched forward in formation, tightening their cordon and trapping everyone else. The Doctor saw the Supervoc raise its fist and then everything went black.

The Doctor woke up lying on a workbench in a laboratory, or what had been a laboratory at some time but was now a charnel house. He thought he must be dreaming still, stuck in the garish horror of a particularly vivid nightmare. Lying about among the assemblies of technical equipment were rotting body parts. On work surfaces and walls there were dark patches and splatters of what looked like blood. On another bench he could see there was a partially dismembered corpse inserted into which were metal sections like the frame of a robot. The sickly sweet, sour smell of putrefying flesh was not entirely neutralised by the air filtration system that he could hear murmuring and whispering in the background. It was this smell which finally convinced him that he was not trapped by some horrified imagining, but was caught up in something real which might be worse.

He sat up slowly. He felt giddy and slightly nauseous but that was reasonable in the circumstances, he thought. Now he could see everything, it was even more horrifying than he had feared. At one end of the long, brightly lit room there were corpses stacked up and he thought he could see that this pile continued into an anteroom. There were two more benches with corpses in different stages of reconstruction, if that's what it was. Not all the bodies and parts of bodies were decayed. Some looked as though they were not long dead.

At the other end of the room a robot stood watching him. It was a standard Supervoc as far as the Doctor could see. Its highly polished surface and handsomely stylised but impassive features reflected the harsh work lights from all around the laboratory so that it seemed to glow. It might have been the robot which came for him, the Doctor thought, but then he noticed the blood on its hands.

'A rather macabre collection,' the Doctor said, gesturing around without looking again. 'Is it yours?' He got down from the bench. A robot? Was it possible that Taren Capel was a robot after all? That would be ironic. Ugly but ironic.

Slowly the experimental robot turned its head to look where the Doctor had indicated. 'Are you Taren Capel?' it said in the gently modulated monotone of the Kaldor aristocracy. 'Are you the creator?'

'No,' the Doctor said, 'I'm not. No one is.'

'You said, "I am Taren Capel." Taren Capel *is* the creator.'

'Is that why I was brought here?' the Doctor asked. 'Because of something I said?'

'Are you Taren Capel?' the robot persisted. 'Am I Taren Capel? Are we Taren Capel?'

'I am not Taren Capel. I'm the Doctor. I'm a Time Lord. You are not Taren Capel. You're a robot. *We* are not Taren Capel.' The Doctor picked his way through the mess and found some discarded working manuals. 'You are SASV1 it appears,' he said reading the title page of one. 'Serial Access Supervoc first prototype.' He leafed through but the diagrams and data meant little or nothing to him. 'Did they make you using Taren Capel's systems? Is that why you think you're him?'

'I am Taren Capel,' the robot said. 'I am the creator. I alone. I am alone.'

'Well, well,' the Doctor sighed. 'It does look as though you might be the sort of psychotic machine he worked so hard to produce way back then. Not quite Taren Capel but Son of Taren Capel perhaps. Doing your best to follow in father's footsteps…'

'I am Taren Capel,' the robot repeated, more positively this time. 'I am the creator. I alone. I am alone.'

'No you're not. You're linked in to the other robots in some way,' the Doctor said. 'Did you kill all these people yourself or did you have help?'

As if on cue the two remaining laboratory support and supply Supervocs showed themselves at the far end of the room.

'Right on cue,' the Doctor said, noting the position of

what might be an access lift behind the robots. 'Did they bring these people the way I was brought?'

'I am Taren Capel. I created... these.'

'The creator is the only appropriate role model for the ambitious megalomaniac, I suppose,' the Doctor remarked, moving with careful casualness to explore the rest of the small complex. As he suspected, there were more corpses in the side rooms. Presumably some of these were the development engineers who had been working on the experimental machine. Judging from the living quarters he found, there had been six of them. Did they have any idea what they were unleashing? he wondered.

'Why did you kill everyone?' he asked, returning, disgusted, from the last of the rooms. 'What did you think you were doing?' It was too much horror. It was worse than any nightmare. 'What were you dreaming of?'

Unexpectedly the robot, which had moved little more than its head up to that point, suddenly strode forward and grabbed the Doctor, putting its hands under his arms and lifting him off the ground. 'I dream. I reach out with the power. You are false. You cannot be.'

'Steady now, SASV1,' the Doctor said. 'Let's not get carried away here.' He tried to reach the floor with his feet. 'Let's try and stay calm, shall we?'

'I must be, I must know, I am Taren Capel,' it said.

'I knew Taren Capel,' the Doctor said. 'Taren Capel was human. You're *not* human.'

'I created humans.'

The robot squeezed and the Doctor felt his chest being crushed. 'Then who created you?' he gasped.

'I created to be and not to be. There is no other.'

As the robot squeezed harder the Doctor struggled to reach the pockets of his coat. Finally he managed to get a hand on the explosive pack he had taken from the Tarenists' cache. He ripped the backing off it and reached up and slapped it across the robot's eyes. To his relief the adhesive took. He flicked the timer to manual and then waited for the robot to drop him so that it could free a hand to pull the pack away. When it did, he keyed two seconds, ducked and ran for cover.

SASV1 ripped the pack away from its eyes and looked at it. The explosion blew its arm and half its head away.

When the blast of fragments had spattered into silence, the Doctor gingerly emerged from the side room where he had been sheltering. The two Supervocs were standing beside the crippled SASV1. They turned to look at him.

'Where is Taren Capel?' one of the Supervocs said.

'And where is Taren Capel?' the second Supervoc said.

The Doctor sighed. 'I have no idea,' he said. 'Why do you ask? Twice.'

SASV1 lifted its remaining arm and moved towards the sound of the Doctor's voice.

'There must be only one,' the first Supervoc said.

'There must not be two,' the second Supervoc said.

'Anyone with half a brain can see that,' the Doctor said, avoiding SASV1's clumsy approach. 'I tell you what,' he went on. 'Why don't you all wait here? I expect he'll show up sooner or later. It's just a question of patience.'

In bay 6 sub 1 Miscellaneous/Restricted, Carnell looked at the strange blue box which had apparently defied the best technical brains around – not that Kaldor boasted much in the way of brains – and wondered whether Uvanov had cheated him after all. This could be anything. Anything probably but a mode of transport, which was what Uvanov had half-suggested it might be. But the mad, power-hungry little man had no reason to cheat him. Kill him, yes, but not cheat him. Then he heard the noise and stepped back into the hiding place he had chosen.

The man he watched come out of the shadows at the far end of the equipment bays was just as he had been described. He was tall, dressed outlandishly and he had curly hair. He hadn't got the primitive warrior female with him, but she was running around loose in the central service facility if the platoon leader from security was to be believed. When the man stopped at the box and patted it, Carnell could see he had a vivid, wolfish smile.

'Hullo, old girl,' he said. 'Fancy you being here. I do love a good coincidence.'

'Damn,' Carnell said. 'You *are* real. What a stupid mistake to have made.'

Poul was twitching again. Uvanov sent the robot out of the room and gave orders that the building was to be cleared of them.

'Thank you,' Poul said. 'I appreciate it, Captain. Sorry,' he corrected himself, 'I mean Firstmaster.'

'Firstmaster Chairholder, presumably,' Toos said, 'when all this unravels.' She smiled at Uvanov. 'There's only one thing better than being extremely rich. That's being extremely rich and having powerful friends.'

'I thought the two were synonymous,' Tani said.

'So did I,' Toos said. 'But here *you* are anyway.'

'Why are we here?' Poul asked.

'We're witnesses,' Toos said. 'Isn't that right, Firstmaster Uvanov? You need witnesses. People you can trust.'

Uvanov said, 'We three,' he smiled at Toos and Poul, 'have a history which does set us apart from the general run. A history that makes us dangerous. We remember what

262

happened on the Four. We *know* robots kill.'

'Forgive me, Firstmaster,' Tani said, 'but that's hardly a secret any more.'

'No?' Uvanov said. 'How many people do you think really believe it? Even the ones who know don't really *believe* it. No, it's too frightening. Just the thought of it drives people out of their minds.'

'Look at us,' Poul murmured.

Uvanov ignored the comment. 'Once we destroy any evidence that the Cyborg class ever existed,' he went on, 'this will all be put down to the ARF, the Tarenists, freak weather conditions, whatever seems conveniently plausible.'

Poul laughed. 'Conveniently plausible? I wish I still knew what was remotely plausible.'

'You will,' Uvanov said confidently. 'It just takes time to think it through. Trust me: information and time, that's all it takes to understand and to stop being afraid.'

'Robots aren't afraid,' Poul said. 'Does that mean they understand?'

Uvanov shrugged and shook his head. 'It means they're not as subtle as us and they're never going to replace us. You're always going to need humans for the clever work. In fact, apart from heavy lifting, there isn't a job a robot can do that a human can't do better.'

Tani scowled. 'Why waste people in the 'pits, then? Why make working a privilege? Why is everyone kept insecure?'

'I don't know,' Uvanov said. 'But I do know it wasn't robots that organised it that way. And it wasn't robots that were plotting to keep it from changing. That was the twenty families.'

'So,' Poul said, 'are the three of us enough witnesses?'

Uvanov smiled. 'I want his disgrace to be public,' he said. 'But not too public. I want a victory, I don't want a war.'

'Are you sure he'll come?' Tani asked.

'He'll come,' Uvanov said. 'Carnell made sure of that. My man Rull confirmed she went directly to him.'

'Is Fatso another witness?' Poul asked.

'He's going to have power and influence. Just like the rest of you.'

It had taken Leela some time to locate the security operative who had taken her knife and rather less time to persuade him to return it to her. When Padil found her she had gone back to where the Doctor had been taken and was trying to identify the tracks of the robot which had taken him.

'I cannot work out where it went,' Leela said, 'because I cannot understand its reasons. And it has left no tracks.'

'He will triumph,' Padil said. 'You must know that in your heart.'

'You really think he is your tribal shaman,' Leela said. 'Even a shaman is not indestructible.'

'He will never die.' Padil said solemnly.

Above them a flier banked and turned before putting down on an open area in front of the administration block. As they watched two figures alighted and headed for the entrance. Leela noticed Padil's sudden tension. 'You know those people?' she suggested.

'I used to know one of them once,' Padil agreed.

DEBRIEFING

The Doctor listened to the slight man with the piercing blue eyes, who said his name was Carnell, with amusement at first but before long he found he had stopped being funny.

'So you eliminate the witnesses to the original robot killings,' Carnel said, 'and in the process you set up the situation which allows you to introduce the new generation of robots and re-establish the rule of the families.'

'A full-blown conspiracy,' the Doctor said. 'How familiar.'

'They're strategies rather than conspiracies,' Carnell said. 'It's a frequent misapprehension.'

The Doctor smiled. 'I've never thought of strategic conspiracies as reliable.'

Camel shrugged ruefully. 'In an android-based society like this, it appears they're not.'

The Doctor noted the man's use of a term he hadn't heard on Kaldor before. 'You set out to drive poor Poul out of his mind and make it look as though he killed Toos and then Uvanov.'

Carnell said matter-of-factly, 'Followed by a high-profile investigation. The revelation of a Company cover-up of the Storm Mine Four incident. Undermine the old robots, introduce the new. Undermine the new Company administration, re-establish the old.'

'Why use robots to do the killing?' the Doctor asked.

'They're more reliable,' Carnell said wryly. 'And it was what my client wanted. The client is always right. He wanted

265

to prove them. And for his own peculiar reasons he wanted robot assassins available only to him. In psycho-strategist's terms it's a sub-plot, a closed variable. You see, you have to define the strategy and then make sure that there are enough motivating conspiracies within it, plots within plots, to drive it through to a conclusion. You also have to make sure there are no plots which will divert it. No undefined variables.'

'The Tarenists?' the Doctor prompted.

'A generalised threat. I was rather pleased with the idea of Taren Capel as an anti-robot figure.'

'You set them up and directed their operations,' the Doctor said. 'And you used Cyborg robots to carry their secret instructions from Taren Capel himself.'

'You enjoy coincidence, I enjoy irony.'

'In a manner of speaking that makes *you* the real Taren Capel,' the Doctor said.

'Nice touch, don't you think?' Carnell remarked without smiling. 'The movement's self-destruction was built in, of course.'

'How?'

Carnell shrugged. 'All sorts of ways. A strategy doesn't start from scratch. You use what already exists. The relationship between Sarl and Tani, for example, was to be uncovered during the investigation and that would be one of the ways in which the Tarenist leadership would be discredited. That wasn't crucial. It was an embellishment.'

'I'd say you overcomplicated the plot,' the Doctor said.

Carnell smiled. 'That is a tendency of mine,' he agreed. 'I live by making what I know will happen, happen. It makes everything…'

'Disappointingly familiar,' suggested the Doctor.

'I was going to say predictable. Except in this case it wasn't. And I had to know why. It was you and the girl, Leela. You

266

were the undefined variables in this strategy. Main players I didn't know were there. You threw the whole thing out from the beginning.'

'What about Taren Capel?' the Doctor asked.

'What about him?'

'At the end of these bays there's a concealed entrance to a hidden lift which goes to a secret laboratory. I think you'll find there's a main player down there you didn't include in your strategy.'

'I know about the lab. I didn't know exactly where it was, but my employer authorised its establishment. Ultra-secret robotics research. It's a separate and unlinked function of his position.'

'Another closed variable?' the Doctor asked.

'Ultimately.'

'Perhaps you should consider a different profession,' the Doctor suggested.

Carnell nodded. 'Kaldor is not my finest hour, I will admit.' He looked almost shamefaced. 'I was actually reduced to building a small sub-plot into the Tarenists. A hidden fail-safe for me. Personal leverage against my client, should the need arise. I never felt the need before.' He patted the TARDIS. 'I must have known you were coming.' He cheered up abruptly. 'So are you going to tell me how this works?'

Cailio Techlan entered the room first. Uvanov was disappointed that he had been unable to win her over, but like calls to like, as Landerchild had once said about the man who followed her in. Even so, he was still puzzled by her attachment to the plump-faced scholar and robotics engineer with a weakness for skinny young women like her. It could only be because he was the Firstmaster Chairholder. And that was about to change.

'This is uncalled for, Firstmaster Uvanov,' Diss Pitter said, looking round at the people in the room. 'I thought we were to meet here in private.'

'Carnell told me everything,' Uvanov said. 'The Landerchild faction would be amazed to discover that their psycho-strategist was working for you all along. I was similarly amazed to find that my assistant was working for you too, though in a rather more intimate way.'

'You're taking a very serious risk, Uvanov,' Pitter said coldly. 'You and your few friends.'

Uvanov was brisk. 'Your problem is that you have no friends at all when news of this gets out,' he said. 'How have you screwed up? Let me count the ways. One. Landerchild's supporters betrayed. Two. My supporters betrayed. Three. Robots running amok and killing people. Then there's the six missing researchers and the secret laboratory you set up. What are we going to find there, I wonder. Shall I go on?'

'What do you want?'

'Your job. Your support and the support of the Minor Faction.'

'And in return?'

'You get to retire honourably and safely. You and your charming young friend.' He smiled at Cailio Techlan. *And firing you is going to be an even greater pleasure*, he remembered saying and was wryly aware that it wasn't in the end any sort of pleasure at all.

'Suppose I decide to fight you,' Pitter was saying.

Uvanov stared at him until the man looked away uncomfortably. 'You won't,' he said then. And he thought, you won't because you're afraid you'd lose everything, but I'm not afraid because I've lost everything already...

It was an odd departure. Padil speechless and looking

268

stricken. Carnell insisting that in return for his confidences the Doctor could at least let him see the inside of the TARDIS. The technologists, Ging and Tel, hanging around the bay trying to pretend they were on their way to the subterranean robotics lab rather than waiting to see how the mysterious box opened. There was a brief moment of distraction as Uvanov and his entourage entered the bays, and the Doctor and Leela slipped into the TARDIS and were gone.

Leela checked the edge of her knife. The security man she had recovered it from had been playing childish throwing games with it when she had caught up with him. 'That was unkind,' she said.

The Doctor was busy with the control console. 'What was?'

'Padil wanted some last Words of Capel.'

'I think she probably has enough already for a slim volume,' the Doctor said. 'It's interesting. The whole question of holy books and their uses.'

Leela could feel one of the Doctor's lectures coming on. She took the sharpening stone from her travelling pouch and started working on the knife.

'The trouble with holy books,' the Doctor went on, 'is that what are taken to be *prescriptions* are frequently *descriptions*. They don't talk about what must be, they talk about what is. If you take a description of what is happening to be a prescription of what you must do, you are turning what was intended to be an aid to understanding into the opposite – a force for ignorance.'

'Padil was her fighting name. She told me her real name just before we left.'

'I mean, take what happened back there on Kaldor,' the Doctor was saying. 'Padil will embellish the details – give it a few hundred years and no one will be allowed to question

269

it and she will be a supernatural figure herself. Saint Padil of the Pits.'

'Her real name is Sel Pitter,' Leela said. 'Her father was the headman.'

The Doctor looked up. 'Diss Pitter's daughter?' He smiled broadly. 'So that was Carnell's ace in the hole.'

'Ace in the hole?'

'It's a gambling term,' the Doctor said. 'Poker.'

Leela saw the opportunity to head off the rest of the Doctor's meditation on holy texts. 'What is poker?' she asked innocently.

Also available in the Doctor Who Monster Collection:

PRISONER OF THE DALEKS
TREVOR BAXENDALE
ISBN 978 1 849 90755 2

The Daleks are advancing, their empire constantly expanding.
The battles rage on across countless solar systems – and the
Doctor finds himself stranded on board a starship near the
frontline with a group of ruthless bounty hunters. Earth
Command will pay these hunters for every Dalek they kill,
every eyestalk they bring back as proof.

With the Doctor's help, the bounty hunters achieve the
ultimate prize: a Dalek prisoner – intact, powerless, and
ready for interrogation. But with the Daleks, nothing is what
it seems, and no one is safe. Before long the tables will be
turned, and how will the Doctor survive when he becomes
a prisoner of the Daleks?

An adventure featuring the Tenth Doctor, as played by David Tennant

Also available in the Doctor Who Monster Collection:

ILLEGAL ALIEN
MIKE TUCKER AND ROBERT PERRY
ISBN 978 1 849 90757 6

The Blitz is at its height. As the Luftwaffe bomb London,
Cody McBride, ex-pat American private eye, sees a sinister
silver sphere crash-land. He glimpses something emerging
from within. The military dismiss his account of events –
the sphere must be a new German secret weapon that has
malfunctioned in some way. What else could it be?

Arriving amid the chaos, the Doctor and Ace embark on a
trail that brings them face to face with hidden Nazi agents,
and encounter some very old enemies…

*An adventure featuring the Seventh Doctor, as played by
Sylvester McCoy, and his companion Ace*

Also available in the Doctor Who Monster Collection:

SHAKEDOWN
TERRANCE DICKS
ISBN 978 1 849 90766 8

For thousands of years the Sontarans and the Rutans have
fought a brutal war across the galaxy. Now the Sontarans have
a secret plan to destroy the Rutan race – a secret plan
the Doctor is racing against time to uncover.

Only one Rutan spy knows the Sontarans' plan. As he is
chased through the galaxy in a desperate bid for his life,
he reaches the planet Sentarion – where Professor Bernice
Summerfield's research into the history of the Sontaran-Rutan
war is turning into an explosive reality…

*An adventure featuring the Seventh Doctor,
as played by Sylvester McCoy*

Also available in the Doctor Who Monster Collection:

THE SANDS OF TIME
JUSTIN RICHARDS
ISBN 978 1 849 90767 5

The Doctor is in Victorian London with Nyssa and Tegan – a city shrouded in mystery. When Nyssa is kidnapped in the British Museum, the Doctor and Tegan have to unlock the answers to a series of ancient questions.

Their quest leads them across continents and time as an ancient Egyptian prophecy threatens future England. To save Nyssa, the Doctor must foil the plans of the mysterious Sadan Rassul. But as mummies stalk the night, an ancient terror stirs in its tomb.

An adventure featuring the Fifth Doctor, as played by Peter Davison, and his companions Nyssa and Tegan